THE
Music OF
Love

Kate McCabe is married with two children and lives in Howth in County Dublin. She is a former journalist and has published several bestselling novels including *Hotel Las Flores*, the *Beach Bar*, *The Book Club*, *The Man of Her Dreams* and *The Spanish Letter*. Kate's hobbies include reading, music, travelling and walking along the beach in Howth while she thinks up plots for her stories.

THE
Music
OF
Love

KATE MCCABE

HACHETTE
BOOKS
IRELAND

First published in Ireland in 2015 by
HACHETTE BOOKS IRELAND
First published in paperback in 2015

1

Cataloguing in Publication Data is available from the British Library

ISBN 978 1 473609655

Typeset in Cambria by redrattledesign.com

Printed and bound in Great Britain by Clays Ltd, St Ives plc

Hachette Books Ireland policy is to use papers that are natural, renewable and
recyclable products and made from wood grown in sustainable forests. The logging and
manufacturing processes are expected to conform to the environmental regulations of
the country of origin.

Hachette Books Ireland
8 Castlecourt Centre
Castleknock
Dublin 15, Ireland

A division of Hachette UK Ltd.
Carmelite House
50 Victoria Embankment
London EC4Y 0DZ

www.hachette.ie

This book is for four very special young ladies:
Karen O'Connell, Elise Patton, Kellie Patton
and Julianna Corkish Patton

Chapter One

Kirsty O'Neill was under pressure. She had managed only five hours' sleep and had been up since seven: she'd had to prepare a presentation for an important client of her busy fashion business. Now it was eleven o'clock, and they were due to meet at one at the Gondola, a pretty little restaurant in Malahide. She had better get a move on, she thought. She glanced up from her desk and saw that clouds were darkening the sky.

She had chosen the Gondola because of its charming location, perched right on the edge of the marina looking out to sea. The last time she had been there, everyone was in jolly mood. She remembered the laughter, the clinking of wine glasses and the sun sparkling off the shining hulls of the yachts. Now it looked as if they would be staring at rain running down the window panes. It wasn't quite the scene she had envisaged.

Kirsty's company was called Allure Fashions and the client was Cecily Moncrieffe, the owner of a string of boutiques specialising in high-end ladies' clothes. Soon after starting her business, Kirsty had persuaded Cecily to take some sample dresses from one of her designers. They had sold well, and the two women had built up a good relationship. Now Cecily was one of Kirsty's main customers.

But their meeting wasn't the only thing weighing on Kirsty's mind that morning. The previous evening she'd had a row with her boyfriend, Robbie Hennessy. He had turned up late for their dinner date, offering some threadbare excuse about a last-minute problem at the office. Then they had gone on to a nightclub where he had proceeded to get drunk and make a fool of himself. Just after midnight Kirsty could take no more. She had left him, still gyrating, while a noisy crowd clapped and shouted encouragement. So far, he hadn't had the decency to call and apologise. She suspected he was still in bed, nursing a hangover. But it was typical of Robbie's selfishness that he couldn't even pick up the phone to say he was sorry.

Kirsty was being forced to face an unpalatable truth. The relationship was in trouble. Robbie was turning out to be one more boyfriend who didn't match up to her high standards. It was the story of her life. She had lost track of the men she had gone out with, believing they would be her soulmate only to discover they had feet of clay. It was a pity: Robbie had many fine qualities and most of her friends thought him a good catch. He was twenty-nine, six feet two, fair-haired, and very entertaining company. He had a smart apartment in the Dublin docklands and held down a good sales job with a social media company called ClickOn. And he was an excellent lover, the best Kirsty had ever encountered.

She had met him nine months earlier at a party hosted by her friend, Angie Dunlop. They had been drawn to each other at once, and Kirsty had spent a pleasant evening in Robbie's company as he entertained her with hilarious stories about his work colleagues and clients and made sure her glass was always filled. When he had suggested they meet again, she had readily agreed and soon they were seeing each other several times a week. Before long, people were referring to them as an item. It was months before Kirsty realised that the whole thing had been a set-up: Angie had pushed her into Robbie's arms because she was the only one of her friends who was still unattached.

It hadn't taken her long to discover that the man of her dreams had an irresponsible streak. She had stopped counting the times when he had promised to do something important and forgotten about it. He had even forgotten her birthday. That particular blunder had put a serious strain on their relationship, which was only patched up after numerous pleading phone calls and the delivery of several large bouquets. The truth was that, despite his good looks and charming ways, Robbie was still an immature schoolboy who hadn't come to terms with adult life.

She would have ditched him permanently but for one thing: she was afraid of losing him. She was thirty-one and very conscious that her biological clock was furiously ticking away. Most of her friends were married or in serious relationships. Several had started families. Kirsty longed to settle down and have her own children. But she was rapidly coming to the conclusion that, if it was ever going to happen, it wouldn't be with Robbie.

She put him out of her mind while she concentrated on her meeting with Cecily. She worked furiously till midday, finished the presentation, then dived into the shower. Kirsty had inherited her mother's good looks. She was slim, with shoulder-length black hair, and stood five feet eight inches tall. She knew that Cecily would be dolled up to the nines, hair immaculately styled, nails polished, skin gleaming with health and vitality. She must be fifty-five if she was a day, but she looked far younger.

Appearing in public was always an occasion for Kirsty to advertise her clothes. It took her ten minutes to choose what to wear. This was a business meeting so she needed something formal but not too severe. She settled for a close-fitting blue dress, by Penny Muldoon, a twenty-four-year-old, not long out of college and one of her aspiring young designers. Then she pulled on a pair of tights, brushed out her hair, applied her make-up and looped a simple gold chain around her neck. Satisfied with her appearance, she stuck the presentation in her briefcase, with her sketches and samples, checked her car keys, opened her umbrella and stepped out into the now pouring rain.

***

It took twenty minutes to drive the short distance from her apartment in Howth to the seaside town of Malahide. By the time she arrived, the rain was easing off and the sky was brightening. Thank God for small mercies, she thought. Perhaps we'll get some sunshine after all.

She found a vacant space in the restaurant car park, switched off the engine and stepped out, taking care to avoid the large puddles that littered the tarmac. She glanced at her watch. It was ten to one. Perfect! It would never do to keep Cecily waiting. As she hurried towards the entrance, her phone began to ring. Damn, she thought. This'll be Robbie at last, with another feeble apology. Well, on this occasion, she would cut him dead. Maybe that would let him know just how upset she was.

She managed to extricate the phone from her bag and clutched it to her ear. But it wasn't Robbie. Instead, she heard a woman's voice: 'Hello, darling.'

'Mum!' Kirsty said in surprise. Just a week ago, she had packed her widowed mother off for a holiday in Marbella. 'What's the weather like today? Sun still shining?'

'All the time.'

'That's brilliant. I hope you're making the most of it.'

'Well, that's why I'm calling, dear. I'm coming home.'

'What?' Kirsty gasped. 'But you've barely arrived.'

'I know, but I've met this lovely man. And I want you all to meet him too.'

Chapter Two

Her mother, Helen, was a major concern to Kirsty. She was a vivacious sixty-four-year-old, who had been a much sought-after beauty in her day. Until quite recently she had been immersed in the activities of her local community in Howth. Her social calendar had been crammed for months ahead, with dinner parties, outings and meetings of the various clubs she belonged to, and the charities she supported: the Peninsula Musical Society, the Heritage Society, the Church Bring and Buy committee, the book club. The list went on. There wasn't an organisation that didn't have Helen O'Neill as a member. She had the energy of a woman half her age and seemed to juggle her many engagements with efficiency and poise, never disturbing a hair on her perfectly groomed head. What was more, she enjoyed every minute. Friends would marvel at her stamina and wonder how she managed to involve herself in so many interests and still find time for her family.

But whenever anyone commented on this, Helen would simply shrug her delicate shoulders. For her, there was no great mystery. It wasn't a chore to sit on a committee and plan a fundraising drive. It was fun and gave her hours of pleasure. Her organisational skills were second to none: she had spent years running her husband James's law office before she'd surprised everyone by marrying her boss while she was still in her mid-twenties.

They had settled into Avalon, a period house on Howth Summit with spectacular views across Dublin Bay. Helen took to her new role with zest and immediately set about refurbishing each of the five bedrooms, plus the large drawing and dining rooms. She hired the best designers and chose all the furniture and fabrics herself. For good measure, she remodelled the kitchen and bathrooms. James let her get on with it, happy to concentrate on his law practice and leave the house to his wife.

When it had been completed, she had turned her attention to the gardens, which had become wild and overgrown. She employed a team of gardeners, who worked to her plans. Within six weeks, the gardens had been licked into shape. The lawns gleamed like smooth green baize. The trees had been trimmed back and stripped of dead branches while the borders were a blaze of brightly coloured flowers and shrubs. Now Avalon was ready to receive guests at the fabulous dinner parties that soon became legendary in the area.

But Helen still hadn't finished. In quick succession, she bore James three children: Deirdre, then Mark and finally Kirsty. When they went to school, she became involved in the local activities that were soon taking up most of her free time. Kirsty's memory of her childhood was of a happy time, filled with parties, picnics and holidays while her mother oversaw everything with effortless grace.

This happy state of affairs might have continued indefinitely but for a tragedy that had occurred six months earlier. One evening, just before Christmas, James came home from work complaining of abdominal pain. He was a fit man who used to boast that he had never been sick in his life. Helen insisted he go straight to bed and made him a light supper of scrambled eggs and toast.

The following morning, after a sleepless night, the pain was worse and she was forced to call in their local GP, Peter Humphries, a family friend. He examined James, gave him some medication to relieve the discomfort and arranged for a consultant to see him immediately.

The consultant had carried out some tests and admitted James to hospital, where he was diagnosed with stomach cancer. Despite the best efforts of specialists and surgeons, he was dead within four weeks at the age of sixty-five.

Kirsty and her siblings were distraught. The speed of events had taken everyone by surprise, including Peter Humphries, who admitted that he had never before witnessed a case like it. Helen was devastated. She seemed to disintegrate before their very eyes. Gone was the energetic dynamo who could take care of half a dozen things before lunchtime. In her place was a frightened woman who seemed unable to cope with the calamity that had overtaken her and rapidly fell to pieces.

As soon as the funeral was over, she recoiled from human contact. She cancelled all her engagements and took to her bed, where she refused to speak to anyone, including her long-time friend Anne O'Malley. By now, Deirdre was married with a young family and Mark was living on the other side of the bay in Blackrock so Kirsty had to look after her mother. She locked up her apartment at Howth harbour and went to live with her at Avalon.

Here, she tried to juggle the demands of her growing fashion business while simultaneously dealing with the administrative problems thrown up by her father's sudden death. Thankfully, she was able to rely on the support of his legal colleagues. Most of her time was taken up with caring for Helen and attempting to nurse her back to health.

It was a slow process and there were occasions when Kirsty despaired of her mother ever regaining her old spirit and vitality. But, gradually, she coaxed her out of bed and into the drawing room, where she would sit for hours gazing out at the garden while tears of grief rolled down her cheeks. It was weeks before Helen was persuaded to accept phone calls and even longer before she finally consented to see Anne O'Malley.

Anne became a regular visitor. She would call in the morning and stay till mid-afternoon, which allowed Kirsty time to catch up with her work. The two women would sit together for hours while Anne brought Helen up to date with local gossip. Kirsty began to see a definite improvement.

By now it was May and spring had arrived. Peter Humphries had suggested that Kirsty should engage the services of a grief counsellor, who recommended a change of scenery. Kirsty took Anne into her confidence and between them they set about persuading her mother to take a short holiday. Kirsty scoured the internet for possible venues, and soon found something she thought might be suitable – a small upmarket holiday complex in Marbella on the Spanish Costa del Sol called Puebla Maria.

It looked ideal. It was a gated complex with twenty-four-hour security. The amenities included a five-star restaurant, two bars, private gardens, a gymnasium and sauna. The publicity photographs pictured guests sipping drinks beside the large swimming pool. When Kirsty showed her mother what she had found, Helen told her to book a two-week stay for Anne and herself.

It was with enormous relief that Kirsty drove them to the airport and saw them safely through security towards the plane that would fly them to Marbella and the sun. Now she could move back into her own apartment and give her full attention to her business and her troubled relationship with Robbie. Each day, Helen rang to keep her informed of developments, and every time Kirsty heard her voice, she sounded happy.

She began to hope that her mother was over the worst, that the black cloud of grief had finally lifted and she was regaining the bubbly energy that had been her hallmark. She had never, in her wildest dreams, imagined that she would receive the news she had just heard. Her mother had met some man and was bringing him back to Dublin.

Kirsty felt breathless with shock. Her parents had been devoted to each other, and Helen had never expressed even the mildest interest in another man. How had this happened? Had she gone mad? Had the sun and the wine addled her brain? And why hadn't Anne been keeping an eye on her?

'A man?' Kirsty managed to say, trying desperately to hide her alarm.

'Yes, dear. His name is Antonio. Oh, he's the most remarkable person. I can't wait for you to meet him, such charm and such good manners. And he's got such a unique talent. You'll be totally impressed.'

'And you're bringing him back to Howth?'

'Yes!'

This was getting worse. Where was she planning to put him? Not in Avalon, surely. She'd have every nosy gossip in the neighbourhood talking about her. Had she taken leave of her senses? Kirsty was about to ask what age Antonio was but thought better of it. She'd find out soon enough. And if her mother was determined to bring him home, it might be best not to argue. She was recovering from an emotional breakdown, after all. Better handle her gently.

Kirsty did her best to sound calm. 'When are you coming back?'

'Tomorrow. Our flight gets into Dublin at half one.'

'I'll meet you at the airport.'

'There's no need. We'll get a taxi.'

'Are you sure?'

'Absolutely. We'll be home around two thirty.'

'Well, I'm really looking forward to seeing you. And meeting Antonio, of course,' she added quickly.

'And we're looking forward to seeing you, too. I'm going to miss the warmth of Spain but it'll be nice to get back.'

They said goodbye and Kirsty cancelled the call. Her mother's announcement couldn't have come at a worse time – just as she was about to have a crucial business meeting with Cecily Moncrieffe. She had no choice but to put aside Helen's startling news and return to it later. Right now, she had to pull herself together and concentrate on Cecily.

She hurried into the restaurant and was promptly shown to a table by the window as she had requested. The sun was now breaking through and the clouds were disappearing. It was going to be a nice day after all, just as she had hoped.

She popped into the Ladies to tidy her hair and touch up her lipstick. It was now almost one o'clock and Cecily was always punctual. Back at the table, she tried to think of the business but the shock conversation with her mother was still reverberating in her brain and she had to struggle to gather her thoughts.

She glanced up when someone entered the restaurant and was greeted by the elegant figure of her guest in the doorway. Cecily was wearing cream linen trousers with an eye-catching coral silk T-shirt. She was perfectly coiffed and made-up, not a hair out of place. The manager glided over to her and guided her to Kirsty's table.

'You look like you've seen a ghost,' Cecily said, as soon as she sat down. 'Have you had bad news?'

'Nothing like that.'

'You can't fool me! You've had a row with your boyfriend, haven't you? I've been there so take my advice and put your foot down. Let him know who's in charge. Somebody has to be the boss in a relationship and it's always better when it's the woman.'

'You're so perceptive,' Kirsty said. If Cecily Moncrieffe wanted to believe her pallor was due to a row with Robbie, that was fine. Much easier than telling her the truth.

Cecily looked out of the window across the marina and the sun sparkling on the sea. 'This is a beautiful little place, such a bright, cheery atmosphere. How did you discover it?'

'A little bird told me.'

'What's the food like?'

'Excellent. I think you'll enjoy it. I picked it especially for you, Cecily.'

'Well, let's find out. Where's the waiter?'

He was by their side in an instant, took their order and returned at once with a fine bottle of Pinot Blanc and a jug of water. Cecily took a sip of the wine and gave a contented sigh. She leaned back in her chair. 'That's certainly getting us off to a good start. Now, down to business. The last creations you gave me sold very well and my clients are looking for more. What have you got to show me this time?'

Kirsty took the presentation from her bag and passed it across the table. 'I've got some really chic designs here. I think you're going to like them.'

Chapter Three

Their lunch ended at three o'clock. Cecily had doubled her previous order and, as her customers were the wealthy and famous, Kirsty's designers would attract a lot of publicity, which, in turn, would generate further orders from other retailers. Both women were delighted with the outcome.

But Cecily was a tough negotiator and it had been nerve-racking. Kirsty had held back some evening gowns, which had been the subject of a recent photoshoot for the *Daily Tribune* fashion pages. They had been worn by an up-and-coming model called Ellie O'Mara and had looked fantastic. The fashion editor, Rachel Maguire, had promised to publish them soon, and when she did, Kirsty expected a flurry of excitement, which would push up the price of the gowns. That was why she hadn't shown them to Cecily. It was a gamble but she was confident she could pull it off.

On a high, Kirsty settled into her silver Aston Martin sports car to drive back to Howth – and her mother's shock announcement rushed back into her mind. Helen had met some man and was bringing him home. Kirsty was still struggling with the news and wished she had asked more questions. But she had been caught off-guard and hadn't had time.

The idea that her mother would take up with a man so soon after her father's death had never crossed Kirsty's mind. Now all sorts of doubts began to creep in. What if Antonio was a confidence trickster who took advantage of older women? She had read about them in the papers. Those predators were sleek and charming and very plausible. And Helen was vulnerable. She was recovering from an emotional breakdown. Kirsty's chest constricted with anxiety. She had to talk to Deirdre and Mark, find out what they thought of it.

By the time she reached her apartment, the anxiety had turned to panic. She sat down at the kitchen table and took out her phone. She started with Deirdre. She had given up her job when her children came along and was usually at home in the afternoon. Her sister answered on the second ring.

'Hi,' Kirsty began. 'Have you got time to talk?'

'It'll have to be quick,' her sister replied. 'I've got to pick up the kids from school shortly. With children, it's all go, go, go. Of course, *you* don't have to worry about that.'

The remark stung, but Kirsty decided to ignore it and press on. 'The reason I'm ringing is that I got a call from Mum this morning. She's coming back from Spain.'

'When?'

'Tomorrow afternoon at two thirty.'

'What? Wasn't she supposed to stay for a fortnight?'

'Yes.'

'Oh, my God, don't tell me she didn't like it?'

'No, that's not it at all. She *did* like it. But you'll never guess what happened – she's met some man.'

She heard her sister choke. 'No way!'

'It's true,' Kirsty went on. 'She's bringing him back with her.'

'Please tell me you're making this up,' Deirdre said.

'I wish I was.'

'I don't believe it. So it's true what they say about Spanish holidays, all that sun, sand and sangria. Oh, this is hilarious. How old is this *hombre*?'

'She didn't say.'

'She certainly didn't waste any time. Well, full marks to her, still pulling men at her age.'

Kirsty's heart sank. She wasn't going to get much support from Deirdre.

'You don't sound very concerned,' she retorted indignantly. 'Mum could be in danger.'

'Don't be ridiculous.'

'I'm serious. We know absolutely nothing about this person. How do we know he's not one of those creeps who prey on lonely women? The Costa is full of them. I'd hate to have Mum taken advantage of in her vulnerable state.'

'Oh, c'mon,' Deirdre said. 'Give her some credit. Mum's not stupid. Maybe he flattered her, made her feel good. What's the harm in that? Every woman likes to get a bit of attention from time to time. It's exactly what she needs to restore her self-confidence.'

'So you're not worried?'

'Why should I be? This might be just the tonic she needs to get over Dad's death. A fling with a man will probably do her a power of good. What's his name?'

'Antonio.'

'I'll wait till I meet him to make up my mind. And I'd advise you to do the same.'

Deirdre brought the conversation to a close, saying she had to pick up the children now. Kirsty felt angry. She had expected her sister to show more sympathy and support. Instead she had scoffed. It was typical of Deirdre: she had always had a selfish streak, even when they were growing up. She was the eldest and had got most of the attention from their father. Now she was totally engrossed in her family. Her life revolved around her husband, Paul, who was a car salesman, and their two boys, Tommy and Shane. When Kirsty had been nursing their mother through her breakdown, she'd had precious little help from Deirdre, she recalled.

Mark was an industrial relations consultant and ran his own company. He was still single but was heavily involved with a young advertising executive called Melanie Smith. Kirsty expected to hear wedding bells any time soon. She rang his number next.

'Hello, Kirsty,' he said, when he came on the line. 'How's life treating you?'

'I can't complain,' she replied. 'I bagged a very important contract today. Cecily Moncrieffe took a large order from me.'

'That's brilliant. Congratulations. You must be thrilled.'

'I sure am.'

'So what can I do for you?'

Kirsty took a new approach with her brother. 'I'm looking for some advice. You have a lot of experience negotiating your way through difficult situations.'

'Well, that's my job.'

'I've got a tricky situation on my hands. There's a woman I know, quite well off, glamorous. She's got herself involved with a man.'

'Is she single?' Mark asked.

'She's a widow.'

'Okay, go on.'

'Some members of her family are concerned that this man might be using her, you know, trying to get his hands on her money.'

'What age is she?'

'Early sixties.'

'Of sound mind?'

'She's had some emotional turmoil recently but I think she's over it.'

'And what age is the man?'

'I don't know.'

'So what's the problem?'

'I've just told you. Some of her family are worried.'

'But why should they be worried? It's none of their business. She's an adult. She can decide for herself.'

'What do you think her family should do?'

'Nothing. If she wants to get involved with some guy, that's entirely up to her.'

'Don't you think they should warn her?'

'What for? Have they any evidence this man is up to no good?'

'Not yet.'

'Then they'd be better off keeping out of it. For one thing, the woman might resent them interfering. It could lead to a family row.'

Kirsty realised she was wasting her time with Mark. He was taking the same line as Deirdre.

There was a slight pause before her brother spoke again. 'Is this woman someone I might know?'

'Yes.'

'Who?'

'It's Mum.'

'For God's sake!' Mark exploded. 'Why didn't you say so at the start?'

***

Kirsty came off the phone feeling totally deflated. Once he'd got over the shock, Mark had promised to consider the situation overnight and call her the next day but his initial response had warned her not to expect any change of mind.

Why were her siblings so blind to the dangers she could see? Her mother had just come out of a breakdown. It would take time to make a complete recovery. In the meantime, she would be prey to loneliness, a sucker for a kind word and a sympathetic shoulder. She was exactly the type of woman the tricksters fastened on. Why couldn't Deirdre and Mark see that too?

She was feeling so downcast that she decided to have a cup of tea. She went into the kitchen and put on the kettle, but before it had boiled, her phone rang. When she picked it up, she saw from the screen that it was Robbie. She was so glad to hear his voice that her resentment over his behaviour disappeared. Robbie was the one person who would certainly see things her way.

'I've been trying to contact you all afternoon,' he began nervously. 'But I haven't been able to get through.'

It was probably true. Kirsty had switched off her phone for the duration of her lunch with Cecily, and since she'd got home, she'd been talking to Deirdre and Mark.

'Look,' he continued, 'I want to apologise. I was out of order last night. I made a total ass of myself. I don't know what came over me.'

'Two bottles of wine and half a dozen brandy chasers were what came over you, or don't you remember?'

'I'm sorry. I want to say that I'm thoroughly ashamed of myself and it will never happen again. I was tired. I've been working too bloody hard recently. I'd like to take you out to dinner tonight to make up. What do you say?'

She sighed. 'I don't know. That kind of behaviour can't go on, Robbie. It doesn't show much respect for me. We need to have a serious talk.'

'It won't happen again. I promise.'

Kirsty had been planning to read him the Riot Act and banish him to the isolation ward to show her displeasure. Now her resolve crumbled. She needed to talk to someone who would listen sympathetically while she poured out her concerns about her mother. Robbie would be ideal. Unlike her siblings, Robbie could certainly be relied on to take her side. 'I'll agree on one condition.'

'Yes?'

'You consume a maximum of two glasses of wine. Understood?'

'Absolutely.'

'Okay, what time do you want to meet?'

Chapter Four

Helen O'Neill emerged onto the bright terrace and shielded her eyes from the early-morning sun. She had just taken a shower and was wearing her bathrobe and sandals. This would be her last view of Puebla Maria, at least for some time. She had settled the bill. They had had breakfast and the taxi would be coming soon to take them to the airport, where Antonio would meet them. Anne was in their room, busily putting the final touches to their packing. Now all Helen had to do was get dressed and leave.

She gazed at the peaceful sight that greeted her: the blue water shining like glass in the swimming pool, the profusion of bright flowers in the borders and hanging baskets, the trim lawns, the palm trees bending gently in the cool morning breeze. She took a deep breath and her nostrils filled with the fragrance of the roses.

Puebla Maria had been the perfect remedy for her depression. She had known it the minute she had clapped eyes on it. The tranquil retreat had provided her with the opportunity she had needed to come to terms with poor James's death, a shock from which, she thought, she would never recover. He had been the only man she had ever loved. He had been her best friend and soulmate for forty years, and when he had died, the future had seemed desolate without him. But, thank God, Kirsty and Anne had encouraged her to take a break in this lovely holiday complex. It had been her salvation.

It had given her a fresh purpose in life: the wonderful Antonio. She smiled when she thought of the first time she had met him. They had been having dinner in the elegant restaurant while, outside the large bay windows, the last of the sun's rays were creeping across the lawn. Because it was the first night of their holiday, Anne had insisted that they have a bottle of wine with their meal. It was a delicious white wine, nicely chilled, and it had helped Helen to relax in her new surroundings.

She had noticed the piano as soon as they sat down and wondered if they were to have live music with their meal. Shortly after they had started to eat, a tall figure in a black dress suit had sat down and opened the lid of the instrument. She hadn't seen him come in and now he had his back to them so she couldn't see his face. He flexed his hands for a moment then touched the keys, and all at once the enchanting melody of 'Für Elise' filled the room.

As she listened, a feeling of stillness and serenity settled over her. When he had finished, a polite round of applause broke out from the diners. The pianist bent to the instrument again and played another Beethoven piece. Helen clapped enthusiastically and prodded Anne to encourage her to join in. This time, he turned to them and she saw his face.

He was a young man, no more than thirty, handsome with jet-black hair and a dark olive complexion. But it was his eyes that immediately drew Helen's attention. They were deep brown and in them she thought she could detect a hint of sadness, as if they reflected some deep inner hurt or disappointment.

He played for the remainder of the meal, an assortment of classical and popular music. Helen was captivated by his skill and virtuosity. Every note was perfect, his touch sure. This wasn't just some amateur hired for the evening to entertain the guests. By the time he had finished, she knew she had been listening to a master. He was the real thing: a truly gifted artist.

Later, when they were sitting on the terrace, watching the stars come out before they retired to bed, she shared her thoughts with Anne. 'Did you enjoy the pianist as much as I did?' she asked.

'Oh, yes,' Anne agreed. 'I thought he was marvellous.'

'I've never heard the piano played like that before,' Helen continued. 'It was absolutely wonderful. I could have listened to him all evening.'

'Me too.'

'I wonder if he might be down on his luck?'

Anne turned to her in surprise. 'Why do you say that?'

'Why isn't he playing in some concert hall? He certainly has the talent and skill. Why is he wasting his time playing for wealthy holidaymakers who don't appreciate him? You saw the looks on some of their faces. They were bored. One old cow actually yawned.'

'Oh, c'mon,' Anne remonstrated. 'Isn't that a little harsh? She might have been tired.'

'That's no excuse. When you're fortunate enough to be in the presence of someone as gifted as that pianist, the least you can do is to show some appreciation.'

* * *

The following morning, they were up early and, after breakfast, set off along the coast to do some sightseeing. They had a light lunch in a nice little restaurant in Puerto Banús and spent the remainder of the hot afternoon reading in the garden in the shade of two large parasols.

When it came time for dinner, Helen insisted that they go down to the restaurant early to get the table closest to the piano. She fidgeted as she waited for the pianist to appear, and when he did, he gave a shy smile of recognition when he saw them and took his seat before the instrument. It was another magnificent performance and again Helen showed her appreciation by applauding loudly.

On the third evening, he spoke to them. When the performance was over, he stopped at their table and bowed politely. 'Did you enjoy the music, Señoras?'

'Enormously,' Helen replied. 'I think you have a wonderful talent. I could listen to you all evening.'

His face broke into a shy smile. 'You exaggerate, Señora. But it is very generous of you to say so.'

'I don't exaggerate. I speak my mind.'

'Your words give me much pleasure.'

'Not as much pleasure as you have given us.'

'Thank you.'

'Won't you join us for a glass of wine?' Helen suggested.

He hesitated.

It occurred to her that he might be forbidden to fraternise with the guests and she was asking him to break the rules. 'If that is allowed,' she added.

'You are very kind,' he replied, pulling out a chair and sitting down.

Anne drew the bottle from its bucket and poured a glass.

He raised it to his mouth and took a sip, then smacked his lips and held the glass at arm's length to view it. 'This is very good wine. Who chose it?'

'I did,' Anne said.

'You have excellent taste, Señora.'

Anne glowed at the compliment.

'A glass of wine is good after a performance,' he continued. 'You know, I am often nervous when I play. A glass of wine helps me relax.'

'You didn't appear nervous tonight,' Anne said.

'That is because the audience has been so warm and ... What is the word?'

'Appreciative?'

'Yes, appreciative. Sometimes the audience isn't interested in my music. Sometimes they chat and laugh. But you have always shown your approval.'

'What is your name?' Helen asked.

'I am Antonio Rivera y Porrón. Every Spaniard has two names, one each for the father and the mother, but it is simpler to call me Antonio.'

'That's very interesting. I'm Helen O'Neill and this is my best friend Anne O'Malley. We've really enjoyed your performance over these past few evenings. You have a great gift.'

He waved a hand. 'Not really. But I do love to play. The music is my life.'

'You speak very good English, Antonio.'

'You think so?'

'Yes, much better than our Spanish. Where did you learn it?'

'Mostly from visitors like you.'

'Do you live here in Marbella?'

'No, in Fuengirola.'

It was another tourist town further along the coast.

'Is that where you were born?'

'I was born in Ronda, a town in the mountains.'

'Do your family live there?'

He shook his head. 'My parents are dead and I have no brothers or sisters.'

It suddenly occurred to Helen that she was bombarding the poor man with questions. But she couldn't help herself. She was intrigued by him and curious to find out all about him. 'Where did you learn to play, Antonio?'

He puffed out his lips. 'It's a long story. I was fortunate to have an excellent music teacher at school. He taught me to play the piano and gave me lessons at his home. But for him I would never have learned to play. My father was a carpenter so we were quite poor. He could never have afforded to pay for my lessons.'

'That's a pity. But now you are a full time musician.'

He lowered his head. 'Not full time. I am fortunate to be able to play here in the evenings during the holiday season. And I'm able to save some money to get by during the winter. I'm not married so I don't have many expenses.'

'Couldn't you get permanent work with a band or an orchestra perhaps?'

He smiled. 'I'm afraid it is not so simple. You see, I have no formal qualifications. I have never trained. I have never been to the music college.'

'But why should that matter? Helen persisted. 'You are a magnificent pianist. Anyone with half an ear would recognise that. Surely if you tried you could find more regular work.'

'I *have* tried, believe me. I would love nothing better than to have a permanent job with an orchestra, but without proper qualifications, it is very difficult.'

Helen frowned. 'That's very unfair.'

He shrugged. 'Perhaps you are right. But that is how it is. Still,' he said, brightening, 'I am lucky. The manager of Puebla Maria, Señor Lopez, is very kind to me. He pays me a good wage and he feeds me in the kitchen. And sometimes I pick up other jobs playing at weddings or communions. Life is not so bad.' He finished his glass, stood up, then shook hands with each in turn. 'Thank you for the wine and for your kind words of encouragement. Now I must take my leave.'

They watched in silence as he walked towards the door and out of the restaurant. To Helen, listening to Antonio had been like hearing something from a child's story book, the talented pianist who could find no work because he was poor. She felt sad.

Chapter Five

The next day, they were up early to go on an excursion to Málaga. They had dressed in light frocks and sensible shoes because the young woman who had sold them the tickets at the reception desk had said walking would be involved and that today would be hot.

The coach arrived at nine o'clock. There were already some passengers on board and the driver stopped at several hotels along the way to pick up more. The coach was almost full when they left the coast road and joined the motorway. From there, they were able to look down at the sea and the little towns dotted along the shore. As they drew closer to their destination they began to see the spires and steeples of Málaga gleaming in the distance.

The driver finally parked near the railway station and the group set off through the streets of the city, the tour guide in front with a furled red umbrella held aloft so she could be easily identified if anyone got separated. They stopped first at the magnificent cathedral, which the guide announced had been built in the sixteenth century. When they had finished inspecting it, they walked through a series of narrow cobbled streets till they reached the Picasso Museum.

Here they stopped again and the guide informed them that Málaga was where the famous artist had been born and spent his early life. They trooped inside and spent half an hour viewing the paintings on display. Then it was off once more to climb the steps to the Alcazaba, an old Moorish fortress that had spectacular views over the city and the sea. Here, the guide announced they would take a break.

By now, it was almost one o'clock and the heat was quite intense. Anne was tired and Helen was peckish. They decided to separate from the tour and find somewhere cool to relax. They told the guide they wanted to do some shopping and would join the coach later for the return journey to Marbella. This was agreed and Anne and Helen set off.

They headed downhill towards the Alameda, a large public garden near the port. It was quiet there, shaded from the sun, and there was a cool breeze coming in from the sea. They found a small bar, with tables and chairs outside, where they sat down and ordered beers and sandwiches.

Anne stretched her legs and uttered a deep sigh. 'This is a relief,' she declared. 'There's only so much sightseeing I can take in one day.' She kicked off her shoes and wriggled her toes in the cool air.

'I fully agree,' Helen replied. 'But it's nice to be able to tell people where we've been when we get home. We don't want them thinking we spent the entire holiday sunbathing beside the pool.'

'Why not?'

'Because it sounds like a waste.'

The beers and sandwiches arrived, and while they ate, they observed the young Spanish couples strolling arm-in-arm under the shade of the trees. The women were slim and dark while the men looked proud and handsome. The sight brought Helen's thoughts back to last night's conversation in the restaurant. She fell silent for a few minutes until Anne woke her from her reverie. 'Something on your mind?' she enquired.

Helen turned to her. 'Yes, indeed. I've been thinking about what Antonio said last night.'

'What exactly?'

'The way he has been treated, the fact that he can't get a proper job because he has no formal training. I think it's very unjust.'

'He didn't seem to be terribly bothered.'

'Nonsense! You heard him say he would love nothing better than to have a permanent job with an orchestra.'

'He also said he thinks he's fortunate to be working at Puebla Maria.'

'He said that so we wouldn't feel sorry for him. You just have to look at him to see how sad he is. Besides, it misses the point. He's got so much talent. It's a shame that it's not available to a wider audience.'

'Well, that's life, I suppose.' Anne sighed.

'Oh, don't say that!' Helen exclaimed. 'I hate that expression. It's so defeatist. It implies that nothing can be done.'

'But nothing *can* be done. He hasn't got the qualifications to become a professional musician. Lots of people would like to fly a plane but they don't have the training.'

'That's different.' Helen was now getting excited. 'What Antonio needs is a patron, someone who will take him under their wing and promote his career. He just needs a break, that's all. I'm certain when people hear how good he is, they'll soon sit up and take notice.'

'And what kind person is going to be his patron, may I ask?'

Helen drained her beer and put the glass down with a thump. 'Me,' she said. 'I'll be his patron.'

Anne stared at her in amazement. '*You?*'

'Why not? I know lots of people who could help him. I met Archie McGonagle once at a party. He's the manager of the Garden Theatre. I'm sure he'd be sympathetic. And I have several contacts in RTÉ. All we would have to do is get him on one of their shows to play the piano and he'd never look back.' She rattled off more names as the idea took hold.

'You mean you'd take him back to Dublin with you?'

'Why not?'

'And where would he stay?'

'At Avalon. Where else?'

Anne's mouth fell open. 'You know you'll have every busybody in the area gossiping?'

'Let them. I've got five bedrooms, for Heaven's sake. He can stay with me while we bring him to a wider audience. He just hasn't been discovered yet. That's what's holding him back.'

'But what if he doesn't want to be discovered?'

'Why do you keep raising objections?' Helen snapped. 'Of course he wants to be discovered. Every artist does. It's the reason God put them on this earth in the first place.'

Anne decided to keep quiet. It was clear that her friend had got the bit between her teeth and wasn't going to be put off. It was the old Helen she knew from before she'd had her breakdown, buzzing with ideas and energy, organising events, dominating committees, getting everyone to fall in with her plans. Maybe it will do her good, she thought. I just hope she hasn't bitten off more than she can chew.

The subject was dropped and, eventually, they made their way back to the coach to find the other passengers boarding. Fifteen minutes later, the driver climbed into his seat, started the engine and began the return journey to Marbella. It was evening now and the sun was sinking fast into the sea, bathing the surrounding coastline in a soft yellow light.

By the time they were back at the resort, the women were looking forward to having a shower and getting dressed for dinner. As they went to their apartment, Helen turned to her friend and said, 'I'll put the proposition to Antonio tonight. I'll wait till he finishes playing, then break it to him. Once I outline my plans, I know he'll jump at the idea.'

Anne still had doubts. 'Are you sure that's wise?' she asked. 'Wouldn't it be better to think it over properly before rushing in?'

'I *have* thought it over,' Helen retorted. 'And my mind's made up. Strike while the iron is hot, that's my motto. There's no time to waste.'

As it turned out, the opportunity to speak to Antonio didn't arise. When they went down to dinner, they discovered that, instead of the pianist, the diners were to be entertained to a display of flamenco dancing.

Helen sat through the meal, glum and disappointed. What made it even worse was the other diners, who seemed to be thoroughly enjoying the colourful spectacle. At the end of the show, the applause was far greater than it had been for Antonio.

The two friends left the dining room and made their way back to their apartment. They had fallen into the practice of relaxing on the terrace before turning in. When Anne suggested a nightcap, Helen said she was tired and wanted to sleep. They went to bed downcast and subdued.

* * *

In the morning, there was another surprise. Overnight, Helen's mood had lifted, and when Anne went down with her for breakfast, she was bubbling over with excitement.

'I spent a good part of the night thinking about Antonio,' she announced, as she smeared honey on a croissant. 'I've been approaching the matter in entirely the wrong way.'

'I did say it was wise not to rush in,' Anne reminded her.

'Well, you were right and I've completely revised my plan.'

'And?'

'Now I know exactly how I should proceed.'

'Go on.'

Helen grinned. 'I'm going to organise a concert.'

'A concert?'

'Yes. Instead of pleading with people to give Antonio a break, I'm going to take matters into my own hands and do it myself. When we get back home, I'm going to hire a hall and he'll give a concert. I'll persuade all my friends to come – and make sure all the important figures in the music industry attend, along with the media. That way, Antonio will be guaranteed oodles of publicity. By the time I've finished they'll be beating down the doors to sign him up.'

Anne was beginning to wish they had never met Antonio. He was taking over the holiday. 'But you've no experience in this sort of thing,' she said. 'You've never organised anything more than a bring-and-buy sale.'

Helen gave her a withering look and reached for the coffee pot. 'If you think I'm going to allow a small detail like that to stop me, I'm afraid you can't know me very well.'

Chapter Six

Now that she had made up her mind, Helen decided to begin at once. After breakfast, she announced that she was not going sightseeing today but instead would spend the time planning her concert. By now, Anne was convinced that the idea was crazy but she was happy to take a break from tramping around cathedrals and ancient monuments. The two women settled on their terrace where Anne stretched out on a recliner with a book while Helen arranged a little table in the shade with a notebook and pen.

She decided to start by drawing up a list of the guests she would invite. In her notebook, she entered the names of her immediate family and friends. Then she moved on to everyone who owed her a favour. Next, she included all those people who might be able to help with publicity and promotion. She knew she would have to be ruthless. Nothing would be allowed to hinder the great work of launching Antonio's career.

She threw herself into the task with zeal, and when she had finished she was surprised to see almost three hundred names on the list of potential guests. Of course, not all of them would be able to come and others would simply buy tickets to please her but would not turn up on the night. However, she now had sufficient information to help her with her next step: choosing a venue.

She jotted down a list of places she thought might be suitable. This was unfamiliar territory but there were certain things she knew would be important. The hall would have to be easily accessible and there should be plenty of parking. The sound system had to be excellent. Most important of all, the venue should be just the right size. If it was too small, it would be cramped and uncomfortable. But if it was too big it would appear empty, no matter how many people came along.

Next, the question of costs. At this point she decided she needed more detailed information. There was a small suite of computers in the lobby beside the reception desk where guests could access the internet. She went down there and spent half an hour firing off emails to various venues, requesting details of accommodation, seating arrangements, hiring fees and availability. On the way back, she checked the entertainments board and was pleased to see that Antonio was scheduled to play the piano once more at dinner.

By now, it was almost lunchtime. So far, everything had gone extremely well. Helen felt she had spent a productive morning and now it was time for a little relaxation. She changed into her swimsuit and went out to the pool where she swam twenty lengths. Then the two women adjourned to the bar for a light lunch of wine and tapas.

'I must admit I'm very pleased with my morning's work,' Helen confessed, as she tucked into a plate of grilled sardines. 'Things are beginning to fall into place.'

'Well, that's good,' Anne agreed. She had decided not to raise any further objections to Helen's scheme. They just upset her and, besides, she never accepted them. But she was alarmed at the speed with which her friend was pushing ahead with her plans when she hadn't even raised the matter with Antonio. So she nodded when Helen reeled off a list of the people she planned to invite and the venues she was investigating. Privately she hoped that Helen wouldn't end up disappointed.

As dinner time approached, Helen's excitement increased. By now, any lingering doubts she might have harboured had disappeared. Not only was she helping a struggling musician gain the recognition he deserved but she was doing what she most enjoyed – organising things. She fussed around the apartment as she got ready and spent an inordinate amount of time choosing which dress to wear and adjusting her make-up. At ten minutes to seven, the women locked up and set off for the restaurant.

'I think I'll tell him tonight,' Helen announced, as they waited for the lift to arrive.

'If you think that's right,' her friend replied coolly.

'The sooner the better. There's so much to arrange and Antonio will be anxious to get to Dublin as quickly as possible.'

The restaurant was filling up. They chose the table closest to the piano and Anne, who was hungry, seized the menu and started to read. But Helen's appetite seemed to have disappeared. She took a glance at the card and opted for gazpacho soup and salad.

No sooner had the ladies been served than a door at the side of the room opened and Antonio appeared. He looked so handsome in his smart dress suit and gleaming white shirt, his eyes bright and his black hair slicked back from his forehead.

He appeared pleased to see the women and smiled to them as he approached.

Once he was seated, he stretched out his hands, bent over the piano and started to play. The notes of 'Clair de Lune' swelled and the diners fell silent. When he finished, a wave of applause went around the room. Tonight's audience seemed more appreciative than previous ones. Helen was delighted for Antonio but also for herself. It confirmed what her instinct had told her from the very start. Now others were recognising the amazing talent in their midst.

Once the applause had died away, Antonio immediately launched into Beethoven's Moonlight Sonata. The room went quiet again. Helen turned to her friend and gave a little smile. Antonio continued to play for almost two hours, and when he finally closed the lid of the piano and stood up to take a bow, another round of applause swept the room. By now Helen was beaming with pleasure. As he approached their table, she got up and clasped his hand. 'You surpassed yourself tonight,' she whispered. 'You were superb.'

'Thank you,' he replied shyly. 'The audience seemed to enjoy it.'

'Won't you join us for a glass of wine?'

'With pleasure, Señora.' He drew out a seat and sat down.

She noticed the beads of perspiration glistening on his smooth forehead. But now that the performance was over, he seemed to relax.

'What have you ladies been doing today?' he asked playfully. 'Did you go sightseeing?'

'We just took it easy,' Anne replied. 'We sat around on the terrace and caught up with some reading.'

Helen had been wondering how she should tell him of her

plan. She decided this was the moment. He had provided the opening himself by asking how they had spent their time. She took a deep breath, then launched straight into the little speech she had prepared. 'Actually, I spent the day working on a project I have in mind.'

'Oh?' Antonio said, turning his attention to her. 'And what is this project about?'

'You.'

'Me?' he replied, with a nervous laugh. 'I don't understand.'

'Let me explain,' she hurried on. 'Since the very first evening I heard you play, I have been wondering how your great gift can be brought to a wider audience. I was very touched by your sad story. And it's scandalous that you should be forced to play to a small gathering like this because of some petty nonsense over lack of formal training.'

Antonio's eyes were now firmly fixed on her as he listened intently.

'Your talent should be available to music lovers everywhere. So I have come up with a scheme which I hope will launch your career on the international stage. I'm going to bring you to Dublin and put on a concert for you there.'

There. She had told him. She sat back with a smile of triumph while she waited for the grateful reaction she expected would greet her declaration.

Antonio's cheeks had gone pale. 'But that's impossible,' he said. 'I can't leave Puebla Maria in the middle of the season. I'd never be employed again. Besides, no one in Ireland has ever heard of me. And where would I stay?'

Helen rushed on: 'You would stay with me. I have an empty house with plenty of room. I'll invite all my friends to the concert. I'll make sure that important people in the music world come. I'll invite the media. I know when people hear you play they will be so impressed that opportunities will immediately open for you.'

But Antonio was violently shaking his head. 'It's no good. It would never work. I can't do it. I'd be put on the black list here in Spain. It would be crazy.'

She took his hand. 'Antonio, let me speak honestly. You could spend the rest of your life playing to small hotel audiences like this but, unless you're incredibly lucky, your career will never go any further. Then, some day, you will be too old to play and the management will let you go. Do you want to look back with regret at the glittering career you might have had, if only you had seized the chance?'

'Of course not.'

'Then please consider what I'm saying. This is an opportunity that might never come again. Don't dismiss it without thinking hard. If you come with me, I promise I will spare no effort to promote your cause.'

But Antonio wasn't listening. He pushed back his chair and stood up. 'I am very grateful, Señora. I know you mean well. But this is too great a risk. There are too many obstacles, too many difficulties. It is impossible.' He bowed politely, turned his back and walked from the room while Helen stared after him, her face crumpled in disappointment.

Chapter Seven

Fuengirola was still buzzing with activity when Antonio got there shortly after eleven o'clock. From the pubs and bars along the seafront, the sound of music spilled out onto the pavement. But Antonio was oblivious to the laughter and merrymaking. A dark cloud of depression hung over him. He couldn't get Señora O'Neill's remarks out of his head. He wished she had left him alone. He wished she hadn't made her offer to bring him to Dublin. Everything was going so well. Why did she have to spoil it?

He knew she was a kind lady but she didn't understand. The manager, Señor Lopez, had been very good to him, giving him a regular job at Puebla Maria and paying him well. He made sure Antonio was looked after. How could he walk out on him when he had been so kind? And at the height of the tourist season, too? He would never be forgiven.

It would also mean giving up the room that had become his home. It was small but he was lucky to have it, and he was comfortable there. If he went to Dublin with Señora O'Neill and the concert failed, he would return to Spain with no job and nowhere to live. It would be madness.

He had been aware of Señora O'Neill and her friend from the very first evening they had dined in the restaurant because they applauded so loudly whenever he finished a piece. It was unusual for the guests to indicate their appreciation so enthusiastically. Indeed, some showed hardly any interest and others were downright rude, talking and laughing noisily throughout his performances.

But the Irish ladies were different. They were enthusiastic. He could tell from the look in their eyes that they enjoyed hearing him play. And then they invited him to drink a glass of wine with them when he had finished and began to ask questions about his background and where he had learned to play. He had seen many tourists come and go to Puebla Maria in the time he had been working there, many glamorous ladies and elegant men. But he had met no one like Señora O'Neill.

Her sincerity had struck him forcefully. He could tell she was an educated lady who knew about music. She was genuinely interested and wanted to help him. And she possessed spirit and determination. Thinking about her made him feel bad. He hoped he hadn't hurt her feelings by his blunt rejection of her offer. Perhaps he should talk to her tomorrow and try to explain better why he had turned her down.

The further he travelled from the seafront, the quieter and more deserted the streets became till at last he came to the outskirts of the town. Finally, he arrived outside a run-down building, paint peeling off the walls and lines of washing strung on the balconies. He searched in his pocket for the key. When he opened the door, the hallway was in darkness. He found the light switch and made his way to the lift, stepped in and rode to the top floor.

Antonio's room was at the end of the hall beside the bathroom. It was quiet and there was no one above him, which was why he liked it. The room consisted of a bed, a narrow desk and a chair, a small fridge, a sink and a stove in the corner. He took off his jacket, hung it neatly over the back of the chair, then went out again to the bathroom, where he had a shower.

When he was dry and in his dressing gown, he put some milk to boil on the stove and made a mug of hot chocolate. He felt tired. It had been a momentous day and so much had happened. When he had drunk his chocolate, he got into bed and within minutes he was fast asleep.

* * *

Bright sunlight filtering through the thin curtains woke him at eight o'clock. He had been dreaming about Señora O'Neill, and the words she had spoken were still echoing in his mind. *Do you want to look back with regret at the glittering career you might have had, if only you had seized the chance?*

Antonio threw back the sheets and got out of bed. He filled the kettle with water and set it to boil. Then he took out his phone and began to make some calls.

* * *

Helen was seated on the terrace of their apartment drinking coffee while she thought about the day ahead. She had been plunged into gloom after the events of the previous night, and Antonio's blunt refusal of her concert. She had felt so certain he would accept.

It had been a disaster. She blamed herself for the way she had handled it. She had been too impetuous, she realised. She should have prepared her approach more carefully, as Anne had suggested. But she had been swept along with the excitement of the idea and hadn't paused to think. She should have been more subtle and slowly planted the idea in Antonio's mind till he felt comfortable with it. But instead she had rushed in, like a bull in a china shop, and frightened him off.

It was such a shame. She knew she would have made a success of the concert. She would have moved Heaven and earth to make it work. And Antonio would have been the winner. Important people would have heard him play – people who were in a position to advance his career and open doors for him. People who could have given him access to the wider audience he deserved. Now he would remain stuck in the hotel restaurant, playing to ungrateful audiences who would never think of him again once they had left Puebla Maria. It was all so sad.

She tried to shake the morbid thoughts from her mind. Today they should take another bus trip and visit Gibraltar. She would put the idea to Anne when she returned from her swim. The trip would take their minds off the events of the previous night.

She glanced over the terrace rail and a strange sight met her eyes. A middle-aged man had come out of one of the apartments wearing a tiny pair of swimming trunks that barely covered him. Now he was spreading a towel on the grass. Surely he wasn't planning on sunbathing. Helen was certain it was forbidden. She was sure she had read something about it in the Rules and Regulations.

Just then her phone began to ring.

'I hope I haven't wakened you?' a polite voice said.

A shiver ran down her spine.

'Antonio?'

'Yes.'

'What a pleasant surprise. No, you haven't wakened me. We've been up for some time.'

'I wanted to apologise. My behaviour last night was very bad and now I regret it. It was because your offer came as such a shock to me.'

'You don't have to apologise, Antonio. It was my fault. I handled it very badly.'

'You forgive me?'

'Of course!'

'Well, that is good because I have changed my mind. I have decided to accept your kind offer, if it is still available.'

Helen's hand shook as she placed the coffee cup down on the saucer. 'You mean you'll come back to Ireland with me?'

'Yes.'

'That's fantastic. I'm so pleased.'

'I have explained the situation to Señor Lopez and he has given me leave to go to Dublin with you. It is inconvenient for him, of course, but he has agreed to keep my job for me. I have also arranged for a friend to take over the tenancy of my apartment. So now I am ready.'

Helen felt dizzy. She could feel the adrenalin surging as she struggled to gather her thoughts. 'Have you got a passport? Is it up to date?'

'I have it in my hand.'

'Excellent.'

'So, when do we leave?'

'Tomorrow. I'll get on to the airline at once and make the travel arrangements. And I'd better ring Reception and tell them we're leaving early. I'll contact you later, Antonio.'

As she was finishing the call, Anne came back from the pool, wrapped in a dressing gown. Helen rushed to her and hugged her. 'You need to start packing. We're going back to Dublin.'

'What?'

'Antonio has changed his mind. He's accepted my offer.'

'But I'm enjoying myself here.' Anne groaned. 'Couldn't we wait for a few more days?'

'No,' Helen replied firmly. 'I've got so much to organise and there's no time to waste. Which reminds me, I'd better call Kirsty and tell her we're coming home.'

Chapter Eight

Kirsty woke with a start and sat up in bed. She had been having a nightmare in which an intruder was breaking into her apartment with a pneumatic drill. She rubbed the sleep from her eyes and looked quickly around the room. It was empty, apart from the naked figure stretched out beside her in the bed. Robbie Hennessy was still fast asleep, his fine, manly torso exposed to the bright morning light seeping in through the curtains. But the noise was getting louder. She leaned closer and saw that Robbie's mouth was wide open and he was snoring.

All at once, her thoughts went rushing back to the previous evening. She had met Robbie after he'd finished work and they had gone to a restaurant in Howth village that was attracting rave reviews. He was still contrite and on his best behaviour. She couldn't wait to tell him about her mother and the strange man she was bringing back from Spain. 'Don't you think it's all very . . .' She had trailed off.

Robbie had been having difficulty in following the story

and wasn't sure how he was expected to respond. 'Romantic?' he suggested.

Kirsty frowned. 'I was going to say suspicious.'

He looked puzzled. 'I'm not sure how you mean.'

'Well, let's say it happened to your mum, how would *you* react?'

'That never would happen to my mum. She doesn't like Spain. She says it's too noisy.'

Kirsty gritted her teeth. Robbie could be very slow sometimes. She wondered if he was still hung-over from the night before. 'Oh, for God's sake, it's got nothing to do with Spain. It's the fact that she's met this man and we know absolutely nothing about him. And now she's bringing him home.'

'Oh, right,' Robbie said. 'I see what you mean. You think he might be leading her up the garden path?'

'I think he might be planning to rob her.'

Robbie looked shocked.

'Right,' he said. 'Now I see where you're coming from. So what do you want me to do? Would you like me to have a quiet word with him? Maybe suggest that he should get the next flight back to España before he has an accident?'

'I'd like you to tell me if I'm overreacting. I've spoken to my brother and sister and they don't seem too concerned. But the way I see it, my mum is very vulnerable. She's just coming to terms with my father's death and along comes this smooth-talking Romeo. Next thing he's wormed his way into her affections and she's installing him in her house.'

'I think you're damned right to be worried,' Robbie said, now that he felt on solid ground at last.

'Can you understand why? When my father died, he left my

mother comfortably off. Besides Avalon, he left her shares and investments. Between you and me, she's not stuck for a few bob.'

'There's a lot of this going on,' Robbie said grimly. 'There was something on Sky News last week about an old lady who was taken to the cleaners by one of these guys – he said he was in love with her. She met him on the internet. Turned out he was operating from a phone box in Lagos.'

'Exactly. It's become a minor industry. The trouble is, I don't know how I should approach it. I don't want to upset her, you see.'

'I understand,' Robbie said, squeezing her hand. 'Well, you've got me right beside you for support. When's he coming?'

'Tomorrow afternoon.'

'Relax. The minute you smell a rat, just tell me. I know some people who'll put the frighteners on him big time. He'll be back in sunny Spain quicker than you can say Fernando Torres.'

Kirsty felt a flood of affection for Robbie. He could be infuriating but at times like this it was good to have him in her corner. She looked up when the waiter approached with their first course. 'Remember what I said, Robbie. Two glasses of wine and no more.'

'Sure,' he replied. 'I can take it or leave it.'

They'd had a pleasant meal of prawn salad and grilled hake. To show his good intent, Robbie had had only a single glass of Chardonnay. Afterwards they had returned to her apartment overlooking the harbour. They had got undressed and he had taken her in his arms. She had felt his breath hot in her ear. They kissed and he began to caress her.

Now she stared at his prone form lying beside her and felt her pulse quicken. There was no doubt about it. Robbie was extremely handsome. A fine coating of blond hair covered his chest and extended along his strong shoulders and arms. His stomach was as flat as a board. She reached out to touch him, then stopped herself.

She hadn't got time for more rumpy-pumpy. She had a very important day ahead and needed to get busy. But, first, she had to put a stop to that terrible snoring before it woke the neighbours. She leaned over and pinched his nostrils between her forefinger and thumb. The noise stopped abruptly and he woke with a start.

'What's going on?'

'You were snoring loud enough to wake the dead.'

'Was I?'

'You do it all the time. It's disgusting.'

'I don't do it on purpose.'

'Talk to your doctor about it. There's treatment you can get.'

The clock on the bedside table said twenty-five past eight. She hopped out of bed and headed for the bathroom.

'I'm under pressure, Robbie. I told you my mum's arriving back from Spain today. If you want coffee, you'll have to make it yourself.'

'How long are you going to be in there?' he asked.

'Five minutes. Go into the kitchen and put the kettle on.'

She stepped under the shower and began soaping herself in the warm stream splashing from the spout. She rinsed herself, stepped out and wrapped a towel around her body.

Kirsty went to the kitchen and made herself some breakfast. As she poured herself a cup of coffee, another thought occurred to her. She must talk to Anne O'Malley. It was important to get her fix on events. Anne had witnessed the whole business at first hand and would be able to give her a blow-by-blow account of exactly what had happened.

Just then her phone began to ring. Mark was on the line. 'I said I'd get back to you about Mum,' he said.

'Yes?' she prompted.

'Well, I've been thinking it over and I've decided I'd better take a look at this Spanish fellow for myself. What time is Mum getting home?'

'She's due at Avalon at half past two.'

'I'll come out and meet them.'

'Have you changed your mind?'

'Let's just say I'd like to run a slide rule over him in case your fears turn out to have some substance.'

'In that case I'll see you there. I expect to be at Avalon around two o'clock.'

She smiled as she ended the call.

She turned to find Robbie beside her, washed, shaved and looking very smart in his elegant business suit. 'I'm off now,' he said, kissing her lightly on the cheek. 'Another day, another dollar. I'll give you a call this afternoon. Byeee.'

He was gone. She heard the front door close and the sound of his car revving up.

She finished her breakfast and went back to her bedroom to get dressed, her mind racing. In a few hours' time, her mother would be arriving home with this Spanish gigolo. Kirsty was convinced it was a monumental act of folly. Not only was she about to make herself a laughing stock in front of all her friends but she was in danger of losing her money as well. As her daughter, Kirsty had to protect her.

It was good to know that Robbie shared her suspicions and had promised to support her. And now her brother had reservations too. If she played her cards right, perhaps everything might work out in the end.

Chapter Nine

Antonio sat in his seat beside the window and watched the coast of Ireland come slowly into view. How green it was in contrast with the brown, sun-baked landscape they had left behind in Spain. Down below, he could see the ocean with white-capped waves rushing towards the sandy shore. As the plane started its descent, he began to make out other shapes – fields and hills, then rooftops.

He had been excited ever since he had made the decision to accept Señora O'Neill's offer to come with her to Dublin. Apart from a visit to Lisbon and another to Marseille, he had travelled very little. He had spent most of his life in the small region of Andalucía where he had been born. He remembered his childhood in Ronda, his father's small carpentry shop and the smell of sawdust.

His father had been a proud man who had worked hard from early in the morning till eight or nine at night, making furniture and repairing carts and ploughs for the neighbouring farmers. He took great satisfaction from his trade and the fine work he turned out. It gave him status in the town, even though his income was small. Besides, there were only three mouths to feed and they never went hungry. His father had expected Antonio to follow him into the carpentry trade. But he had reckoned without Señor Alvarez, the music teacher at the local school.

Señor Alvarez was a gentleman, tall, with a dark moustache. He always dressed well in a neatly tailored suit and waistcoat, and had spotted Antonio's talent when he was very young and encouraged him. 'You have a fine ear, Antonio,' he would say. 'And the music is in your head. That is a rare gift. You should nurture it. Not everyone is so lucky.'

His kind words had made Antonio feel special. He looked forward to Señor Alvarez's lessons – he enjoyed them far more than maths and geography. Music came easily to him. It wasn't a chore. There was an old piano in the music room and Señor Alvarez had taught him to play. As Antonio got older, the teacher began to invite him to his home.

He lived in a fine house at the edge of the town. It had a sitting room and in it was the teacher's great joy – a maple-wood piano. On his very first visit, Señor Alvarez had sat down and run his fingers lovingly over the keys, then played a local folk tune. It was astonishing. The piano was far superior to the one they had at school, and the sound it made was like nothing Antonio had ever heard before. He felt his senses swell as the notes echoed in the room. When he had finished, Señor Alvarez stood up and invited Antonio to take his place.

The boy sat down nervously and spread his fingers as the teacher had shown him. Then he began to play a short piece he had learned at school. At the end Señor Alvarez had clapped and shaken Antonio's hand. 'That was beautiful,' he said. 'Like the breath of the angels.'

After that, Antonio began to spend more and more time at the teacher's house. His playing grew increasingly confident as his skill improved. Each morning when he woke, he looked forward to the day ahead and longed for the time he would spend with Señor Alvarez when school was over. The teacher moved from simple tunes to more difficult melodies until eventually Antonio was playing pieces by Beethoven and the other great composers.

But his absences from home were causing tension. His father was anxious for Antonio to help him in the carpentry shop. 'Why waste time with that piano?' he would say. 'What is the use of it?'

'I enjoy it,' Antonio replied. 'Señor Alvarez says I have talent.'

'But how will it put bread on the table?'

Antonio had no answer to that so he tried to put it out of his mind. But it wouldn't go away, and as time went by, he began to encounter another difficulty. One day, the music teacher sat down beside him. 'I have taught you all I can,' he confessed. 'If you want to improve, you must go to the music college. I know some people there. I will speak to them and write you a letter of recommendation. You will have no difficulty being accepted.'

Antonio knew that his teacher was paying him a great compliment. But he also knew it was impossible. The fees for the music college were far more than his father could ever afford even if he agreed to let him go.

'I will never go to college,' he said.

The teacher nodded, as if he was able to read Antonio's mind. 'I understand. It's sad. But you must continue to play.

You can come here to my house anytime you want. The piano will always be here for you.'

When he was sixteen, Antonio left school and began to work full time at his father's shop. But at every opportunity, he visited his teacher and the piano. By now, his father was anxious to retire and hand the business over to his son. Antonio could see that a crisis in his life was approaching. He had to decide whether to devote his life to the carpentry shop or to music.

When he was alone, he spent anxious hours debating his future. Antonio knew that his father would be bitterly disappointed if he didn't follow him into the shop. But he also knew that he would never be happy unless he was playing the piano. The words of Señor Alvarez were constantly in his ear: 'You have a rare gift. You should nurture it. Not everyone is so lucky.'

One day, he sat down with his father and told him of his decision. His father looked sad as Antonio explained that he couldn't continue to work in the carpentry shop. 'So what will you do?'

'I will go to Málaga and find work playing the piano.'

'I wish you well, my son. If only I had the money, you could learn more and be happy.'

Tears had welled in Antonio's eyes and he had turned his face away.

A few months later, his father had sold the shop to another carpenter from the nearby town of Antequera. He got a good price and was able to retire. Antonio packed his bags, said farewell and moved to the big city beside the coast.

He began to pick up work playing in bars and restaurants. The money he earned was poor and he had certain expenses to pay. He had to dress well and, of course, he had to find somewhere to live and feed himself. He managed to rent a room from a friend of the man who owned one of the bars where he played and he used the small sum of money his father had given him to tide him over. But he lived a hand-to-mouth existence, and doubted he would be able to survive as a pianist. There were many nights when he went to bed hungry.

Gradually, though, word spread about his talent and he picked up more work, playing at wedding receptions and birthday parties for wealthy shopkeepers and business people, who liked to add a touch of class to their celebrations. Antonio's situation began to improve.

Then one day he received news that his mother had cancer. He hurried back to Ronda to be by her side. When he saw her, he barely recognised the bright, cheerful woman who had raised him. She seemed to have shrunk and her face, which was always smiling, was now thin and wrinkled. Despite the best efforts of the doctors who attended her, the disease progressed rapidly and she died.

Antonio was heartbroken. He was an only child and his mother was very dear to him. His father was shattered. He stopped going out to the café to play cards with his friends and stayed inside his house all day.

Antonio felt guilty that he was away in Málaga while his father was alone in the little house and constantly reproached himself for rejecting the carpentry shop. About sixteen months later, he received a phone call from the parish priest to tell him that his father, too, was dead – struck down by a heart attack. Now he was totally alone in the world.

He inherited his father's little house and the money he had saved from the sale of the carpentry shop. One of the neighbours wanted to buy the house. Antonio knew he was offering less than it was worth. But it didn't matter. He had decided to leave Ronda for good. The town held too many sad memories for him. But before he left, he visited Señor Alvarez. They went into the parlour and the old music teacher invited him to play the piano. He sat down, touched the keys and began. When he eventually stood up, Señor Alvarez shook his hand. Antonio said goodbye and left Ronda for ever.

He continued to play in the bars and restaurants of Málaga, using the money he had inherited to supplement his income. But it was a precarious existence and Antonio dreamed of a regular job with better pay and more appreciative audiences.

Then he had a stroke of fortune. A smartly dressed man started to call into one of the bars where he played. He would sit at a table near the door, drinking a glass of wine while he listened to Antonio perform.

One evening, he introduced himself as Lopez and said that Antonio had been recommended to him by several people who had heard him play. He was the manager of the Puebla Maria holiday resort in Marbella, he said, and wanted to hire Antonio to entertain the guests in the evenings while they were having dinner. 'This is a regular job, six nights a week, for the whole summer season. What are you earning here?'

Antonio told him.

'I'll double it,' Lopez said. 'And I'll give you dinner, as much as you can eat. What do you say?'

'I accept,' Antonio said.

He began to play each evening at Puebla Maria. The restaurant there had a fine upright piano with a magnificent tone. He played for two and a half hours and afterwards he went into the kitchen where the chef let him choose whatever he wanted to eat and gave him a bag of chops and chorizo sausages to take home. It was the best job Antonio had ever had.

That had been three years ago. Señor Lopez had kept his word and Antonio had played the long summer season at the resort ever since. In the winter, when the tourists had left, he continued to find work playing in bars. His life was fine. He could manage. He wasn't a wealthy man but he never went hungry and he had his music. He was contented with his lot. Now he had given it up to go to a strange country where he knew no one except Señora O'Neill and her friend Señora O'Malley.

Over the public-address system, the pilot was instructing the passengers to fasten their seatbelts in preparation for landing. Helen turned to him and smiled. 'We're almost there, Antonio. How do you feel?'

'Happy,' he said.

Chapter Ten

By half past nine, Kirsty had dressed and breakfasted. She poured another cup of strong coffee and went into the spare bedroom, which she had converted into an office. This was where she ran her business. It contained a scanner, printer, laptop computer and a wall of shelving, littered with drawings and photographs of waif-like women modelling stylish clothes.

She sat down at her desk and stared at the yachts bobbing up and down in the harbour. Now she had the peace and quiet she needed to give her full attention to the issue that had been dominating her thoughts ever since she had heard her mother was coming home: how to deal with the interloper who had charmed his way into her affections and who was now about to be installed in her house.

The main thing was to work out a strategy. If she could only get her siblings to support her, they might be able to call a family council and convince their mother of the disaster that threatened if she proceeded with her crazy plan. But she would have to persuade her brother and sister and, so far, the omens were not good. Deirdre seemed to think the whole escapade was a great joke, although there were signs that Mark might be waking up to the dangers now that he knew the family money might be at stake. There had always been a venal streak in Mark where cash was involved.

But, whatever happened, she must avoid a confrontation: it would irritate her mother and cause her to dig in her heels. Instead, she would have to conceal her feelings and pretend to welcome Antonio. In the meantime she would observe him at every opportunity and gather evidence. And when she was ready, she would pounce. But it was going to be difficult.

If she had her way, she would have Antonio on the next plane back to Spain as soon as his feet touched Irish soil. But that wasn't possible. She had no choice but to bide her time and play a longer game. Eventually, the Spaniard would show his true colours and Kirsty would seize her opportunity. She just had to be patient.

Once she had made this decision, she felt better. She made a few phone calls to her stable of designers, then sent some emails. It felt good to be working. It kept her mind occupied while the arrival of the Málaga flight drew closer. She worked steadily through the morning until half past one when she stretched and stood up from her desk. She wanted to get to Avalon early so she could air the rooms and be ready to welcome her mother with a smile.

She went into the bedroom to put on her make-up and pick up her handbag. As she emerged, the phone began to ring.

'Hello, Kirsty,' Cecily Moncrieffe began. 'Have you got a moment? I just want to run over some details of what we agreed yesterday so that we're both on the same page. It will save a lot of hassle later.'

Kirsty's heart sank. This was the last thing she needed right now. She willed herself to be calm. Cecily was her most important client and she had just placed a large order so she couldn't afford to upset her. She waited patiently while the older woman checked the various garments she had ordered and added a few more to the list.

Then, just as Kirsty thought the conversation was about to end, Cecily launched into a long and rather scandalous tale about rival boutique owner Trixie Lefarge. Kirsty glanced at her watch and saw the minutes ticking away. If she didn't get off the phone soon, she was going to be late. Then suddenly she heard Cecily say, 'Of course, you will keep all this to yourself, won't you? I wouldn't tell you except I know you'll be discreet. Now, I really can't sit here gossiping all day. I've got work to do. Goodbye.'

Kirsty heaved a sigh of relief. Free at last. She locked up the apartment, went out to the carport and settled into the driving seat of her Aston Martin. Two minutes later she was driving up the hill towards Howth Summit.

**

Avalon was one of the most prestigious houses on the hill and could be seen for miles around. It sat on a promontory overlooking the sea and was approached by a winding driveway that rose steeply until suddenly the house came into view. When Kirsty arrived at a quarter past two, Mark was waiting for her at the front door. 'I thought you said two o'clock,' he began, as she stepped from the car.

'I had a last-minute call from an important client,' she replied. 'I couldn't be rude.'

'I've been here since ten to two,' he complained, glancing at his watch.

Kirsty gave him an apologetic grin, then walked towards the front door. Mark was thirty-three and had inherited their father's features. He was five feet eight, the same height as Kirsty, with fair skin and freckles. He followed her into the house where she was already opening the windows. The house had only been closed for a week but a musty smell was gathering.

'What are you doing?' he asked.

'Letting in some fresh air. We want to create a good impression for our visitor.'

He gave her a strange look. 'I didn't know you cared so much. Yesterday you sounded like you didn't want him here at all. You said you suspected he was trying to get his hands on Mum's money.'

'I still do.'

'How much is involved, do you think?'

'Oh, several million at least, if you include the house.'

'That much?'

'Maybe more when you count the shares and investments. But you said it was none of my business and Mum could do as she pleased.'

He began to shift his ground. 'Well, in a general sense that's true. She's an adult. But that doesn't mean we should stand idly by if we think this guy's up to no good. We have a duty as her children to protect her.'

'So you *have* changed your mind,' Kirsty said.

Mark shifted from one foot to the other, clearly uncomfortable. 'I didn't realise it was Mum you were talking about. You just said it was a woman you knew. It's different when it comes to family. That's our inheritance at stake. I must say, I'd be appalled to see it going to a stranger.'

'Those are my views precisely.'

'But we have to be fair. We know nothing about the man. I think it's only right that we should give him the benefit of the doubt until we have evidence to the contrary.'

At that moment, they heard a car approaching. Kirsty checked her watch and saw it was now twenty past two. Perhaps the Málaga flight had arrived early. But when she rushed outside it was her sister's car she saw coming up the drive. That was unexpected. It stopped beside Kirsty's, the door opened and a chubby leg appeared, quickly followed by Deirdre.

Kirsty stared at her. She was the eldest, and Kirsty found her slightly intimidating. Deirdre had always bossed the others when they were children. She was definitely putting on weight again. It's preparing meals for three young children that does it, she thought. Too much temptation. But she knew it was a touchy subject so she said nothing.

'Am I on time?' Deirdre asked, looking around. 'Mum's not home yet?'

'We're expecting her at any moment.'

'Good. I thought I'd just nip over and see her. I'll pick the kids up from school on my way back.'

As she spoke, Mark came out of the house.

'So, the whole family's here,' Deirdre declared. 'This is a nice welcoming party. Mum will be pleased.'

'I've come to lend a hand,' Mark replied defensively. 'I'm sure she'll be tired after the journey.'

'You're quite the devoted son, aren't you?'

Mark ignored the barb. 'And why are *you* here?'

'To get a peek at this *caballero* she's bringing back. I wonder what he looks like. I must say, I find the whole business hilarious. Imagine pulling a bloke at her age. It just goes to show it's never too late.'

'Let's hope the neighbours don't share your view,' Kirsty said caustically. 'I don't want to see Mum making a fool of herself.'

'Oh, give us a break!' Deirdre groaned. 'You're taking the whole thing far too seriously. Who cares what the neighbours think? It's none of their damned business. If Mum is happy, so am I. She's been through a hard time, poor thing. She needs something to cheer her up.'

It's a pity you didn't show the same consideration when I was nursing her through her breakdown, Kirsty thought bitterly. I could have done with your support. But she was distracted by the arrival of yet another car. A blue taxi had turned into the drive. The little group fell silent as it approached, stopping outside the garage. The driver hopped out and opened the back door. First Anne got out, then Helen, both of them sporting suntans. Then a third figure appeared.

Kirsty gasped. The man who emerged was dressed in a dark suit. He was tall and slim, with olive skin, brown eyes and well-groomed black hair. He was easily the handsomest man she had ever seen. She glanced at Deirdre and saw that her mouth had fallen open. She was staring at him with unconcealed admiration. It confirmed Kirsty's worse fears. This guy was too good to be true.

He just had to be a gigolo.

Chapter Eleven

Helen stood for a moment, surveying her surroundings. The roses were coming into bloom and two fat blackbirds were pecking at the lawn, which, she noticed, could do with a trim. It was amazing how quickly the grass grew at this time of year. Across the bay she could see the spires of Dún Laoghaire sparkling in the sun. Spain had been wonderful but it was good to be back in Dublin.

She had always found travelling very stressful and today had been no exception. They had been up early to take a taxi to the airport. Then there had been the inevitable queuing at the security checks and Passport Control, although the staff had managed everything very efficiently. While she rested with Anne, Antonio had gone to fetch coffee and muffins, which they had consumed before they boarded their plane. Now she was at home.

And there was a reception committee to welcome her! Deirdre and Kirsty were hurrying to meet them while Mark paid the taxi driver. What a pleasant surprise, Helen thought, to have all my children turn out to greet me.

'Hi, Mum, it's great to have you home again.' Kirsty hugged her mother and kissed her cheek, then turned to Anne and kissed her too. 'Lovely to have you back, Anne.'

'Yes,' Deirdre agreed. 'And look at the lovely colour you've got. You're as brown as a berry. How was the holiday?'

'It was wonderful. I'll tell you all about it later. But, first, I want you to meet Antonio. He's the reason we came home early.'

The dark-haired man was waiting at the edge of the group. Helen drew him forward. Up close, he looked even more stunning. He took Kirsty's hand in a firm grasp and smiled as he bent to kiss her cheek politely. Then he turned to her sister.

'You must be Deirdre,' he said. 'Your mother has told me about you.'

Deirdre stared at him, like a rabbit caught in a car's headlights. 'You're very welcome to Ireland,' she stammered.

'Thank you,' he replied.

'And, finally, this is my son,' Helen continued, as Mark joined them, carrying their luggage.

Antonio made a little bow and shook Mark's hand. 'It is my pleasure,' he said.

He certainly has excellent manners, Kirsty thought. No wonder he charmed Mum.

Helen clapped her hands. 'So now that you've all been introduced, I suggest we go inside and have a nice cup of tea while I tell you all about my idea.'

Kirsty watched the others troop through the front door and into the large drawing room. Deirdre was still engrossed in the Spaniard, her eyes firmly fixed on his face. Mark seemed distinctly ill at ease. Only Anne seemed resigned to the situation. 'I'll go and put the kettle on,' she said, and headed for the kitchen.

Kirsty went after her. 'I've been dying to talk to you,' she said, closing the door and lowering her voice. 'What on earth is going on?'

'It's this project your mother's got hold of.' Anne was taking cups and saucers from the cupboard.

'What project?'

'I'd better let her explain it. She'll tell you when the tea is ready. But I want to make one thing quite clear. I had nothing to do with it.'

Kirsty looked at her suspiciously. 'And who is Antonio?'

'A musician.'

'A *musician*?'

'She met him at the complex where we were staying. He played the piano in the restaurant.'

'My God, how did he persuade her to bring him here?'

'Oh, he didn't,' Anne replied. 'It was the other way round. The whole thing was her idea. In fact, he turned her down at first, then changed his mind.'

Kirsty's face fell. This was even worse than she'd imagined. The idea of her mother chasing after some piano player of half her age sounded too awful for words. It was so demeaning. What on earth had possessed her? 'Why didn't you stop her?' she demanded. 'You're her best friend. I would have expected you to keep an eye on her.'

'Are you kidding? You know what your mother's like once she gets an idea in her head. I didn't want to come back. I was enjoying myself. But once she'd made up her mind, there was no stopping her.'

'What do you know about Antonio?'

'Very little.'

'Is he married? Has he got a wife anywhere?'

'He didn't say.'

'Listen, Anne, you've got to help me. I'm worried about her. She's not in the habit of picking up strange men and bringing them home. I wouldn't like anything bad to happen to her.'

'Relax, she's fine. The holiday did her good. In fact, I think she's got her old spirit back again.'

Kirsty was anxious to question Anne further but just then the kettle boiled. It would have to wait till later. Anne filled the teapot and handed it to Kirsty, along with a tray of cups and saucers and biscuits, and they went to the drawing room.

Talking to Anne had only increased Kirsty's concern. There was no way her mother would have brought a complete stranger back to Avalon unless something dramatic had made her do it. Somehow the Spaniard must have persuaded her.

They found Helen seated on the sofa, Antonio beside her, smiling broadly. She waited till the tea was poured, then began to speak. Every face in the room fastened on her.

'No doubt you're all wondering what Antonio is doing here. So, I'll get straight to the point. On our very first evening at Puebla Maria, Anne and I went down to dinner and there we had the most amazing experience.' She smiled at her friend for confirmation. 'Antonio was playing the piano for the guests and, from the very first note he struck, we realised we were listening to something unusual. As he continued to play, it dawned on me that we were in the presence of a unique talent. We were listening to a very rare phenomenon – a truly gifted musician.'

At these words, Antonio blushed and lowered his head.

'Each evening when we went to hear him play, my conviction grew stronger. When we spoke to him and he told us his story, I was struck by the terrible injustice of his situation. Because of an accident of birth, Antonio's family had no money to allow him develop his great talent by going to music college. As a result, he was compelled to earn his living by playing for tourists at a holiday resort.'

Kirsty glanced at Deirdre to gauge her reaction but her eyes were still glued to the Spaniard. Meanwhile, her mother had launched into an impassioned speech about the obstacles that Antonio faced and how his lack of musical training prevented him playing in the great concert halls of the world where he rightly belonged.

Suddenly a light bulb went on in Kirsty's head. She had been trying to figure out how Antonio had pulled off this remarkable coup and now she had the answer. The crafty Spaniard had inveigled his way into her mother's affections by playing on her sympathy for the underdog. It was a clever trick. It had got him to Dublin and right into Avalon. And unless she did something to stop him, it wouldn't be long before he was raiding her mother's bank account.

'I was very moved by Antonio's predicament,' Helen went on. 'I wanted to do something to help him. An idea began to form in my head. I decided to bring him here to Howth and launch his musical career in Ireland. So I'm going to organise a concert for him. I'll invite all the important people in the music business and I know when they hear him play they'll recognise his genius.'

There was a hush in the room. Kirsty couldn't believe what she was hearing. Not content with installing the Spaniard in the family home, her mother was going to organise a concert for him? She was out of her mind.

At that moment, there was the sound of a chair scraping on the floor. Kirsty saw her sister stand up, gather her handbag and hurry from the room. She went after her and caught up with her in the hall.

'So now you understand,' she said triumphantly.

Deirdre stared at her. 'What are you talking about?'

'Antonio! He's wormed his way into Mum's confidence. He's an imposter. He's after her money. That cock-and-bull story about being an impoverished musician is a load of nonsense. He's only just arrived and already she's planning to put on a concert for him. You recognised it too.'

'Quite the contrary,' her sister replied. 'I thought his story was very moving. Mum has my full support. I think what she's doing is tremendously generous.'

Kirsty gasped. 'So why did you walk out?'

'I told you earlier. I've got to pick the kids up from school.'

Kirsty returned to the drawing room, feeling totally despondent. Helen had finished speaking and was now in a huddle with Anne and Antonio. Mark was standing by the window, staring out over the lawn. When she entered, her mother came to meet her. 'Is Deirdre all right?' she asked. 'She left in a hurry. She wasn't ill or anything?'

'No, she's gone to pick up the boys.'

'Of course – I'd forgotten. With all the excitement, my mind is distracted. Now, what did you think of my little announcement?'

'I was ...' Kirsty struggled to find the right words '... completely bowled over.'

Her mother beamed. She draped an arm around Kirsty's

shoulders and drew her closer. 'That's fantastic. I knew I could rely on you, darling. There's going to be a lot of work to do. Something like this doesn't happen without a great deal of planning. You've got to chase after people and twist their arms.'

Kirsty opened her mouth but no words came out. She was so shocked that she couldn't speak. Helen was now in full flow.

'It's all in a wonderful cause and I'll be calling on you for support. I expect you to use your influence with people in the fashion industry. Once they're on board, others will follow. Your brother has already pledged to help in any way he can.'

At that moment, Mark turned from the window and looked in their direction. Kirsty felt her stomach churn. So, she was on her own. Her mother was about to be the victim of a massive confidence trick and she was the only one who could see it. 'I have to leave now,' she said abruptly. 'I've got some calls to take care of.'

'That's all right. You mustn't neglect your business,' Helen said, giving her a little hug. 'It's been a busy day so we're all going to take a little rest now. But tomorrow the project starts in earnest. You can expect to hear from me.'

Kirsty left Avalon, got into her car and started back down the hill. She felt so frustrated she could have wept.

Chapter Twelve

As soon as Kirsty got to her apartment she went straight into the kitchen, opened the fridge and poured a large glass of chilled white wine. She took it into her office, sat down at her desk and stared out of the window at the harbour. She had read in a magazine that it was bad to drink when you were upset but this was an emergency. And by the way things were shaping up, there were going to be plenty more in the days ahead.

She was shocked at her siblings' response. Mark had turned out to be a proper snake in the grass, but Deirdre was in a different category: she had clearly been in awe of Antonio from the moment she had met him. Her mouth had dropped open as if she was a giddy schoolgirl in the presence of a rock star. It had been embarrassing to watch her. She wondered what her husband, Paul, would have thought if he had seen her.

No, she wasn't surprised at her sister's foolish reaction although she was very disappointed. But Mark was another matter. He had given her to believe that he shared her suspicions of the Spaniard and what he was up to. He had agreed with her that their inheritance could be at stake. He had said he would be appalled to see it go to a stranger. And then he had signed up for this crazy notion to put on a concert to launch Antonio's career.

Her mother had definitely taken leave of her senses. It was one thing to organise a bring-and-buy sale for the local school but a concert? Who did she think she was – Bob Geldof? Had she any idea what was involved and how much it would cost to hire a hall, get tickets printed and arrange advertising and publicity? She was looking at thousands of euros just to set it up. And who was going to come? Nobody in Dublin had ever heard of Antonio. Even in Spain, his homeland, he had made his living playing to tourists in a holiday resort.

The whole thing was madness. Why was she the only one who could see that? Even Anne O'Malley, who could usually be relied on to be sensible, seemed to have fallen for it. Kirsty took a mouthful of wine as a further thought occurred to her. From the moment she had received the phone call saying her mother was bringing a man home, she had sensed that something wasn't right. Cutting short your holiday and inviting a complete stranger to live in your house wasn't the behaviour you would expect of a rational person.

Now the doubts were multiplying fast. Had her mother really recovered from her breakdown? Had her mind been fully restored? Was she, perhaps, a little unhinged? She wondered if she should call Peter Humphries and tell him what was going on.

She groaned as another thought struck her. Her mother was expecting her to assist with this mad venture. Well, she was going to put a stop to that. She would tell her to take her name off the list. Kirsty couldn't in all conscience assist her mother in making a total fool of herself. It was time to revise her strategy. She had decided to be pleasant and avoid confrontation but things were rapidly getting out of hand. She would start by calling her brother and having a serious talk with him.

He answered immediately.

'O'Neill Consultancy.'

'It's me, Kirsty. Where are you?'

'On my way back to work.'

'We need to talk,' she said.

'Fire away.'

'Why have you changed your mind about this imposter piano player? Why have you agreed to Mum's deranged notion to organise a concert for him?'

'*What?*'

'You heard me. Mum said you had pledged to support her.'

Immediately, he went on the defensive. 'So I did. What's the big problem?'

'Everything. It's delusional. She'll never get it off the ground. She's going to waste her time and money. But that's only the start. Can't you see how this guy is insinuating his way into her confidence? He's already living in her house. Now she's organising a concert for him. Next thing, they'll have a joint bank account. I thought you agreed with me that our inheritance is at stake.'

'Hold on a minute,' Mark interrupted. 'I also said we should give him the benefit of the doubt. So far I've seen nothing to make me suspicious. He seems a genuine sort of guy. He's down on his luck and Mum has agreed to help him. What's wrong with that?'

'He's *using* her. Surely you can see what he's up to. He's playing on her sympathy. That's how these gigolos work.'

'Calm down, Kirsty. You're jumping to conclusions. Believe me, if I saw anything to make me uneasy, I'd be right on your side, but I trust Mum's judgement. She's not the fool you take her for.'

'But that's the point. Her judgement's impaired. She's recovering from a breakdown after Dad's death. She's in no fit state of mind to be making big decisions like this.'

There was a pause.

'Do you realise what you're saying, Kirsty?'

'Of course I do.'

'You're suggesting she's mad. That's a terrible thing to say about your own mother.'

'I didn't say she was mad. I said her judgement was impaired.'

'It amounts to the same thing. I have to say her behaviour seems perfectly rational to me.'

'So you're going to help her with this?'

'I'm going to lend a hand with publicity, fundraising and stuff like that. I think what she's doing is very noble. She's helping a poor musician launch his career. I think that's very generous. If there were more people like Mum, the world would be a far better place.'

Kirsty gave up. She was fighting a losing battle. Talking to her brother was like having a conversation with a brick wall. 'But we know absolutely nothing about him,' she wailed. 'We don't even know if he can play the piano.'

She disconnected, drained her glass and poured another. By now, she was getting desperate. Things were going from bad to worse. Was Antonio some kind of witch doctor? Not only had he mesmerised her mother but he appeared to have cast a spell over Deirdre and Mark as well. She stared out of the window at the seagulls scavenging in the litter bins along the pier as she tried to decide what to do next. She needed to talk to someone who was impartial and professional, someone who had not been taken in by the slick Spaniard and his charming ways. She needed to talk to Peter Humphries. He was the family doctor. He could be relied on to give a balanced opinion.

His secretary quickly put her through.

'Hello, Kirsty,' he said. His voice was soft and reassuring and she immediately felt secure. Here at last was someone who would understand her point of view. 'How is your mum enjoying her little holiday? I take it the weather's fine down there in Spain.'

'She's home.'

'Already?' She heard the note of concern in his voice. 'Wasn't she supposed to go for two weeks?'

'That was the plan. But something happened to bring her back. That's what I wanted to talk about.'

'Go on.'

'She met someone down there, a young Spanish musician. He played the piano in the holiday resort. She's brought him back with her.'

'Really?' Dr Humphries sounded surprised.

'Yes, and she's installed him at Avalon.'

'How long is he staying?'

'Indefinitely.'

'What?'

'She claims he's a musical genius and she's cooked up this plan to launch his career. She's going to organise a concert for him.'

The doctor listened patiently while Kirsty continued her story, concluding, 'So, you see, I'm a little worried, particularly after Mum's recent illness and my father's death and everything. I thought I'd ask your advice. You don't think her behaviour is a bit odd?'

'That depends. Is she displaying any other signs? She hasn't taken to her bed like the last time?'

'No. It's just the opposite. She's boiling over with energy and ideas. She can't wait to get started.'

'Do you want me to visit her?'

'No,' Kirsty said quickly. 'You're not supposed to know she's home. She'd realise I've been talking to you. I really wanted to find out if I should be concerned for her mental state.'

'Why do you say that?'

'Well, this is very strange behaviour to say the least.'

'I'm not sure I would fully agree with you.'

'No?'

'Not really. In fact, from what you've told me, this plan of hers might be just what she needs to recover. It's shaken her up and got her motivated again. You know how busy your mum used to be before your father died. Well, it sounds like she's getting back to her old self again.' He paused for a moment. 'This concert project might do her a power of good.'

Kirsty ended the call feeling totally defeated. She had run out of road. Nobody seemed to share her conviction that this bizarre business was going to end in tears. As for her suspicions about Antonio, she hadn't even dared to raise them with Peter Humphries for fear that he would laugh at her.

She looked at the bottle of wine that sat before her on the desk. She'd had two glasses already and if she had another she'd be blitzed. What she needed was someone to comfort her, listen to her woes and offer her support.

She lifted the phone again and rang Angie Dunlop.

Chapter Thirteen

Angie Dunlop was a slim, petite blonde, who worked hard at looking younger than her thirty-two years. She dressed in short skirts and tight blouses, and had succeeded so well that often she was refused admission to nightclubs and had to produce her driving licence to prove her age.

Kirsty had known her since she was fifteen. They had met at secondary school, gone to teenage dances together, consoled each other when adolescent crushes turned sour and remained close pals right through their college years. Now Angie was a senior negotiator with the RightHouse estate agency, which was gradually getting back on its feet after the recession. Kirsty regarded her as her best friend.

It was six o'clock when she pulled into the apartment block in Clontarf where Angie lived. Her friend opened the door and brought her straight into the lounge.

'Drink?' she asked, raising an eyebrow. 'You sounded frazzled on the phone.'

'I'd better not. I've had two glasses already and I've got to drive back to Howth.'

'Tea, then?'

'Yes, please, and make it strong.'

Angie disappeared into the kitchen and Kirsty glanced around the lounge. It was stylishly furnished with light, airy fabrics and bright pictures on the white walls. Angie had always possessed good taste and an eye for decoration. A few minutes later, she returned with a tray containing teapot, cups, saucers and plates and a large chocolate cake.

Kirsty opened her mouth to protest but her friend silenced her. 'Don't even attempt to argue. If I read your mood correctly, you're in need of some TLC and this is just what the doctor ordered.'

'Not my doctor. He'd strike me off his list if he knew I was eating this stuff.'

'Then don't tell him,' Angie replied, taking a knife to the cake and cutting two large slices, one of which she passed to Kirsty. This was followed by a mug of tea.

'Now,' she announced, 'before we begin, let me enquire about our mutual friend, Mr Robbie Hennessy. How is he behaving himself?'

Kirsty made a face. 'You know what he's like. You introduced us. I'm beginning to think you sold me a pup.'

Angie raised an eyebrow. 'What's the problem?'

'There are so many, I don't know where to begin.'

'Don't get too high and mighty,' Angie said. 'Robbie's a great catch. He's handsome and he's excellent at his job. He'd make anyone a very good husband. I know for a fact that Samantha O'Leary had her sights set on him before you whisked him away.'

Samantha O'Leary was an aspiring model with a fearsome reputation for stealing other people's boyfriends. There was a string of women lining up to tear her eyes out.

'You left out one important detail,' Kirsty told her.

'What?'

'He hasn't grown up yet.'

'Then it's your job to train him.'

'I'm not sure I have the energy.'

'We all have flaws. If you ask me, Robbie is better than most of the men I see around. If he was Mr Perfect, he would have been snapped up long ago.'

'He's just so irresponsible. What I want in a man is someone I can rely on, someone who'll take care of me. In this relationship, I'm the carer. There are times when I feel like his mother. He even forgot my birthday, for God's sake.'

'Maybe you should have a good chat with him.'

'I'm sick of talking to him. It just seems to go in one ear and out the other.'

Angie shrugged. 'Well, I don't have to remind you that you're not getting any younger. I get scared sometimes when I look around and see all these young things turning up at the clubs. Some of them look as if they've just changed out of their school uniforms.'

Kirsty shuddered. This was a sore topic. 'Tell me about it. I see it all the time in the fashion business.'

'Well, my advice is to hang on to Robbie. He'll settle down eventually. Some men just take longer than others. How's the cake, by the way?'

'Too good.' Kirsty put down the plate. 'Anyway, I didn't come here to talk about Robbie. I came to talk about Mum.'

'Go on.'

'You know she was off in Spain?'

'You told me.'

'Well, she's brought a guy back.'

Angie rolled her eyes. 'Really? What's he look like?'

'Very handsome – tall, dark, smouldering Latin looks.' She paused as she thought of Antonio's beautiful eyes. 'To be honest, he's an extremely attractive man.'

'Good for her,' Angie said approvingly. 'What's he do?'

'He's a musician. He plays the piano.'

'And what's his name?'

'Antonio.'

'Sounds very interesting. She didn't waste any time, did she? How long is your father dead?'

Kirsty frowned. 'I sincerely hope it's nothing like that. Mum's convinced that Antonio is a musical genius who's just waiting to be discovered. She's taken him under her wing. She's planning to organise a concert to launch his career.'

'So what's bothering you?'

'Can't you see it? I'm worried he's taking advantage of her. My mum got a terrible shock when my father died so I convinced her to go to Spain to recuperate. She's only just got there when she meets Antonio and a few days later she cancels the holiday and brings him back home with her. The really scary thing is, we know absolutely nothing about him, apart from some story he told her about being too poor to go to music college. And that could be a load of codswallop for all we know.'

'You've got a point,' Angie said. 'I can see why you're worried. I'd be worried too.'

'The trouble is,' Kirsty continued, warming to the subject, 'nobody agrees with me. My sister is entirely under his spell.

My brother thinks it's all very noble, and Mum's doctor says it will probably do her good. Meanwhile, I'm terrified I'm going to get a phone call some morning to say her bank account has been cleaned out, he's skipped back to Spain and Mum has to sell the house.'

Angie was nodding thoughtfully. Then she reached out and gently patted Kirsty's knee. 'I can see why you'd worry. I think you're being very responsible. I'm amazed that no one else has spotted the pitfalls.'

Kirsty felt enormous relief. So she wasn't alone. Good old reliable Angie was in her corner. She heaved a sigh. 'Thanks, Angie, I knew I'd get some straight talking from you.'

'Well, that's what friends are for.'

'So what do you think I should do?'

'Can't you talk to your mum, point out the dangers to her?'

'I don't think so. She's besotted with Antonio and I don't want to have a row with her, not in her frail state. She's even roped me in to help organise this damned concert.'

'Well, then, you've got to get ammunition. You said you know nothing about him. Can't you find out?'

'How do you mean?'

'Maybe he's done this sort of thing before. Maybe he has a history of preying on vulnerable women. And this story about his impoverished background, surely that can be checked out. If you can get some dirt on him you can bring it to your mother and she'll have to listen to you. And if she won't you can go to the police.'

'You think so?'

'Well, that's what I would do in your situation.'

'And how do I get this information?'

'There are agencies that deal in that sort of thing. You know, for people who suspect their spouses are cheating on them, stuff like that. They have ways of digging up dirt. Why don't you check the web? I'm sure they advertise.'

'Thank you, Angie. You're a treasure.'

'There's no need to thank me. It's always good to talk to people.'

'You're so right. Now, you know what? I'll have another slice of that cake.'

* * *

Benny Taylor looked like a pale imitation of Philip Marlowe. He was thin, with a pinched face and a prominent nose. He wore a striped suit, button-down shirt and tie, with a trilby. He looked up when Kirsty came through the door of his tiny office at the top of a rickety building at the back of Grafton Street. She had got his name from the internet and made an appointment to see him.

The private detective stood up and shook hands. Kirsty was half expecting him to open a drawer in his desk and take out a bottle of Old Kentucky bourbon.

'Pleased to meet you,' he said. 'Take a seat and tell me what's bothering you.'

Kirsty sat down. 'It's about my mother. She's brought this man back from Spain.'

Benny Taylor nodded, took out a notebook and listened while she told him about Antonio. Occasionally, he wrote in the notebook. When she had finished, he leaned back in his chair. 'So you want me to find out if he's straight, is that it?'

'Exactly. You see, we know absolutely nothing about him.'

'You don't have to tell me. I get cases like this all the time.

Now, I'm going to need his full name, place of birth and any other information you might have. I'll also need a photograph.'

'Will you have to go to Spain?'

Benny Taylor waved his hand. 'Naw, we've got people over there can do that.'

'How much is this going to cost?'

'Depends how much work is involved.'

'So, do you think you can help me?'

'Sure. That's my job.'

'One last thing, this business is urgent. I need a result as soon as possible.'

'I hear ya.'

'Okay,' Kirsty said. 'I'll get back to you as soon as I can.'

She left the office and went down to the street. Tomorrow morning she would visit Avalon and try to find the information the detective required. Getting Antonio's basic details mightn't be too difficult although a photograph could be tricky. But she would give it her best shot. She set off to the car park with a spring in her step. For the first time since she'd heard of Antonio, she was beginning to feel good.

Chapter Fourteen

It was a glorious morning. From her desk in the drawing room, Helen looked over the garden, shining in the sun. She could see some weeds appearing in the flowerbeds and daisies sprouting on the lawn that would have to be removed before the grass could be trimmed.

The garden had always been her responsibility, one of the many household tasks she enjoyed. She found it very therapeutic to watch things grow. But when she had become ill, Kirsty had hired a man from the village to do it. Helen would give him a call now and ask him to tidy things up. She would have done it herself but she didn't have the time: she had Antonio's concert to organise.

She allowed her eyes to travel down the lawn as far as the tree house where the children had played when they were young. James had built it for them one balmy summer weekend and they had spent many joyful hours cheerfully clambering up the rope ladder and looking out to sea.

Deirdre had bullied the other two, she remembered. She

was the eldest and always insisted that she was the leader and should be first to climb the ladder. There had been many fights and arguments over that tree house and tears wiped away. But they had been happy times, and all the memories she had of those days were pleasant ones. But that was the past. James was dead and the children had gone their separate ways. Now she was alone.

Well, not quite alone. She still had Anne and other friends, and the children kept in regular touch, particularly Kirsty, who had been a proper Florence Nightingale, nursing her through her illness after James's death. She knew what James would have liked her to do. He wouldn't want her to brood and mope and grieve. She had done that, and where had it got her? It had made her ill and almost landed her in hospital. No, James would want her to be busy, just like she had always been. He would want her to put her grief aside and get involved. He would want her to extend a helping hand to others less fortunate than herself.

That had been James's philosophy. He had always insisted that people like themselves, who were comfortable and successful, had a duty to those who had not been so lucky. And it was why she had decided to take up Antonio's case. Anne had thought she was mad when she'd told her, although she'd kept it to herself. But Helen knew.

Once she had heard Antonio's story, she had known what her response should be. He had so much talent that it would be a scandal if he was to spend his life confined to restaurant diners, half of whom didn't even want to listen to him. He deserved a wider audience of people who would recognise his talent and appreciate it. That was the task she had set herself, and she would do everything in her power to fulfil it.

She would let nothing stand in her way, and when her job was done, she would gracefully withdraw and leave him to enjoy his success.

She took a sip of tea and replaced the cup on the little table beside her. Yesterday had been hectic, first the travelling, then the business of introducing Antonio to the family and telling them of her plans. She had been a little apprehensive about that. It was only when Antonio had agreed to come and they were on the plane that she had fully appreciated what she was taking on.

It could have turned out badly. What if they had rejected him? What if they had scoffed at her idea for a concert? What if they had tried to stop her? There were so many things that could have gone wrong, things she hadn't even considered in her haste to get Antonio to Dublin.

But she needn't have worried. It had all gone extremely well. The family had supported her plan, welcomed Antonio warmly and agreed to help her. She had been particularly pleased with Kirsty's response. She worked in the fashion industry, which was full of celebrities and glamorous personalities. If Kirsty could persuade some models and designers to come on board, it would give the project an enormous boost.

After they had all left, Helen had spent the afternoon tidying up the house and getting Antonio unpacked and settled in. She had given him the guest bedroom. When he had walked into the en-suite bathroom, his eyes had opened in wonder as if he had never seen anything so splendid. It was the same with everything else in the house. He had been so impressed. But, then, Antonio had had an impoverished childhood and Avalon must look like a palace to him. Well, he had better get used to it. Once Helen was finished and

Antonio was launched on the world stage, gracious living would become second nature to him.

Last evening, she had taken him for dinner to the best fish restaurant in Howth. The head waiter had fussed over them and given them a table by the window where they could look out at the trawlers tied up in the harbour and the gulls swooping for scraps. Helen couldn't escape the other diners' inquisitive glances, drawn by Antonio's striking presence. He was such a tall, handsome young man that it was inevitable people would notice him, particularly the women.

It had amused her to realise that he might have been taken for her lover. She'd been forced to suppress a smile. But if Antonio was aware of the attention, he hadn't let it show. His manners had been impeccable. They had had grilled lobster and new potatoes, and by eleven o'clock they had been back at Avalon. By then, Helen was exhausted. She said goodnight and went straight to bed where she immediately fell into a deep sleep.

Now it was half past ten and Antonio hadn't appeared yet. But Helen was anxious to begin. Her laptop had pride of place on the desk. Beside it, she had a notebook, a pen and her phone. She was ready. It was time to begin her project. She took up the pen and started to write.

She began with a list, as she always did when she was organising some event. It concentrated her mind to get everything down on paper. At the top of the page she wrote 'PIANO' in capital letters. Before she did anything else, she would have to get hold of one because Antonio would want to practise for his concert.

They had owned a very good piano when the children were small and Helen had wanted them to learn. But, despite a succession of music teachers, none of them had shown any interest and, in the end, she had been forced to accept that they didn't have the talent so the piano was sold. Well, she would have to get another and it had to be one of the best.

She had no idea what pianos cost nowadays so she switched on her laptop and called up the search engine. The computer was such a useful tool. This was the second she had owned and they just kept getting better and faster. Pages of material came up. After several minutes spent sifting through them, she hit on a site called The Music Store. It had a Dublin address and a telephone number. Helen dialled and got a man who said his name was Smith.

'I need to purchase a piano,' she said.

'Certainly, madam. Have you any particular model in mind?'

'Not particularly, but the piano must be very good.'

'Well, you've come to the right place,' Mr Smith said. 'We offer a selection of first-class pianos including high-quality models, such as Bechstein, Fazioli, Bösendorfer—'

Helen interrupted: 'What price would I expect to pay?'

'Our pianos range from fifteen thousand to a hundred thousand euros.'

It sounded like an awful lot of money. She realised she was getting out of her depth. She hadn't a clue what sort of piano was required. 'I want this piano for a concert I'm organising. What would you advise?'

'For a concert, madam, I would recommend the very best. Perhaps you would like to come in and have a look at what we have. That might help you to decide.'

'That's a very good idea. How soon could you deliver?'

'That depends. If we have the model in stock we can deliver in the Dublin area in a matter of days. If we have to import the piano, it would take longer.'

'How much longer?' she asked.

'Several weeks.'

'That wouldn't do,' Helen said. 'I'm going to need it sooner.'

'May I ask who I'm speaking to?' Mr Smith suddenly said.

'O'Neill, Mrs Helen O'Neill.'

'Mrs O'Neill, why don't you come in and talk to us? I'm sure we can work something out. Do you know where to find us?'

'I have your address.'

'Just ring and let us know when you're coming. I'll make sure to be on hand to assist you.'

'Thank you.' Helen disconnected the call.

She felt a little pang of unease. This was going to be more difficult than she had thought. She had planned to buy a piano and surprise Antonio. But what if she bought the wrong one? Now it looked as if she would have to consult him. She would have to take him into The Music Store and let him decide for himself. And what if they didn't have anything that suited?

Before switching off the computer, she decided to go into her inbox and check for replies to the emails she had sent from Puebla Maria, seeking information about venues. There were only two replies and both said the venues were solidly booked for the next six months. Oh dear, she thought. This is getting very complicated. She had barely started on her project and already the problems had begun.

At that moment, the door opened and Kirsty came into the room. What a lovely surprise, Helen thought. She had been so absorbed in the business of the piano that she hadn't heard her car come up the drive.

'Good morning, darling,' she said, getting up to embrace her daughter. 'It's lovely to see you.'

'I just thought I'd drop by and see how you were doing. Sleep all right?'

'Like a log.'

'That's good. Where's Antonio?'

'He's still sleeping. I think he's exhausted, poor man. Would you like a cup of tea?'

Kirsty shook her head. 'I won't be staying long.'

A thought occurred to Helen. Maybe Kirsty could help her. 'You don't know anything about pianos, do you?'

'Not really. Why?'

'I'm trying to buy one for Antonio to practise on. I've been talking to a man in a shop in town and he told me they cost anything up to a hundred thousand euros.'

* * *

Kirsty's breath caught. So it's started already, she thought. A hundred thousand for a piano and he's only been here a day. If it goes on at this pace, he'll have her in the bankruptcy court in no time. 'I can't help you there, Mum,' she said, pulling out a chair and sitting down. 'But I'm absolutely fascinated by Antonio. Tell me more about him. What's his full name?'

'Antonio Rivera y Porrón. Did you know that Spaniards have two surnames, one each for their father and mother?'

'How intriguing,' Kirsty replied, filing the name away in her memory. 'And where exactly is he from?'

'A town called Ronda. It's not far from Marbella where we were staying.'

'Ronda,' Kirsty repeated. 'And what did his parents do for a living?'

'They were poor. His father was a carpenter. That's why Antonio didn't get to music college. They just didn't have the money.'

'How sad,' Kirsty said.

'Yes, it is, but I aim to put it right, and I'm really pleased you're going to help. You know lots of people in the fashion industry and they're exactly the types we need to bring on board. If we could get some of them to endorse Antonio, it would give the concert a great push.'

Kirsty could feel they were drifting into dangerous waters. She would have to steer the conversation back onto safer ground. 'I'll do what I can, of course.'

'That young model, Samantha O'Leary, she's the sort of person I have in mind. She's always on the television chat shows. You know her, don't you?'

At the mention of Samantha O'Leary's name, Kirsty felt her blood pressure rise a notch. She recalled what Angie had said about the woman's designs on Robbie.

'She's not the sort of person you want, Mum.'

'Oh, why not?'

'She's much too temperamental. She throws tantrums, shouts and screams when she doesn't get her way. I think she'd do more harm than good.'

'Oh. Well, in that case we'd better leave her out. But you know lots of other people. Whenever we get an opportunity, we must sit down and draw up a list. I've got some contacts already in the theatre world and RTÉ. I find lists are a very good way of concentrating one's thoughts.'

Just then they heard footsteps approaching and Antonio appeared, wearing one of Kirsty's father's old dressing gowns. He had shaved and his hair was damp as if he had just stepped out of the shower. Kirsty caught her breath. He looks even sexier than before, she thought.

'Good morning,' he said, kissing her cheek and staring

soulfully into her eyes. Despite herself, she felt a thrill of excitement run along her spine. 'It is so nice to see you, Kirsty. Have I interrupted a private conversation?'

'No, I just dropped in to see Mum.'

He turned to Helen and kissed her too. 'I'm sorry that I slept so long,' he said. 'I was just so tired.'

'Well, I'm glad you're up,' she said. 'I've just been telling Kirsty that I've been trying to buy a piano.'

'Why do you want to do that?'

'So you can practise for your concert. But when I made enquiries, I realised I know absolutely nothing about them. Now you're awake, you can advise me. But first let me get you some breakfast.'

Suddenly, Kirsty had a flash of inspiration. Here was the opportunity she was looking for. 'Don't go,' she said. 'I want to get a photograph.' She delved into her bag and pulled out her phone. 'Now, Antonio, just sit on the sofa beside Mum.'

'But I'm not even dressed yet.' He laughed.

'That doesn't matter. This is just for the family.'

He sat down beside Helen, took her hand and smiled.

Kirsty quickly framed the picture and snapped them. 'That's wonderful,' she said. 'See how good you look.' She showed them the photo, then put the phone in her bag. 'Now I really must go,' she said. 'I've got an awful lot of work to do.'

'You work too hard,' her mother said.

* * *

What a stroke of luck, Kirsty thought, as she drove away. Sooner or later, Benny Taylor will dig up all the dirt I need to expose Antonio for the charlatan he is.

Chapter Fifteen

'You don't have to buy a piano,' Antonio said, after Kirsty had gone. They had moved out to the sunlit patio and he was enjoying a breakfast of scrambled eggs that he had insisted on cooking.

'But I thought you'd want to practise. Surely for something as important as your first concert you'll need to prepare.'

He smiled. 'You've never done this before, have you?'

'Not a concert,' Helen admitted. 'But I've organised lots of other events.'

'If you don't mind me saying so, I think you are starting the wrong way round.'

Helen stared at him. 'Really? So how should I start?'

'First you should hire the hall. I'm sure the proprietors will have a piano that I can use. Anyway, I won't have to spend much time practising. A few hours should be enough. You see, I have the music here.' He tapped his forehead.

'Are you sure?'

'Absolutely.' He took Helen's hand and looked into her eyes.

'You and I should have a little talk. I am very grateful for what you are doing for me. You have brought me here to your home. You have undertaken to organise this concert. But I don't want you to spend your money on me.'

'I don't mind. I want the concert to be a success.'

'But *I* mind,' Antonio said. 'You are providing me with my opportunity. That is more than enough. Now, instead of worrying about a piano, why don't we start by finding a suitable venue?'

'If you're sure it's the right way.'

'It *is*. Once we have the venue, everything else will fall into place, you'll see.'

Helen's spirits revived. She had begun to feel a little overwhelmed although she didn't want to admit it. But talking to Antonio had reassured her and suddenly she felt a burst of energy overtake her. 'I'll begin at once,' she said. 'I'll ring Anne and ask her to come over. She'll have plenty of ideas, I'm sure.'

Antonio finished his breakfast, got up and carried his plate and cutlery off to the kitchen.

'Leave them in the sink,' Helen shouted after him. 'I'll look after them.'

'No. You are not my servant. I am very capable of washing up. I do it all the time when I'm in Spain.'

A few minutes later he was back. He had put on a pair of hiking shorts and a light jacket. A pair of sunglasses was perched on the end of his nose.

'Where are you going?' Helen asked, surprised.

'I am off to explore this beautiful place where you live. Now, please advise me where I should go.'

* * *

Helen smiled to herself as quiet descended again over the house. What an adorable man, she thought. He just improves in my estimation the more I get to know him. And to think he was stuck in a rut in Marbella until I heard him play. But her thoughts were interrupted by the doorbell.

She found Anne O'Malley in the porch. 'What a coincidence. I was about to call you.'

'I thought I'd nip over and see you. Has Antonio settled in yet?'

'Oh, yes. He's gone for a walk.'

'Why don't we go out to the patio and have a little chat?'

The two women settled themselves in the sun and Anne stretched her legs. 'Now, tell me how you've been getting on.'

Helen told her about her initial enquiries about a piano and Antonio's insistence that they start by finding a venue.

'He's quite right,' Anne replied. 'But to help us choose one, we have to know how many people will be coming.' She paused. 'You're finding this more difficult than you'd thought, aren't you?' she said kindly.

Helen lowered her eyes. 'A little,' she agreed. 'But that just makes me more determined. Come hell or high water, this concert will be a success.'

'So why don't we start at the beginning again? You drew up a list of potential guests before we left Spain, didn't you? Once we've decided on a guest list we'll know what size of venue we require.'

Helen searched through some papers and pulled out several sheets held together with a staple. 'There are almost three hundred names here,' she said, handing the sheets to Anne, who began to study the list.

'The lord mayor?' she muttered. 'The minister for culture?

The chairman of the National Concert Hall? And who's this? Victoria Mulcahy?' She looked up at Helen.

'She's a big wheel in the Arts Society. I was introduced to her at a function I was attending with James. She's very nice. We had quite a pleasant chat.'

'These are all very busy people,' Anne continued. 'Do you really think they're going to come to a concert by someone they've never heard of?'

'We won't know until we invite them.'

'I don't,' Anne said firmly.

Helen was disappointed. She wasn't used to Anne disagreeing with her and telling her what to do. 'It's just a provisional list,' she admitted. 'I put down everyone I could think of.'

'So maybe you should be more realistic. Why don't you pare it down to those you *know* will come? Then you'll have a better idea what size of venue will be required.'

'But I want a big attendance for Antonio's concert,' Helen protested. 'The whole idea is to get influential people to hear him, people who can help his career. I don't want him coming all the way to Dublin to end up playing for thirty people. He could do that every night at Puebla Maria.'

'Listen to me,' Anne said. 'If you don't get this right, he won't be playing for anyone. He'll be going back to Spain totally disheartened and you'll have wasted your time and money. So let's get this list down to manageable proportions. That means people you know can be persuaded, browbeaten or blackmailed into attending.'

Helen scowled. Then she sighed. 'Okay. Let's get started.'

They divided the list into two and worked steadily till it was early afternoon, when Helen said she needed a break.

They went back indoors. 'How is Kirsty taking all this?' Anne wondered.

'Oh, she's totally on board with it. In fact, she was here this morning. She's going to help me rope in some fashion people to help with publicity.'

'And is she happy about Antonio coming here to stay?'

'Of course. Why shouldn't she be?'

Anne thought of the hurried conversation she'd had with Kirsty the day before when Antonio arrived. She certainly hadn't seemed happy then.

'I think she likes him,' Helen continued. 'She took a picture of us on her phone.'

'Well, that's good,' Anne said. 'It's nice to have everyone pulling together. Now let's press on with the guests, shall we?'

* * *

It was after five o'clock by the time they finished, and they had managed to thin out the list to a hundred and seventy, whom Helen insisted were all people she was sure would come.

'We're making progress,' Anne said. 'We might even push the number up to two hundred. And now we have a better idea what size of hall we're going to need. That's our next task.'

'You've been very helpful,' Helen said.

'Forget it. I'm your friend, remember, and that's what friends are for. Now we need to think about possible venues. I'll come back in the morning and we'll start working on it.'

Helen walked with her to the door and saw her drive away. I'm so lucky in the people I have around me, she thought, as she returned to the drawing room. She was still a little disappointed that her plans for a grand concert were receding but she was forced to accept the logic of Anne's argument.

At the end of the day, the size of the attendance didn't matter. What was important was the calibre of those who came and the influence they could wield. She was confident of one thing: once they heard Antonio play, she would be pushing at an open door.

She heard a key in the lock and he came into the hall. He looked refreshed after his walk, his dark eyes gleaming with excitement.

'So you didn't get lost,' Helen joked.

'Not at all. I had a wonderful time. It is true what I have read about Ireland. The scenery here is fantastic. And now I am hungry.' He put down a grocery bag.

'What's this?'

'Our dinner. I want you to pour a glass of wine and go and relax. I am going to cook us a delicious Spanish meal.'

'Oh, how nice,' Helen said. 'May I enquire what it is?'

He grinned. 'Paella.'

Chapter Sixteen

Kirsty was so excited after her visit to Avalon that she drove straight into town to the detective's office.

'That was fast,' he said, picking up the photo and studying it. 'Good-looking bloke. I'm not surprised your mother fell for him.'

'It's not that kind of relationship,' Kirsty said sharply.

The detective smiled. 'Not yet. I'll bet he's also very charming and has excellent manners – holds the door open for her and passes little compliments, that sort of thing.'

'How did you know?'

'I've seen his type before,' Benny said.

'So, what happens now?'

'I'll email this photo to my colleagues in Spain, along with the other information. That'll get them started. I'll talk to you as soon as I've got anything to report.'

'Remember what I said. This is urgent.'

'You don't have to tell me. The sooner I get the dope, the sooner I get paid.'

She returned to her car and drove back to Howth. Benny Taylor had been rather too familiar with his remarks about her mother, she thought. He was a bit of a low-life, really, with his spiv suit and trilby. She wished she didn't have to deal with him. But he seemed to know his job, she'd give him that. And he'd certainly got the measure of Antonio. Now that she had set the ball rolling she relaxed a little.

When she got home, she went straight into her office and spent the afternoon dealing with business. By five o'clock, she was hungry and realised she hadn't eaten since breakfast. She decided to round off the day by having dinner with Robbie.

* * *

At that moment, Robbie was thinking of Kirsty. He was sitting back in his office with his feet up on the desk while he chewed a pencil and stared into space. He had just concluded a deal with a major client that could net ClickOn around a quarter of a million euros and make his boss very happy. It would also earn Robbie a handsome bonus.

He wondered if he should tell his boss now or wait till the deal was signed. So far, all he had was a verbal agreement. Better to wait, he decided. If I tell him now and it doesn't go through, he'll be really pissed off. If I don't tell him, he'll be none the wiser. The client had sounded very keen on the phone but Robbie had been there before. Nevertheless, his gut instinct told him that everything would be fine. A thought struck him. He should take Kirsty out tonight and celebrate.

He was growing very fond of her. She was his type of woman: classy, sharp, intelligent and very easy on the eye. He knew that several of his friends were envious. He could tell from the way they looked at her whenever he and she were out together. But that was part of the fun. Robbie felt proud to be seen in public with a woman like Kirsty. It was a positive reflection on him that he was able to have such a clever, attractive female on his arm.

But, like every woman he had ever known, Kirsty could have her moments. And she'd been acting very strangely since the Spanish bloke had appeared on the scene, worrying about him ripping off her mother. If Robbie had his way he'd hire a couple of heavies to take the Spaniard up the Dublin Mountains and have a serious talk with him. But Kirsty didn't want any rough stuff. She was all for dealing with this in her own way. Anyway, it was her business: why should Robbie care?

Then there'd been that incident about her birthday. What a fuss she'd kicked up over that. If she'd forgotten *his* birthday, he wouldn't have blinked an eye. He often forgot it himself. Birthdays didn't mean anything to him. But Kirsty had carried on as if he'd knocked over an old man and stolen his walking stick. He'd never heard the end of it.

And the way she went on about his drinking – anyone would think he'd got an alcohol problem. He enjoyed a couple of beers in the evening but what was the harm in that? He worked hard all day so surely he was entitled to let his hair down a little. Every bloke he knew did that.

Robbie sighed. He'd never understand women. Their brains were wired differently from men's. Take Samantha O'Leary, the model: she didn't mind his drinking. She thought it was great fun. He had run into her one night in Crazy Joe's nightclub before he'd met Kirsty and she'd been positively encouraging him to hammer the vodka shots till he could barely stand.

And she wasn't a bad-looking woman either with her nice blonde hair and hot little figure. No wonder she was all over the tabloids and never off the television. He'd spent a very pleasant evening with Samantha and the only downside he could remember was that she was a bit slow in the intellectual department. All her chat had been about film stars and page-three girls. It had got a bit boring after a while. He never got bored with Kirsty.

At that moment, his phone rang and when he picked it up he heard her voice. Immediately, all thoughts of Samantha O'Leary disappeared. An evening with Kirsty would be the perfect ending to his day. He would tell her all about the deal he had clinched.

'What are you doing?' she asked.

'I'm about to knock off.'

'Me too. I was thinking we might have something to eat.'

'Great!'

'Why don't you come out to Howth? We'll have a nice dinner somewhere. Afterwards we might go back to my place for a nightcap.'

'I'm on my way,' Robbie said, reaching for his jacket.

* * *

They went to a new restaurant that had opened in Main Street. Kirsty seemed to know a lot of the diners. They waved to her as she and Robbie passed their tables.

'I'm hungry,' she said, once they had sat down.

'Me too. I could take a bite out of a baby's arse.'

Kirsty frowned.

'I'm sorry', he said quickly.

She reached out and gently stroked his arm. 'Don't take it badly. I'm thinking of you. I don't like to see you letting yourself down in company. Now, what shall we order?'

Robbie went for steak and Kirsty chose roast Wicklow lamb. They ordered a bottle of Beaujolais.

'How did your day go?' she asked.

Robbie brightened at once. 'Extremely well. I pulled off a great deal. It's worth about a quarter mill to the company.'

She smiled. 'That's fantastic. Well, done, Robbie.'

'Thank you.'

'Your boss must be delighted.'

'He doesn't know. I haven't told him yet.'

'Why not?'

Robbie explained that he was waiting till the contract was signed just in case anything went wrong.

'Clever,' Kirsty said approvingly. 'That shows intelligence. Anyone else would have gone rushing off to broadcast the news. When will you know for certain?'

'Maybe tomorrow.' Robbie lifted the bottle of wine and poured them each a glass. 'It will mean a nice little bonus for me, couple of thou. I'll celebrate it with you. Perhaps we might go for a little holiday somewhere.'

'That would be lovely,' Kirsty said. 'But I won't be able to go anywhere for a little while.'

'Oh?'

'I've got to wait for the results of a little scheme I've hatched.'

Robbie looked baffled. 'What sort of scheme?'

She leaned closer and lowered her voice. 'I've hired a private detective to investigate the Spanish guy my mother brought home.'

'How do you mean investigate?'

'I want him to find any skeletons Antonio might have hidden in his cupboard. And when I do, I'll take the information to my mother and that will be the end of him.'

'Why beat about the bush?' Robbie said. 'Why don't you do what I suggest? Just let him know he's not wanted, and if he'd like to keep his front teeth, he should make himself scarce.'

'Because I don't want anything nasty. It would just upset my mum.'

'And what if you don't find any skeletons, what will you do then?'

Kirsty smiled. 'Oh, we'll find skeletons, all right.'

* * *

It was almost ten o'clock when they left. Robbie had consumed most of the bottle of wine, plus a large brandy to round off the meal, but he wasn't drunk. They walked the short distance down the hill to where Kirsty's apartment was located beside the harbour. It was dusk and a large yellow moon was reflecting off the sea near Ireland's Eye. The gulls were kicking up a racket along the pier.

Once they were inside, the frantic undressing began. Robbie kicked off his shoes and trousers and helped her pull off her dress. Then his lips were on her mouth and Kirsty closed her eyes. Robbie had many faults but this was one thing he was especially good at.

Chapter Seventeen

The following morning at seven o'clock, Kirsty was wakened by the loud ringing of her phone. She looked around the untidy room. There were clothes strewn all over the floor. Robbie's boxer shorts were suspended from the bedpost while his socks were rolled in a ball in a corner of the room. Meanwhile, their owner lay curled up in bed, mouth wide open, snoring loudly. Kirsty grabbed the phone and headed for the quiet of the kitchen.

'Hello,' a voice said. 'I hope I didn't get you up.'

'Who is this?'

'Rachel Maguire.'

'Oh, Rachel, I'm sorry,' Kirsty apologised. 'I didn't recognise your voice. Don't worry, you didn't wake me. I was already up. I'm in my kitchen right now, looking out the window at another beautiful day.'

'The reason I'm calling so early,' Rachel continued. 'That photoshoot we did with O'Mara wearing your evening gowns? It's in the paper this morning. I thought I'd alert you.'

Kirsty's heart leaped. 'That's brilliant. I'm delighted. Thanks, Rachel.'

'No need to thank me. I just hope you like it. We're all very pleased in here.'

Kirsty ended the call and dashed into the bathroom. She had a quick shower, pulled on a pair of jeans and a T-shirt and drove to the village. There were only a few early birds in the Centra store and the newspaper rack was deserted. She grabbed a copy of the *Tribune* and flicked through it till she came to the fashion pages.

The photographs of Ellie O'Mara had been given a full-page spread in gorgeous colour and they looked fantastic. The model was wearing a number of evening gowns created by Kirsty's young designer, Penny Muldoon. Rachel had cropped the pictures to give a stunning effect and had written a bold strapline across the top: *New Summer Designs from Kirsty O'Neill.* She felt her pulse race as she stared at them. This was the sort of publicity that money couldn't buy.

She paid for several copies of the paper and went back to the apartment, making a mental note to send Rachel some flowers as a thank-you gesture. When she came through the front door, she found Robbie standing naked in the kitchen waiting for the kettle to boil.

She kissed his cheek. 'Robbie darling, there's been a very big development. I need you out of here fast. I'm expecting a lot of important business calls.'

'I hear you,' he said, making himself a mug of coffee. 'Give me fifteen minutes and I'll be gone.' He set off for the shower, taking the coffee with him.

She watched him go. Once the retailers saw the *Tribune*

they'd be calling to make enquiries and she needed all her wits about her.

Robbie was soon back, shaved and dressed.

'Would you like some toast?' she asked.

'No, I'd better be on my way.'

He gulped down the remains of his coffee and Kirsty walked with him to the front door.

She put her arms around him and kissed him on the mouth. 'I'm sorry to rush you like this, Robbie.'

'It's all right. I understand. Business is business. Have a great day. I'll be in touch.'

She closed the door firmly behind him and returned to the kitchen.

Just then her mobile began to ring. She glanced at the clock on the kitchen wall. It was ten to eight. The calls were starting early. She took the phone into her office along with some coffee, sat down at her desk and answered.

'Good morning,' a voice said. 'It's Cecily Moncrieffe.'

'Cecily! How nice to hear from you.'

'Let's cut out the crap,' Cecily snapped. 'You didn't play fair with me.'

Kirsty adopted a shocked tone. 'Whatever do you mean? How can you say that?'

'I've got the *Tribune* fashion shoot in my hands. Why didn't you show me those gowns when we had lunch the other day?'

Kirsty took a deep breath. 'Because someone else has shown a strong interest in them.'

'To hell with that. Who is it?'

'You know the rules, Cecily. I can't possibly tell you.'

'Have they made a firm offer?'

'Not yet.'

'Nothing is sold till the money changes hands. Who designed those gowns?'

'Penny Muldoon.'

'You've sold me some of her stuff before. Now tell me what you want for them.'

Kirsty gave a sigh and mentioned a figure she plucked from the air.

'Okay,' Cecily said. 'I'll pay it, and I'll guarantee to take all Penny Muldoon's creations for the next eighteen months. How does that sound?'

'But you haven't seen them yet.'

'I trust that girl. I like what she does. I think she has a future in this business.'

'You're putting me on the spot, Cecily.'

'If you can't stand the heat you shouldn't be in the kitchen.'

'Okay, okay, let me consider it. I'll ring you tomorrow.'

'Don't leave it any later. This offer won't be on the table for ever.'

There was a click as Cecily disconnected.

Kirsty punched the air. Dealing with Cecily Moncrieffe could be like playing high-stakes poker in a Las Vegas casino but she had held her nerve and her bluff had paid off. Now she had squeezed a very lucrative offer out of her. She decided to send Rachel a bottle of vintage champagne with the flowers. She reached for the mug of coffee on her desk. It had gone cold. She got up and went into the kitchen to make some more.

There was a fantastic adrenalin buzz at a time like this when she had some exciting new clothes to sell and the shops were keen to buy. It made up for the long weeks of waiting and planning. But it was also very wearing on the nerves. Kirsty had a suspicion that her business was approaching a crossroads and she would soon be forced to make some very hard decisions about its future.

Cecily's offer was extremely generous. And she had promised to take Penny Muldoon's work for the next eighteen months without even seeing it. Penny would be over the moon when she heard. Kirsty liked dealing with Cecily. She was a sharp business woman who could do a lot to grow Kirsty's business. And she possessed one other crucial quality: once she struck a deal, she always kept her word.

If Kirsty negotiated an exclusive contract with Cecily, it would remove a lot of pressure because she would have a guaranteed market for her garments. But it would mean cutting out other retailers and would give Cecily a very important weapon. She would have a stranglehold over Kirsty.

It was a genuine dilemma. Kirsty felt as if she was walking a tightrope. If she made the wrong decision, she might regret it. But she had no time to think about it now because the phone was ringing again.

***

It continued to ring right through till the afternoon as people who had seen the *Tribune* coverage called to ask if the garments were available to buy. She dealt with each enquiry pleasantly, explaining that she had a firm offer, which she was considering, and inviting the callers to submit their own. She also used the opportunity to explain that she had other young designers apart from Penny Muldoon whose garments were available.

It was early evening before the calls petered out. Kirsty was exhausted and she was hungry. She had eaten almost nothing all day. As she was preparing to finish up, her phone sounded again. This time it was Robbie.

'Hiya, honey,' he began. 'What sort of a day have you had?'

'Exhausting,' she replied.

'I've got some good news. That deal I told you about, well, it's come through. The contract arrived this afternoon. My boss is over the moon. I've just been handed a bonus of five grand.'

'Congratulations. That's fantastic.'

'Yes, I'm extremely chuffed. I thought you and me might hit the town and celebrate. Champers all the way. What do you say?'

Right now, a night guzzling champagne with Robbie was just about the last thing she wanted. She was going to have to turn him down. 'I can't, Rob. I just haven't got the energy. I'm planning on having an early night. Why don't we do it some other time?'

She could hear the disappointment in his voice as he said, 'I'm sorry to hear that.'

There was a buzz and the phone went dead.

Kirsty went into the bathroom and filled the tub. She was sorry to have disappointed Robbie but she just didn't have the energy for a night on the town. She luxuriated for half an hour and put him out of her mind. Afterwards, she made herself a tuna sandwich and ate it with some salad she had in the fridge. By ten o'clock, she was tucked up in bed, fast asleep.

Chapter Eighteen

It was eight o'clock and a brand new day. The sun was shining and, after a shaky start, Helen was impatient to push ahead with the concert. She assumed Antonio was still asleep, but as she passed his bedroom, the door was open. She called his name and got no answer. Perhaps he's gone for an early-morning walk, she thought. She had given him a key and told him to come and go as he pleased because she wanted him to feel at home in Avalon.

She went to the kitchen to put on the kettle. When she looked out of the window she saw him at the bottom of the garden, on his knees pulling the weeds from the lawn and putting them into a large bin bag. He looked up and smiled when she rattled the window. She pointed to the kettle in her hand and he stood up to walk back towards the house.

'You were up early,' she remarked, when he came in. 'Did you sleep all right?'

'I was asleep as soon as my head was on the pillow.'

'I'm about to make breakfast. Would you like tea or coffee?'

'I will have whatever you are having.'

'No,' Helen insisted. 'You're my guest. You must choose.'

'In that case, I'll have coffee, please.'

'And what about food? Would you like me to make an omelette?'

'That would be nice. But why don't you relax and I will make the breakfast?'

'No. I've already started and, anyway, you cooked dinner last night, remember?'

He shrugged. 'A paella isn't much.'

'Now don't try to fool me,' she said, putting the breakfast things on the table. 'It was a lovely meal.' She poured the coffee and a few minutes later put down two omelettes. They began to eat.

'You decided to weed the lawn?'

'I thought I would tidy up the garden.'

'Don't you need to be careful with your hands?'

He shrugged. 'It's nothing. I am wearing gloves. Perhaps I should have asked your permission?'

'Not at all. I'm delighted. Normally I'd do it myself but I'm so busy organising the concert.'

'Then I shall be happy to do it. The exercise will be good for me. I will enjoy it.'

'In that case, fire away.'

He gave her a strange look. 'Fire?'

Helen leaned back in her chair as a fit of laughter shook her. 'You're so funny, Antonio. It's just an expression. It means you have my full agreement.'

He smiled and nodded. 'I am truly fortunate to have met you, Helen. Not only are you organising my concert but you are also teaching me to speak proper English. What a lucky man I am.'

***

At ten o'clock, Anne arrived, carrying a smart leather briefcase.

'Where do you want to work?' Helen asked.

'Let's use the drawing room.'

Outside in the garden, Antonio had finished weeding the lawn and was now trimming the hedge. He waved when he saw Anne. 'I see you've put him to work,' she remarked.

'It was his idea. He volunteered.'

'At least it keeps him occupied. I'm sure he must find everything very strange, poor man. Is he getting homesick yet?'

'I don't think so. He rarely mentions Spain, although he did make us paella for dinner last night.'

'So he can cook too. Is there no end to his talent?' Anne opened her briefcase and took out a large notepad and pen. 'I've jotted down a few venues that might suit and a list of phone numbers. I suggest we start ringing them and get a feel for prices.'

'Good idea.' Helen was eager to get started.

It was lunchtime before they had exhausted Anne's list. They had found three places that sounded suitable and had made appointments to view them that afternoon. Helen informed Antonio that they would be away for a few hours and reminded him to make sure to lock up and take his key if he was going out. They got into Anne's car and headed into town.

The first place was a hall at the top of Parnell Street that was used for trade union meetings. The caretaker was waiting and was eager to show them around. It was about the right size for the expected audience and it was clean and tidy but Helen immediately spotted a problem. There was nowhere to park.

When they mentioned it to the caretaker, he said there was a public car park half a mile away. But Helen still had doubts. Not all of the guests would want to walk that distance. In any case, what were they supposed to do if it was raining?

They thanked the caretaker and said they would get back to him if they decided to proceed, then set off to look at the second venue on the list. This turned out to be a community centre used by local voluntary groups. At first sight, it was exactly what they were looking for and had ample parking outside. But alarm bells began to sound when they learned that the hall next door was used for basketball practice seven nights a week. Anne thought of a ball bouncing off the wall while Antonio tried to play the piano, not to mention the excited cries of the athletes. It would be impossible. By now, their hopes were fading.

'Don't worry,' Anne said, as they settled into the car for the short drive to Rathmines and the church hall she had selected. 'There has to be a venue somewhere that will suit. Perhaps the next one will be what we want.'

'What's the church called?'

'St Matilda's.'

When they got there, they left the car in the adjoining car park and were met by the church warden, a thin man with a stoop, who took out a key and opened the door of the church. Inside they were met with a reverential stillness. It was a beautiful old building. As the warden led them down the aisle, the women glanced in admiration at the polished pews, the stained-glass windows and the high ceiling. At last they came to a door. He pushed it open and they found themselves in the hall.

It was a bright, cheerful room, used during the day as a nursery school so there were rows of little tables and chairs and a shelf with books and toys. The two women looked around before exchanging a glance. Their expressions said it all. The hall would have been perfect except for one thing. It was far too small. They would never get their expected audience in here along with a piano.

The warden stood silently while they turned to him and slowly shook their heads. 'It's just not large enough,' Anne explained. 'We're hoping to have up to two hundred people at our concert.'

'What a pity,' the man replied mournfully. 'We hoped it would suit you. We have a fundraising drive under way for a new organ and the fee for the use of the hall would have come in handy. But there you are, it can't be helped.'

He led them back out to the car park and shook their hands. 'Good evening, ladies. Have a safe journey home.'

They drove back to Howth in near silence, their disappointment almost palpable. As Anne was dropping Helen off at Avalon, she took her friend's hand and looked into her eyes. 'Don't be downhearted. We've got to think positive. We'll start again in the morning.'

But her words failed to lift Helen's spirits and she was in a gloomy mood as she opened the front door and stepped into the house. She was met at once with an appetising aroma coming from the kitchen. When she went in, she found Antonio at the stove wearing her apron and holding a wooden spatula.

'What's going on?' she asked.

'I'm preparing dinner. Now why don't you go and get changed

into something comfortable? When you return everything will be ready.'

She began to protest but Antonio shooed her out of the kitchen and returned to the stove.

It took her fifteen minutes to slip out of her clothes and into a pair of slacks and blouse. When she got back to the kitchen he had set the table and poured two glasses of wine.

'What are you cooking?' she enquired.

'It's a dish from my home town of Ronda, chicken with peppers and onions and rice. Are you hungry?'

Helen had eaten nothing since breakfast. 'A little.'

'Then sit down and drink some wine. This will be ready in a minute.'

Helen did as he said while he transferred the food onto hot plates and joined her at the table. He lifted his glass and touched it against hers. '*Buen provecho.*'

'What does that mean?'

'"Enjoy your meal." Now tell me how your visit went.'

Helen lowered her head. 'Not very well, I'm afraid.'

'I'm sorry to hear that. What was the problem?'

'We looked at three possible venues. One had no parking, another was too noisy and the last one was too small.'

'So? Dublin is a big city. There will be somewhere else. It doesn't have to be too grand. I don't mind.'

'But I want it to be right, Antonio. This is your big occasion. And the venue is important. I want everyone who comes to be impressed by your performance. Now I'm beginning to wonder if . . . ' She didn't finish the sentence as tears welled in her eyes and rolled down her cheeks.

He took out a handkerchief and gently wiped them away.

'Don't be sad. Tomorrow is another day. Now eat your food before it gets cold.'

As they ate, Antonio told her of the busy day he'd had. Not only had he weeded the lawn and trimmed the hedge but he had also found time to cut the grass and walk into the village to buy the ingredients for dinner.

'You don't believe in being idle, do you?' Helen said.

He shook his head. 'Time goes too fast,' he replied. 'It is best to be doing useful things.'

They moved back to the drawing room and talked for a while till Helen said she was tired and was going to bed. She went to her room and stood at the window, gazing out at the night sky. Antonio was a kind, self-effacing man, not brash or proud or boastful. It was beginning to look as if she might have raised his hopes and brought him to Dublin on a fool's errand. Unless they found a suitable venue for the concert, no one would hear him play. How was she going to tell him the terrible news?

She got undressed and slipped between the sheets. Just as she was drifting off to sleep, her phone began to ring. This will be Kirsty, she thought. I haven't heard from her all day.

But when she answered, she heard Anne's voice. 'I was so excited that I had to ring at once to tell you.'

'Tell me what?' Helen asked.

'I think I've found the very place for the concert. It was staring us in the face and we didn't see it.'

By now, Helen was wide awake again. 'Where?'

'Not the hall but the church itself. It's such a beautiful building and it's exactly the right size. It would be perfect. The concert should be held in the church.'

Chapter Nineteen

Robbie entered Crazy Joe's nightclub and made a beeline for a seat at the bar. It was drinking time and he was there to celebrate, even if he had to do it on his own. He had nailed down a lucrative contract for the firm and he was the golden boy. Pity more people didn't appreciate that fact.

After leaving work he had gone for a meal to a burger restaurant near his office. It had been a joyless experience, eating on his own while all around him cheerful couples were laughing and being happy together. One pair in the corner, who looked like tourists, were even feeding each other forkfuls while they gazed soulfully into each other's eyes. Robbie had felt like an outsider, lonely and abandoned.

He had his bonus cheque tucked away in his wallet. He hadn't found time to lodge it in his bank account yet but he would do that first thing tomorrow morning. As he had studied the menu, he'd realised just how hungry he was. He'd been so busy that he'd only managed a sandwich at his desk. As for breakfast, that had been a mug of coffee and a goodbye kiss from Kirsty.

When the waitress came, he ordered a bowl of fried chicken wings and the triple Mexican burger with chilli sauce and fries. He decided to add a salad. It was important to get his greens and, besides, it came with a tasty mustard dressing that he liked. A half carafe of red plonk rounded off his order.

As he ate his meal, he thought again of his plight. Across the room, another young couple had sat down and were busy taking selfies while she cuddled closer to him and kissed his ear. Robbie looked away in disgust. Wouldn't you think Kirsty would have had the decency to come and eat with him? Would that have been too much to expect on this night of all nights?

He had finished his meal and paid the bill, making sure to leave a generous tip for the pretty waitress. They worked hard, those poor girls, on their feet all day and taking abuse from awkward customers, most of whom never left them even a red cent. He went downstairs to the Gents and studied himself in the mirror. His handsome face stared back at him. He would go out and sample the action in Crazy Joe's nightclub.

He sat now on a stool at the bar with a Bombay Fizz in his hand. It was early but the place was filling. The night is young, Robbie told himself, and filled with promise. The cocktail caused a warm, comforting glow to spread from his chest up to his head. It was cosy down here in Crazy Joe's and he felt good. He was among friends – just a pity Kirsty wasn't here to share it with him. Yes, he thought, as he downed the Bombay Fizz and nodded to the barman to give him another. I think I'm in the right place.

'Expecting many in tonight?' he asked, as the man put the fresh drink in front of him.

'It's the same every night. This place will be jammers by midnight.'

'The way I like it,' Robbie replied, passing a ten-euro note he'd got earlier from an ATM and telling the barman to keep the change. He was feeling flush. He'd got a cheque for five thousand euros in his wallet.

He looked around when the sound machine came on. It was playing an old Rolling Stones number. Robbie tapped his hand on the counter in time with the beat. A couple of girls got up and started dancing together but he was in no hurry. There'd be plenty of opportunities later. In the meantime, he'd work on getting a nice buzz going.

'Another?' The barman pointed at his empty glass.

'Why the hell not?'

He slapped another ten spot on the counter and watched as the barman poured. He glanced at his watch. It was eleven o'clock. Kirsty would be getting ready for bed. A thought came into his head. He would ring and let her listen to the music on his phone. He took out the phone and dialled her number.

'Hello?' a drowsy voice said.

'Hi, it's me. Just checking you're all right. Grab an earful of this.' He held the phone out to catch the blast from the speakers. 'Recognise it? "Walking the Dog", one of your favourites.'

'Robbie? Where are you?'

'Crazy Joe's. I'm celebrating my success with that contract.'

'You woke me up. Is this your idea of a joke?'

'Not at all. I just wanted you to know I was thinking about you.'

'Well, now you've told me, can I please get back to sleep?'

'Of course, honey. Sweet dreams.'

There was a buzz and the phone went dead.

* * *

By midnight, the place was packed with heaving bodies and Robbie could no longer see the dance floor. Not that it mattered. It was the atmosphere he enjoyed, the feeling of peace and tranquillity that had settled over him despite the roar of the crowd. All around, he could see shapely young ones with their short skirts and tight T-shirts and the heady aroma of their perfume. Yes, sir, he was in the right place and he was feeling no pain.

There was a period when he seemed to drift off. When he came to again, it was half twelve and someone was talking to him. He forced himself to focus and found himself looking into a large pair of laughing blue eyes set beneath a crown of soft blonde hair. Her face was familiar but who the hell was she?

'It's Robbie, isn't it?' her teasing voice said. 'I thought I recognised you. Robbie Hennessy?'

'That's me,' he said, forcing a smile onto his face.

'You remember me, don't you?'

'Of course I do.' He was getting it now. She was the model who kept talking about film stars. 'How could I ever forget you? You're ...'

'Samantha O'Leary. I met you here a couple of months ago.'

'I remember, Samantha. We had a fantastic night. You were great company.'

'Thank you,' she simpered. 'Are you with someone?'

'Not tonight, honey.' He sat up straight and gave his best impression of a seductive smile. 'Tonight I'm free as a bird and on the town. Why don't you join me?'

He got up and offered his stool. 'I'm about to have another Bombay Fizz. Can I get you one?'

'That would be nice.'

The barman was over at once with the drinks. Robbie felt

himself come alive again. It was all happening exactly as he had hoped. The beautiful Samantha was practically throwing herself at him. It was like shooting fish in a barrel. If he played his cards right, he wouldn't be going home to an empty bed tonight.

'Where's your girlfriend?' she asked.

'Girlfriend? Who said anything about a girlfriend?'

'Well, a snappy-looking guy like you must have a girlfriend. Maybe more than one,' she said, with a coquettish grin.

'She's washing her hair,' Robbie replied, and they both laughed.

'So what are you doing here?' she persisted.

'Celebrating.'

'Oh?'

'I just pulled off a big contract for my firm, ClickOn. It's a social media company. Took a lot of hard work but I got there in the end.'

'Wow!' she said, looking impressed.

'So I thought I'd hit the town. I was just about to order a bottle of bubbly. What would you say to that?'

'I wouldn't say no.' Samantha leaned closer.

The barman came as soon as Robbie raised his hand. That was one of the benefits of tipping. You got grade-one service.

'Bottle of Dom Pérignon,' Robbie demanded, with the authority of a man who drank champagne every morning for breakfast. 'And two glasses.'

'Right away.'

'You must work very hard,' Samantha said, stroking his arm.

'I'm just lucky.'

'I don't believe in luck. You get results through hard work and application.'

'That sounds like something you got out of a self-help manual.'

Samantha laughed uproariously. Meanwhile, the barman had put down two glasses and was struggling to get the cork out of the bottle. There was a loud pop and the champagne spurted out. A group further along the counter gave a cheer. Robbie smiled in appreciation. He was the man of the moment, the centre of attention. And he was loving it. It was only his due.

Samantha took a gulp of champagne and started to cough.

'Go down the wrong way?' Robbie asked, clapping her on the back. 'You've got to drink it slowly.'

She laughed, took out a handkerchief and dabbed her eyes.

'You'll get used to it,' Robbie assured her. 'Here, have some more.' He topped up her glass. He was on a cloud. This was the life.

'You're a very handsome man,' Samantha purred.

'You're not a bad looker yourself.'

The sound system was blasting out a raucous reggae number. 'Here,' she said, grabbing his arm and dragging him onto the floor. 'You don't want to sit there all night looking like a lemon. Let's dance.'

Chapter Twenty

Anne was so excited that she couldn't wait to get to Avalon. When she arrived soon after nine o'clock, Helen let her in and they went to the drawing room. She had the windows open, and outside in the garden, she could see Antonio painting the tree house. He waved when he saw her.

'He never stops, does he?' she said.

'He just likes to keep busy.'

'You can send him over to my house when he's finished doing jobs for you.' Anne laughed. 'I'll find plenty more for him.'

'The church.' Helen was anxious to get straight down to business. 'You think it might be suitable?'

'I certainly do. It's so obvious I'm surprised we didn't think of it sooner. First, St Matilda's is small. It probably seats about two hundred people, which is perfect for our purpose. Second, it provides a beautiful setting with the stained-glass windows and the fine architecture. Third, it has easy access and ample parking. And last but not least, it has a high ceiling, which means the acoustics should be very good.'

'But will the vicar agree?'

'I don't see why not,' Anne said. 'It's not unusual for concerts to be held in churches. And it's not going to be punk rock so the neighbours won't be complaining. Besides, they're short of money. The warden said they need funds for a new organ.'

'What's his name?'

'John Watt. Why don't I ring him now and ask him?'

'No,' Helen said. 'I'll do it. It's time I got back into the driving seat.'

Anne dialled the number and handed the phone to her friend.

There was a ringing tone and then Helen heard a refined male voice.

'Is that Mr Watt?'

'Speaking.'

'My name is Helen O'Neill. Forgive me if I'm disturbing you.'

'Not at all. Aren't you one of the ladies who came to view the church hall yesterday?'

'That's correct.'

'I was sorry to hear that your trip was wasted. My warden tells me the hall was too small.'

'Yes, unfortunately it was. But we've had second thoughts and now we have a new proposal to put to you.'

'Oh?'

'We were wondering if we might hire the church instead?'

She heard a short intake of breath.

'The church?'

'Yes. How many people does it hold?'

'We've had two hundred and fifty worshippers on some occasions.'

'In that case, it would certainly be large enough. We're

hoping to put on a piano recital and your church would be ideal.'

There was a slight pause while Helen waited anxiously.

'I've never had a request like this, Mrs O'Neill. Before I can decide, I should consult some others.'

'I can assure you that the church wouldn't be disturbed in any way,' Helen hurried on. 'We would leave it exactly as we found it. And we're prepared to pay you a reasonable fee. I think this is what could be called a mutually beneficial arrangement.'

'When do you plan to hold this recital?'

'We're still at the planning stage but hopefully it would be within the next fortnight.'

'You've taken me by surprise. Perhaps we should sit down together and flesh this out a little more.'

'That's perfectly agreeable. We're available at any time.'

'Let me look at my diary.'

There was a short pause and then he was back again. 'I have a meeting of the vestry committee at two o'clock. I could see you at four. Would that give you enough time?'

'Plenty.'

'In that case, I shall look forward to meeting you, Mrs O'Neill. The vicarage is right beside the church. You can't miss it.'

'We're looking forward to meeting you too, Mr Watt. Goodbye.'

She gave Anne a big smile and raised her thumb. 'You heard that. He'll see us at four.'

Just then, Antonio came in from the garden. He wiped his hands on a rag, then went straight to Anne and kissed her on both cheeks. 'How are you, this morning?' he asked, his dark eyes sparkling with good humour.

'I'm very well, thank you. We think we might have found the ideal venue for your concert.'

'Really? That is very good news. Where is it?'

'It's a beautiful little church in Rathmines.'

'A church?'

'St Matilda's. It's the perfect place. We're going to talk to the vicar this afternoon. In fact ...' she turned to Helen '... why don't we bring Antonio with us and he can see it for himself?'

'That's a splendid idea.'

'Mind you, it's not agreed yet,' Anne hastened to add. 'We still have to persuade the vicar. But I think when Helen and I get to work on him we'll manage to bring him around.'

The two women exchanged a smile. Since the conversation with Mr Watt, Helen's excitement and confidence had returned.

Antonio was smiling too. 'I think when you two ladies get together you could even persuade the Pope to let you have the Sistine Chapel.'

'Now why didn't I think of that?' Helen laughed.

* * *

They set off in Helen's car at a quarter to three. She wanted to allow plenty of time in case they got caught in traffic. Three-quarters of an hour later they arrived in Rathmines, parked near the church and went for a short walk.

'You should lead the discussion,' Anne said to Helen. 'This is your project. If you need support, Antonio and I can come in.'

This was agreed and at five minutes to four they were ringing the bell of the vicarage, a small building beside the church with ivy climbing its old stone walls. The door was opened by a bright, middle-aged woman who introduced herself as Mrs Watt. She led them into a cosy study where the vicar was waiting. He was a tall man with sandy hair, dressed in a dark suit and clerical collar. He shook hands warmly while his wife withdrew.

'We've never done this sort of thing before,' he explained, as soon as they were settled. 'I've spoken to the vestry committee and they have mixed views about your proposal. Some of them are quite nervous. Tell me exactly what you have in mind.'

Helen had already rehearsed her arguments. She began by explaining how she had first met Antonio and recognised his musical talent. 'He really is a very gifted pianist. I thought it was a terrible pity that more people couldn't hear him play so I decided on a plan to bring him here to Dublin and organise a concert.'

Antonio sat shyly with his head lowered, but as she continued, Helen could see the vicar warming to her plan.

'We've looked at several venues but so far we haven't been able to find a suitable place. Then we saw your church and realised it would be perfect. The church won't be disturbed. All we need to do is erect a small stage, which can be quickly dismantled again. We won't need a sound system because the acoustics should be very good. If you agree, you'll be assisting in a great work of charity.'

The vicar rubbed his hands together. 'I'm beginning to see merit in your proposal.'

'There is one other thing you might consider,' Helen pressed on. 'I understand you're raising funds for a new organ?'

'That's right.'

'If our concert is a success, you might consider using the church for similar events in the future.'

'That's an excellent idea,' Mr Watt said, making a note on a pad beside his desk. 'Now may I ask what level of fee you have in mind?'

'We haven't worked out all the financial details yet but we're hoping to have up to two hundred guests. If we charged twenty euros per ticket we would raise four thousand euros.'

She exchanged a glance with Anne. 'We would be prepared to donate the entire receipts to the church organ fund, minus some small expenses such as the hire of a quality piano and equipment.'

At this news, Mr Watt positively beamed with pleasure. 'That puts an entirely fresh complexion on the issue. Indeed, I might even be able to help you with the piano. One of our parishioners is a keen pianist. I might be able to persuade her to let you use her instrument for the recital, subject to Antonio's approval, of course.' He smiled at the young Spaniard.

'You are very kind,' Antonio said. 'Is it possible for me to see the church?'

'Why, of course.'

Mr Watt took a key from his desk and called his wife to say that they were leaving for a few minutes. Then they all trooped out of the room and walked the short distance to the church. Once they were inside, Antonio stood for a few minutes, taking in the polished wooden pews, the high vaulted ceiling and the sunlight streaming in through the stained-glass windows. At last, he turned to Mr Watt.

'This is a beautiful building, Señor. It would be an honour for me to play here.'

Eventually they took their leave of Mr Watt, who promised to contact them after he had spoken to the vestry committee again.

'You were brilliant, Helen,' Anne said, once they had settled into the car for the drive home. 'You really should have been a diplomat. The way you handled the vicar was a pleasure to watch.'

'Yes,' Antonio agreed. 'You were excellent.'

'Let's hope he can sell the idea to his committee,' Helen replied.

When they got home, she insisted they all have tea and scones, but when she set off towards the kitchen, Antonio took over. 'I'll do it,' he said. 'You sit down and relax.'

When she and Helen were alone, Anne said, 'He's really very domesticated, cooking, tending the garden and painting the tree house. You'll miss him when he goes back to Spain.'

'Yes.' Helen sighed. 'I will. He's a real dote.'

They sat in the drawing room, drinking tea and looking out at the lawn while they waited for Mr Watt's reply. To pass the time, they engaged in small talk but everyone knew there was only one subject that mattered. If the vicar turned them down they would have to begin their search again. And there was no guarantee they would get anywhere as good St Matilda's.

It was almost six when the phone rang. Helen immediately picked it up and clasped it to her ear. The others watched nervously.

At last they heard her say: 'Thank you very much, Mr Watt.'

She switched off the phone and turned to them. 'That was the vicar.'

'And?' Anne gasped.

'He's agreed to let us have the church.'

They hugged each other. Helen walked to the sideboard. She returned with a bottle of sherry and three glasses. 'I think this calls for a celebration,' she said, and pulled the stopper from the bottle.

Chapter Twenty-one

Robbie opened his eyes and a searing pain shot through his skull, like someone was sticking burning needles into his brain. He groaned and pulled the duvet over his head. After a few minutes he peeped out again. He could make out the contours of his bedroom. Thank God I'm somewhere safe, he thought, as a wave of relief swept over him.

Next thing was to get out of bed. His knee trembled as he placed his right foot on the floor and paused to see if it would support him. He waited for a minute, then gingerly placed the other beside it. Praying that he wasn't going to fall over, he stood up and took a few tentative steps, holding onto the dressing table for balance.

He made it as far as the bathroom and looked at himself in the mirror. He was shocked at the sight that stared back at him. His eyes were bloodshot, his skin was yellow and beads of sweat were breaking out on his forehead. I look like a beached whale, he thought, as he fumbled in the press for a packet of paracetamol. His hand shook as he took out two and swallowed them with a glass of water from the tap.

He sat down on the toilet seat to rest. By now, the sweat was cascading down his cheeks like a river and nausea swept over him. He reached for a facecloth to wipe away the sweat, lost his balance and toppled over onto the floor. I'm having a cardiac arrest, he thought, as he stared up at the ceiling and felt his heart trying to burst through his chest. I'm going to die on the bathroom floor. What am I going to do?

Gradually, the nausea passed and he felt a little better. This time, he managed to get into the kitchen and switched on the kettle. It gave a whistle as it boiled. Robbie heaped three spoonfuls of coffee into a mug, then added hot water and milk. He took several huge gulps.

Slowly the fog began to lift. His head sank into his hands. How the hell did I get myself into this state? He tried to piece together the events of the previous night. He could remember loud music, laughter and flashing strobe lights. It had to have been a nightclub but which one? And how had he got there?

He decided to start at the beginning and work from there. He could recall leaving work and going to a burger joint. He was out to celebrate because he had landed a contract and had the bonus cheque for five grand in his wallet. At this thought, cold terror seized him. He stood up and careered back to the bedroom, where he began frantically searching for his jacket.

He found it lying in a heap in the corner and rifled through the pockets till at last his fingers grasped the wallet. He opened it, and there was the cheque signed by the company secretary, exactly where he had put it for safe-keeping. He raised it to his lips and kissed it with joy.

Just then his phone rang. When he picked it up, his boss was on the line. 'Where are you?' he demanded. 'Aren't you coming in today?'

Robbie felt the burning needles again. He glanced at his watch and saw it was five past ten. He should have been at work since nine.

'I've got food poisoning,' he croaked. 'I've been sick all morning. I was hoping it would pass.'

'Maybe you should see a doctor,' his boss said, his tone softening a little.

'Right now, I can't move from the bed.'

'You sound bad. Do you want me to send someone round to see you?'

'No, no,' Robbie said. 'I might take a cab to the doctor this afternoon. He'll give me something for it.'

'What about tomorrow?'

'I'll be at my desk even if I have to crawl in. That's a promise.'

'So we can expect you here at nine?'

'On my mother's grave.'

He terminated the call, closed his eyes and fell back on the bed, exhausted.

Eventually, he managed to get up again and made his way into the bathroom where he stood under the hot shower for fifteen minutes, shaved, put on a dressing gown and went back to the kitchen. He made more coffee, scrambled some eggs and forced himself to eat. As he sat down, he noticed a note propped against the salt cellar. He stared at it. Where had that come from? he wondered, as he opened it and began to read.

It looked like it had been written by a child.

Darling Robbie, Thank you for a wonderful night of passion. I will never forget it as long as I live. What a strong virile lover you are. Now that I have found you, I will never let you go. I will call you later to arrange another rendezvous. I can't wait. With all my love,
Samantha
Xxx

Suddenly the events of the previous night rushed into his mind. After the burger joint, he had gone to Crazy Joe's nightclub. He remembered the Bombay Fizzs, the champagne, the laughter, the music . . . and Samantha O'Leary appearing out of the crowd, like a seductive nymph. He must have brought her back here and made love to her in his bed. And now she was threatening to pursue him.

'Oh, no!' He groaned. Another thought made his blood freeze. If Kirsty ever got to hear of this, all hell would break loose. His brain was on fire again. He threw his head back and screamed.

* * *

Kirsty had been up since half past seven. She had slept well and now she was buzzing with energy. She had decided to accept Cecily Moncrieffe's offer for Penny Muldoon's evening gowns. But before she confirmed it, she should ring Penny to tell her.

She went into the kitchen and had breakfast – porridge, fruit and toast spread with honey. At nine o'clock she went into her office and rang the young designer. 'Are you sitting comfortably?' she asked.

'Yes – what is it, Kirsty?'

'I've got some very good news.'

'Yes?'

'You saw the spread in the *Tribune* yesterday?'

'Of course I did. It was brilliant. I thought Ellie O'Mara looked magic. I tried to ring you several times but your line was constantly engaged.'

'That was because I was dealing with a lot of clients eager to buy your gowns. As you can imagine, it wasn't easy. Swimming with sharks would be a doddle compared to negotiating with some of those people. Anyway, I've got an excellent offer from Cecily Moncrieffe, which I'm inclined to accept. But first I wanted to get your reaction.'

'You know I trust you, Kirsty. If you think it's a good offer then go right ahead and take it.'

'Don't you want to know what it is first?' She explained what Cecily had offered.

Penny gasped. 'That's absolutely fantastic. I'm over the moon.'

'That's not all. She's agreed to take all your stuff for the next eighteen months, sight unseen.'

'You're kidding me?'

'No, I'm not. This is practically unheard of, except for the very top dress designers. But she likes your things, Penny. And this offer will give you peace of mind. It'll allow you to get on with your work safe in the knowledge that you've got a guaranteed buyer.'

'So what are you waiting for? Call her at once and accept before she changes her mind.'

Kirsty laughed. 'I'm going to do that right away and this evening I'm going to take you out for dinner to celebrate.'

'I feel dizzy. I can't believe this is happening to me.'

'Well, it is. Congratulations, Penny. You deserve it. Now I'd better go. I'll call you later about dinner.'

She disconnected with a smile on her face. It was refreshing to hear the girl's reaction to her achievement. It was in marked contrast to the arrogance of some fashion prima donnas, who regarded success as their entitlement. She took a sip from the coffee mug on the desk beside her and prepared to ring Cecily.

* * *

'I'm going to accept your offer,' she began, when the boutique owner was on the line.

'I should certainly think so,' Cecily replied. 'You're a smart woman. You know you won't do better.'

'That wasn't the reason.'

'Oh? What was?'

'Loyalty. I thought about what you said. You helped me when I was starting out. I felt I owed you something. And I also think it will be good for Penny's career.'

'Oh, give over,' Cecily said. 'You'll have me weeping in a moment. Now, we need to sit down and finalise things, the sooner the better. When are you free?'

'Whenever you are. I'll make myself available.'

'Why waste time? We can meet tomorrow for lunch.'

'Okay.'

'I'll book that place we went to the last time.'

'The Gondola in Malahide?'

'I liked it.'

'Fine. What time?'

'One o'clock.'

'Excellent. See you tomorrow.'

So far, so good, Kirsty thought. Now I'd better organise tonight's dinner with Penny. This was a special occasion so she should push the boat out a little, somewhere special and maybe a bottle of champagne. She thought immediately of Malibu, an upmarket spot on Dawson Street that was attracting the movers and shakers. Penny would like it. Kirsty rang at once and got one of the last tables for eight o'clock. Then she rang Penny back and gave her the details.

She spent the rest of the morning dealing with paperwork and emails, and by one o'clock she was free. She decided to walk up the hill and visit her mother. She changed into jeans and a stout pair of shoes, then set off along the cliff path to the Summit.

It was a glorious day. Along the path, the wild flowers and heathers were coming into bloom. Down below, the waves were lashing against the cliffs. Across the bay, she could see the rooftops of Dún Laoghaire gleaming in the sun. The only sound to disturb the stillness was the squawking of the gulls. When she reached the top, she sat down for a moment to catch her breath and admire the wonderful view. Then she continued on to Avalon.

When she arrived she found her mother, Anne and Antonio gathered around a little table on the patio. Helen had a large pad in her lap and was busily taking notes. They stopped talking when she arrived.

'Good morning,' she said. Her eyes travelled along the smooth lawn, and the neatly clipped hedges. 'I see you've been busy. The garden looks beautiful.'

'Oh, that wasn't me,' Helen replied. 'That was Antonio. He also painted the tree house.'

The Spaniard smiled at her, and she felt a momentary flutter, but instead of returning his smile, she turned away.

She still hadn't come to terms with her mother's crazy scheme. Privately, she was hoping it would all fall through and the Spaniard would be despatched home as soon as possible.

'How are your plans for the concert coming along?'

'Beautifully,' Helen replied. 'We had a really good piece of luck yesterday.'

'Yes,' Anne put in. 'We've managed to secure the perfect venue, a beautiful little church in Rathmines – it's ideal.'

'A church?'

Antonio nodded. 'The atmosphere is exactly right and the acoustics are so good that even a little mouse could sound like Pavarotti.'

He smiled at his joke but, once again, Kirsty didn't respond. He might have wormed his way into the affections of her mother and Anne but she wasn't so easily fooled by his charm. 'Isn't that a rather unusual venue?'

'Not at all,' Anne replied. 'It's been done before.'

'What happens now?'

'This is when the hard work begins,' Helen said excitedly. 'We have to finalise our guest list, then persuade as many important people as we can to come. In the meantime, Mr Watt is arranging a piano for Antonio so he'll have to go over there and try it out. If it's not suitable, we'll have to hire another one.'

'Who is Mr Watt?'

'The vicar, darling. So you can see we're going to be extremely busy. Remember, I'll be calling on you for help. Your sister has already volunteered and so has your brother.'

'I'll do what I can, of course I will,' Kirsty said, without conviction.

She stayed for half an hour. Antonio offered to make her tea, which she declined. At last, she left to walk back to her apartment. She could see that she had underestimated her mother. But instead of feeling pleased for her progress with the concert, a heavy gloom had settled over her.

The Spaniard was succeeding spectacularly in his plan to ingratiate himself with Helen. Kirsty had observed how he fussed over her and Anne. He had cleared up the garden, painted the tree house and was quickly becoming part of the household.

If she didn't act quickly, he would have achieved his objective. She made a mental note to call Benny Taylor and hurry him up. The sooner he got the dirt on Antonio, the better.

Chapter Twenty-two

A hum of chatter hung like a warm cloud over Malibu when Kirsty and Penny arrived for dinner at eight o'clock. The restaurant wasn't one of those quiet retreats where lovers could conduct a discreet rendezvous, safe from prying eyes. It was the complete opposite, a place for celebrities to strut and be seen, which was why the two women were shown to a table tucked away in a corner, suitable for diners who hadn't had the foresight to book well in advance.

The sleek waiter handed them two menus, then disappeared back into the well-dressed crowd. Kirsty had to stretch her neck to look around the room but she quickly spotted several personalities. A popular television chat show host was holding forth to a group of awed companions at a table in the centre. Nearby, an aspiring actress was pretending to be bored while she strove desperately to attract attention. Across the room, a prize-winning photographer was deep in conversation with a famous publisher.

Kirsty started as her eyes came to rest on a plump, flame-haired figure who inspired fear and loathing throughout the ranks of the Dublin glitterati – Susie Kelly, the middle-aged showbiz columnist with the *Trumpet*, the city's scandal rag. Every day, her column was studded with personality gossip: who was going out with whom, which singer was breaking up with her boyfriend, who was going into rehab. She cultivated an image of the all-seeing, all-knowing journalist from whom no secret was safe. In reality, she relied on a network of spies and informers who fed her titbits of information, which she hammered into short, snappy paragraphs guaranteed to put the fear of God into anyone unfortunate enough to cross her path. But for many readers, her column was the first thing they turned to when they picked up their daily copy of the *Trumpet*.

Tonight she was wearing an outrageous white dress studded with large black spots, a string of fake pearls and a ridiculous hat with a drooping ostrich feather. Her companion was a slim, effete young man in a blazer, with a handkerchief poking out of the breast pocket, and cavalry twill trousers. They probably believed they were projecting an image of glamour and fashion but, to Kirsty, they seemed outlandish.

'Who's that dreadful-looking woman?' Penny asked, lowering her voice.

'Someone you should pray never to meet,' Kirsty replied.

'Why?'

'Because she's not a very nice person.'

'What's her name?'

'Susie Kelly.'

'The gossip columnist?'

'Exactly.'

'Funny, I always thought she was younger.'

'That's because she's been using the same photograph on her column for the past thirty years.'

At that moment, Susie Kelly turned and stared across the room towards Kirsty, as if she realised they were talking about her. Kirsty lowered her head and pretended to read the menu.

'Enjoying yourself?' she whispered to her young companion.

'Enormously, I've never been here before. It's interesting to watch all these famous people. Isn't that Peter Lawlor, the photographer, over there?'

'That's right.'

'They really look quite ordinary when you see them up close.'

'They *are* ordinary. They've got the same problems as the rest of us and maybe some more. But they like to pretend they're special. Maybe it makes them feel superior, but I find the whole thing boring. Now you'd better decide what to eat before the waiter comes back.'

Penny, who looked as if she hadn't had a decent meal in weeks, scanned the menu and chose a pasta dish with prawns to be followed by grilled lamb chops with baby potatoes and broccoli. Kirsty, who wasn't particularly hungry, opted for chicken salad, then ordered the champagne.

'Now that you're becoming famous yourself,' she went on, 'you'll probably come here more often.'

The waiter arrived with the bottle, removed the cork unobtrusively and poured some, fizzing, into their glasses.

Penny blushed. 'I'm not famous.'

'Not yet but just wait till Cecily has finished with you.'

'I'm not sure I'd want to be famous, at least, not *too* famous. I wouldn't want that awful Susie Kelly poking into my affairs.'

'It really depends how you handle it. Just try to keep your

head and be yourself and you should be all right. Those summer gowns really attracted a lot of publicity. That was why Cecily was so keen to sign you up. She believes you've got a bright future and so do I.'

Penny clasped Kirsty's hand. 'I know this deal is a big opportunity for me and I don't think I've thanked you sufficiently. I hope I won't let you down.'

'You won't, and you don't have to thank me. I'm simply doing my job. Like I said, you've got talent. If Cecily hadn't snapped you up, someone else would. But remember one thing. This is a very competitive business and you're only as good as your current designs. You've got to keep doing it again and again. There will always be other designers breathing down your neck.'

'I know that already.'

'Then you should go far.'

At that moment Penny's first course arrived.

'When will the deal be signed?' Penny asked, taking a sip of champagne.

'I'm seeing Cecily tomorrow to finalise everything. I'd expect it all to be wrapped up pretty quickly.'

'And then what?'

'You start working on your next collection.'

'I already have. I'll send you some sketches tomorrow. You can show them to her.'

'That's my girl,' Kirsty said, patting her wrist. She glanced across the room to find that Susie Kelly had shifted her attention to a woman in a blue dress sitting at the next table. She had felt uncomfortable being under the journalist's gaze. Now she felt as if a potential threat had just passed.

It was after eleven when they left Malibu to go home. The restaurant was still buzzing and there was a queue of people hoping to get in. They found a line of taxis waiting along Dawson Street, hopped into one and gave their directions. Penny lived in Clontarf, which was on the way to Howth so the taxi dropped her off and Kirsty continued on to her apartment.

When she got in, she checked her phone for messages and decided to turn in. As she was drifting off to sleep, the thought occurred to her that she hadn't heard from Robbie all day. He was probably recovering from his night on the town. There was no doubt about it: he was getting more erratic.

* * *

The following morning she was up at eight o'clock. When she drew the curtains she saw that the sun was out again. It was going to be another beautiful day. She made some breakfast, went into her office and spent the rest of the morning working at her desk. At midday, she began to get ready for her lunch with Cecily Moncrieffe. As she was coming out of the bathroom her phone rang. It was Angie Dunlop. She sounded sombre.

'Please sit down,' she began.

'Why?' Kirsty asked, immediately suspicious.

'Because you're not going to like what I have to say.'

Kirsty lowered herself into a chair with a sense of foreboding. 'Okay, I'm sitting down now. Tell me the worst.'

'I got a call this morning from a pal who was in Crazy Joe's two nights ago.'

'And?'

'Your friend was there.'

'Robbie Hennessy?'

'The very same.'

'I knew that already. He called me.'

'Wait till I'm finished. He was very drunk. He was lowering Bombay Fizzs and champagne to beat the band.'

'I knew that too.'

'Did you know that he left with someone?'

Kirsty steeled herself for the worst. 'Who?'

'Samantha O'Leary.'

She felt the breath leave her body. 'I don't believe you.'

'Unfortunately it's true. I did warn you. That girl is never content with one guy when she can steal somebody else's. She collects men like other women collect shoes. Anyway, I thought I'd better tell you before someone else does. Now you'll be prepared.'

Kirsty wasn't listening any more. She put the phone down as her blood ran cold. The thought of Robbie humiliating her like that before a crowded nightclub was the last straw. And with Samantha O'Leary? It was just too much to bear.

Suddenly, the lunch with Cecily didn't seem appealing any more.

Chapter Twenty-three

Antonio stepped out of a taxi on Rathmines Road and began walking in the direction of St Matilda's Church. The vicar had called that morning to say that the piano had been delivered and Antonio was on his way to inspect it. Everything was moving at remarkable speed after the initial setbacks. Now they had secured the perfect venue for the concert. Antonio knew he would feel entirely at ease playing to an intimate audience in the beautiful old church. He would be relaxed and able to deliver his very best performance. The knowledge gave him a warm feeling of confidence.

He thought how kind everyone had been since he'd arrived in Ireland. Helen had been wonderful, making him feel entirely at home in her beautiful house. She had even given him a key and treated him as a member of the family who could come and go as he pleased. And the others, Anne, Deirdre and Mark, had been equally welcoming. They had all rowed in behind Helen promising to support her effort to launch his career.

The only one who had showed any coldness was Kirsty. She

was a beautiful woman, and he found her very attractive, but she had never been as friendly as the others. Indeed, Antonio could sense a degree of hostility from her. She kept her distance and rarely spoke to him. She was strong, he could see that, and proud. He wondered if he had done something to offend her. Then again, he thought, perhaps it was nothing to do with him. Perhaps it was a personal problem she had. Or maybe she was having trouble with her work.

He put the thoughts from his mind as he approached the front door of the vicarage and pressed a large button set into the wall. He heard a bell echoing inside the house. A moment later, footsteps were approaching. The door swung open and Mr Watt was smiling at him. 'Come in, come in,' he said. 'You're precisely on time. We're all waiting for you in anticipation.'

Antonio followed him along a carpeted corridor to the study where they had met before. Inside, a small grey-haired lady was waiting. Mr Watt made the introduction. 'This is our parishioner, Mrs Gilbert. She is the lady who has kindly loaned us her piano.'

Mrs Gilbert stood up and shook Antonio's hand. 'I've heard all about you from Mr Watt. I'm told you're a wonderful pianist and I can't wait to hear you play.'

Antonio felt himself blush, as he always did when people praised him too much. 'Thank you for your kind words, Señora. It is true I love playing the piano. But I will leave you to decide whether I am as good as you have been told.'

Mrs Gilbert smiled. 'You're certainly not arrogant,' she said. 'I like that in a musician. Too many are full of their own importance. So let's go and find out how well you can play.'

By now, the vicar's wife had joined them and the little party trooped the short distance to the church. Mr Watt took a key from his waistcoat pocket and they went inside. Antonio stood for a moment to absorb the atmosphere once more. The church was still, and when they spoke their voices echoed around the walls. The light from the windows cast a bright radiance over the scene and lent an air of solemnity. He let his gaze travel along the aisle till it came to rest at the altar. There, just below the pulpit, was the piano. He could tell at once, even before he inspected it, that it was a high-quality instrument.

'Come and see it,' Mrs Gilbert said, drawing him down the aisle.

It was a Steinway, made from polished spruce. He ran his fingers along the smooth surface, then turned to Mrs Gilbert, who was waiting for his reaction.

'It's beautiful,' he said. 'The best I have ever seen.'

'Thank you,' she said, clearly delighted. 'It belonged to my mother. She was a piano teacher. I inherited my love of music from her.'

'I had a wonderful teacher when I was a little boy,' Antonio told her. 'He taught me all I know.'

'So, now, let us hear the result of his good work. You must play for us, Antonio.'

He sat down before the piano and drew a deep breath, then flexed his hands. There was an expectant silence and his fingers touched the keys. Liszt's 'La Campanella' soared to the high roof of the church while his audience listened, enthralled. When he had finished, he bowed to them, and they responded with warm applause.

'That was superb,' Mrs Watt said, plainly impressed by Antonio's playing.

'Yes, indeed,' the vicar agreed. 'A really excellent performance.'

'But you must play something else,' Mrs Gilbert urged.

This time he played Brahms' 'Lullaby'. As he finished, the response was even more enthusiastic.

'I'm truly impressed,' Mrs Gilbert said, her eyes gleaming. 'You have a rare talent. I've heard dozens of pianists but none as good as you.'

Antonio was blushing again. 'No, no. It is simply that the piano is such a fine instrument and the acoustics are so good. They improve the sound.'

'Nonsense,' Mrs Gilbert said. 'Even those advantages wouldn't mask a poor performance. I know a great pianist when I hear one.'

'Thank you, Señora, and you too.' He bowed politely to the vicar and his wife. 'You have all been so kind.'

'You will probably want to practise before the concert,' Mr Watt continued. 'You may have the use of the church any time you wish. Just ring in advance and let me know when you're coming. Now, we would like to invite you to the vicarage for afternoon tea. I'm sure Mrs Gilbert will want to have a good long chat with you.'

* * *

Kirsty returned from her lunch with Cecily Moncrieffe at half past three, still in a rage with Robbie Hennessy. She couldn't get him out of her mind. Indeed, it was all she could do to concentrate on what Cecily was saying as her thoughts kept straying to Angie's call. Several times during the meal, Cecily had leaned across the table and examined her closely. 'Are you feeling all right, Kirsty?'

'I'm fine.'

'You certainly don't look it. Perhaps you've been working too hard.'

'No,' Kirsty replied, plastering a smile onto her face. 'I'm just a bit tired – too many late nights.'

'You should slow down. Take it from me, I know. You need to be alert in this business otherwise people will take advantage of you.'

'Yes,' Kirsty said, sitting up straight. The last thing she wanted was Cecily thinking she was losing her grip. If word got out that she was wilting under pressure, it would be professional suicide. Now she wished she had postponed the lunch till a later date but Cecily had been anxious to get the deal wrapped up and so had Penny.

As a result, the meal was a disaster. There had been none of the wit and humour that had characterised their previous lunch in the same restaurant. Kirsty couldn't get away fast enough.

Now that she was home, she could barely remember what they had discussed and the terms of their agreement. It was all down to that reptile Hennessy who couldn't keep himself under control. She imagined the news spreading round town like wildfire and her enemies laughing with glee. The very thought made her heart sink.

She went into the kitchen, put the kettle on and made a strong cup of tea. She sat down beside the window where she could look at the harbour as she turned the situation over in her mind. The break-up had been coming anyway. She had known that for some time. Robbie wasn't the sort of man any woman would want to be saddled with for long. Apart from good looks and certain strengths in the bedroom, he was a total liability. She should never have got involved with him in the first place.

Now, to any observer, it would appear that he had dumped her for Samantha O'Leary. That was the story everyone would fasten on when the tongues got wagging in the Dublin watering holes. It made her look like a loser and Kirsty hated that. The humiliating thought of people whispering behind her back made her feel sick.

Just wait till he calls to apologise, she thought. I'll let him have it with both barrels. His ears will be sore for weeks. Then a terrible thought struck her. What if he never called at all? What if this wasn't just a one-night stand as she suspected? What if he had fallen for Samantha O'Leary and started parading her around town for the whole of Dublin to see? How was she going to handle that?

But even that was nothing compared to the knowledge that she had failed once again. Robbie Hennessy was just the latest in a long line of disasters. Why couldn't she form a proper relationship? Why was she always drawn like a magnet to the wrong men? She wasn't getting any younger, as Angie had reminded her, in her blunt, no-nonsense way. Was she doomed never to meet a decent man and fall in love?

Her thoughts drifted to Antonio. Here was a man she might have been interested in if the situation had been different. He was very attractive, with dark, Latin good looks and there was no disputing his charm and excellent manners. She felt herself starting to daydream then pulled herself up short.

What was she thinking of? The guy was a crook, busily sneaking his way into her mother's affections so he could rob her. If she didn't stop him soon it would be too late to save her mother from making a fool of herself. She lifted the phone and dialled Benny Taylor.

'It's Kirsty O'Neill.'

'Yes, Miss O'Neill.'

'I'm calling to talk about Antonio Rivera.'

'What about him?'

'He has my poor mother eating out of his hand. He'll have her life savings if he isn't stopped. What have you managed to find out about him?'

'Nothing so far.'

'*Nothing?*'

'I've got men checking him out but he appears clean.'

'He can't be! You'll just have to try harder.'

'We're trying as hard as we can.'

She was rapidly running out of patience. This was turning out to be one of the worst days she could ever remember. 'Listen.' She sighed. 'There's a lot riding on this. Would you please pull out all the stops?'

Chapter Twenty-four

'Debbie McKenzie? It's Helen O'Neill here. How are you?'

'Oh, Helen! I'm very well, thank you,' Debbie replied. 'And how are you? I thought you went off to Spain for a little holiday.'

'Well, that's the reason I'm calling. I'm back and I've brought a young Spanish friend with me. His name is Antonio Rivera and he's a very gifted pianist. I'm organising a recital for him.'

'Really?' Debbie sounded surprised.

'Yes. This is going to be a very big occasion and I knew you'd want to be there. He's absolutely brilliant. I've set aside some tickets for you.'

'Where is it?' Debbie asked, cautiously.

'A pretty little church in Rathmines, called St Matilda's. We chose it especially for the ambience and acoustics. This is going to be a wonderful evening, Debbie. You won't want to miss it.'

'I'm sure it will. What date?'

'June the third, at eight o'clock. I should tell you that the attendance is strictly limited to two hundred guests.'

'How much are the tickets?'

'Twenty euros each. We're keeping the price as low as possible, just basically covering our costs.'

'Oh, no,' Debbie said suddenly. 'Did you say June the third? I think that's the night Regina Donleavy has organised her bridge tournament and I've promised to go to that. Look, put me down as a maybe. If I can wriggle out of the tournament, I'll get back to you.'

'Don't leave it too late, Debbie. I expect these tickets to go pretty fast.'

Helen finished the conversation and shook her head at Anne. 'You can strike her off the list. She won't be coming.'

The two women were sitting at a table in the drawing room. They'd had a very busy morning. They had already located a printer who had agreed to produce the tickets and flyers for the concert, and would also print the programme once Antonio had decided what he was going to play. He had left earlier to go back to Rathmines to see Mrs Gilbert. Now Helen and Anne were working their way through the list of potential guests. It was midday and so far they had managed to contact forty of the hundred and seventy names. But the results had been mixed. Helen was taken aback to discover that some of those she had considered certainties to come had turned her down. As a result, they had managed to sell just thirty tickets.

At one o'clock, they decided to have a break and retire to the patio to take stock of the situation.

'I have to admit that I'm a little discouraged,' Helen confessed. 'I was expecting a much better response. Georgina Gordon refused to come on the grounds that her doctor had advised her to avoid crowds. Did you ever hear such a lame excuse? And after everything I've done for her. She could have made a donation at least but I've always known she was a skinflint.'

'It's early days,' Anne replied, cheerfully. 'Sales are bound to pick up once word gets around.'

'They'd better – or Mr Watt will be very disappointed, not to mention Antonio.'

'And we still have to get working on publicity. That will give the concert another push. Have you spoken to Kirsty? Didn't she promise to help?'

'I'll ring her this evening, Mark and Deirdre too.'

'Do that. Now let's have a nice cup of tea and then we'll get back to working the phones.'

* * *

By five o'clock when they decided to finish for the day, they had managed to contact another thirty names on the list and the ticket sales had crept up to fifty. A further twenty people had said they might come and would confirm later. It was an improvement but still a long way short of the two hundred guests that Helen had promised Mr Watt.

'I've been a little too easy-going in my approach,' Helen said. 'Perhaps it calls for a firmer touch.'

'How do you mean?'

'You mentioned blackmail when we first discussed this. Tomorrow I'll start reminding people of all the favours I've done for them in the past. I'll shame them into buying tickets if I have to. I'm going to fill that church by hook or by crook.'

When Anne had left, saying she'd be back again the following morning at nine o'clock, Helen started ringing the children. She began with Deirdre, who sounded harassed when she answered the phone.

'It's Mum, darling. I'm ringing about the concert. We have almost everything organised.'

'That was quick.'

'Well, we don't want to waste time. We've arranged a lovely venue and we've even managed to get Antonio a beautiful piano.'

'How is he?'

'He's fine.'

'Tell him I was asking for him. I must pop over and see him soon.'

'I'm sure he'd be delighted to meet you again. Now, the reason I'm ringing. We've got to sell the tickets and I thought you might lend a hand.'

'How do you mean?' Deirdre asked defensively.

'I'd like you to ring your friends and encourage them to come. Tell them it's for a very special cause. I know you can be persuasive, Deirdre. I expect you to sell these tickets.'

'I'll do my best, Mum, but you know how busy I am with my boys.'

'But they're at school during the daytime.'

'Yes, but I'm not just sitting here twiddling my thumbs. I've got the washing and shopping and cooking and cleaning.'

'You don't need to tell me,' Helen said tersely. 'I did it, too, or had you forgotten? Now, I'm going to set aside thirty tickets for you.'

'Thirty? That sounds like a lot. How much do they cost?'

'Twenty euros each. Speak to your neighbours and the parents on the school committee. The tickets are being printed as we speak, along with a little flyer of the event. I'll get them over to you as soon as they arrive.'

'I'll see what I can do,' Deirdre said, without much enthusiasm.

'You weren't listening to me,' Helen replied firmly. 'I said I *expected* you to sell them. I'm investing a lot of time and energy in this event and I am relying on my family to help me. That includes you.' She finished the call and uttered a loud sigh. There was a selfish streak in Deirdre. She was the eldest and James had spoiled her. But on this occasion Helen expected her to do her duty.

The next call was to Mark. He answered on the first ring. 'O'Neill Consulting.'

'It's me.'

'Mum!' he said, brightening. 'I thought you were a client I was expecting.'

'No, just your mother, darling.'

'How are you? How is Antonio? Have you organised your concert yet?'

'One question at a time,' Helen replied. 'I'm quite well. As for Antonio, he has settled into Avalon and has proved very useful. He's tidied up the garden for me and enjoys cooking us Spanish dishes for dinner.'

'He sounds like the ideal house guest.'

'He is. Now, as regards the concert. We're making great strides. We've got a venue. It's a lovely old church in Rathmines. Antonio is over there right now, discussing his programme with the lady who is loaning us her piano.'

'My God, you've certainly been busy. I'm very impressed.'

'We're only at the beginning, darling. We've got to make sure that people come and that's why I'm calling you. You said you'd help.'

'Of course,' Mark said.

'Well, I'm allocating thirty tickets for you to sell. They cost twenty euros each and I hope you can persuade your friends and customers to buy them. We want to fill that church for Antonio's concert.'

'No bother,' Mark said. 'It'll be a pleasure.'

'Thank you,' Helen said. 'I'll get the tickets to you as soon as they're printed. In the meantime you can be thinking of the people you're going to approach. I appreciate your support.'

'Not at all.' There was a brief pause, then Mark continued, 'You said Antonio's settled in at Avalon?'

'Indeed he has. He loves Howth. He goes out walking over the East Mountain most days.'

There was a slight pause. 'Does that mean he might stay?'

'What a strange question. Why do you ask?'

'I was just wondering . . .'

'We've never discussed his future plans,' Helen replied. 'Right now we're concentrating on launching his career and getting more people to hear his amazing talent.'

'Quite right,' Mark replied. 'Just let me have the tickets whenever they're ready. I'm sure I'll manage to sell them all.'

'Excellent,' Helen said. 'I'll be in touch.'

She put the phone down and stared into space. She had known she could depend on Mark, unlike his older sister. But he had raised a question that hadn't even occurred to her. What *was* Antonio going to do when the concert was over? She had vaguely supposed he would return to Marbella, but what if he decided to stay on in Dublin?

Well, she'd be quite happy to have him as a permanent guest. She enjoyed his company and he was absolutely no trouble. Indeed, it was quite useful to have a man around the house again.

Her final call was to Kirsty. She hadn't heard from her today and she was relying on her to use her contacts to drum up publicity.

'I'm ringing about the concert,' Helen began.

'Yes?'

'We haven't discussed this properly but I did mention the possibility of getting some publicity. You know so many influential people.'

'You've got me at a very bad time,' Kirsty replied rather brusquely.

'This won't take long, darling. Now, I know you said she wasn't very nice but she does seem to be all over the television and the newspapers and I think she might be very useful if we could get her on board.'

'Who are we talking about?' Kirsty asked.

'That young model with the blonde hair, Samantha O'Leary. I wonder if you might give her a ring and ask if she can help us out.'

There was a groan and suddenly the line went dead.

Chapter Twenty-five

Kirsty had been up since eight o'clock but she hadn't slept well. She had simmered down a little overnight but she was still burning with resentment at Robbie's behaviour. After a light breakfast, she had checked her email and text messages, turned off her phone and gone back to bed. Work could wait. She didn't feel like talking to people today.

Tucked up in bed, she wallowed in self-pity. Her pride had taken a blow. No man had ever dumped her before. Whenever it came to ending relationships, she had always taken the initiative. And it was made worse because it had been done in public by someone as shallow as Robbie Hennessy. It showed how far she had allowed her standards to slip in pursuit of a man.

There had been a time when Kirsty was so particular about choosing partners that she had been known among her friends as the Ice Maiden. Any man she consented to go out with had had to meet certain very strict criteria. Anyone over the age of thirty-five was too old, and anyone earning less than eighty thousand a year was too poor. She had even checked out the model of car any candidate drove. And this was before it came to looks.

Her men had to be taller than she was and they had to be well-built. No one overweight was even considered. They had to be handsome and in possession of a good head of preferably dark hair, although she might make an exception for a fair-haired man if he was particularly good-looking.

Other qualities included good bedroom skills, charm, a sharp sense of humour and a generous personality. Also very high on her list was intelligence. Robbie wasn't stupid. He was good at his job, but he would never win the Brain of Ireland competition. The fact that she had agreed to go out with him underlined just how low she had sunk.

Thinking like that just made her feel worse. She needed someone to cheer her up so she waited till five o'clock and rang Angie. 'I'm sorry I cut you off yesterday.'

'That's all right.'

'I was just so incensed at that rat embarrassing me like that, especially with someone like Samantha O'Leary.'

'I understand. You were in a state of shock. Your reaction was perfectly reasonable. I'd have done the same.'

Good old Angie, she thought. I knew I could rely on her.

'How are you feeling today?' her friend asked.

'I'm getting over it. I'm not going to curl up and die, if that's what you mean.'

'That's the spirit. Tell you what, why don't you drop down and see me? I'll pick up another chocolate cake on my way home from work.'

'That sounds brilliant.'

'I'll be home in an hour and we'll have a good old natter. Talking things over never did any harm.'

'You're on,' Kirsty said, throwing back the duvet and getting out of bed.

She had a shower and got dressed. Before leaving her apartment, she checked again for messages. There were several texts from clients and one each from Cecily Moncrieffe and Penny. They would have to wait till tomorrow. She locked up, went downstairs and got into her Aston Martin. Twenty minutes later, she was pulling up outside Angie's apartment.

'You look fantastic,' Angie said, when she opened the door.

'No need to butter me up,' Kirsty told her. 'I didn't even put on any lipstick.'

'You don't need make-up.'

'Oh, give me a break!' Kirsty started to laugh.

They went into the lounge.

'Wine?' Angie asked.

'I'd prefer tea.'

'Coming up. Just make yourself at home.'

Angie went to the kitchen and soon reappeared with a tray and a pot of tea. She handed Kirsty a plate and fork and proceeded to cut several large slices from the tempting chocolate gâteau she had bought.

'Where do you get these wonderful cakes?' Kirsty asked, placing a slice on her plate. 'The last one we had was delicious.'

'I buy them at a little French pâtisserie on Vernon Avenue.'

'I must try it some time.'

'Nothing beats comfort food when your spirits are low,' Angie said, settling down opposite her on the sofa. 'I must say I applaud your attitude, stiff upper lip and all that. Just put it behind you and start again. Has Robbie tried to contact you yet?'

'My phone's been off all day but he hasn't left any messages.'

'What are you going to do when he does?'

'You're making a large assumption. I might never hear from him again.'

'You will. Mark my words, once he's sobered up he'll realise the terrible blunder he's made and be back to you like a shot.'

'What would you recommend? Should I chew his head off or give him the silent treatment? Or should I simply put the phone down?'

'Do I assume you're not taking him back?'

'Are you mad? When Daniel got out of the lion's den, did he go back in?'

Angie smiled. 'In that case, I'm inclined towards the silent treatment. If you bawl him out, he'll know you're upset. Just let him grovel for a while, then tell him it's over. Keep your poise. Don't argue. Tell him not to contact you again and then finish the conversation. That will leave him feeling he's the loser.'

'You're a genius,' Kirsty said. 'That's exactly what I'll do.'

Angie took a mouthful of cake. 'I never said this before but I don't think you and Robbie were really suited. He's not your intellectual equal, in my opinion.'

'What?' Kirsty said, almost choking. 'You set me up with him, for God's sake. You said he was a great catch. Now you're telling me we weren't really suited.'

'I was only trying to do you a favour. You'd just ditched the accountant you were going out with.'

'Charlie Frazer.'

'That's him. I thought he was quite dishy. He had nice eyes. What did he do wrong?'

'Nothing. I just got bored. He had no conversation beyond

figures and statistics. Having dinner with him was like reading the *Financial Times*.'

Angie laughed.

'What really upsets me,' Kirsty said, 'is that everyone is going to believe that *he* ditched *me*.'

'Who cares what people think? It's your peace of mind that counts. Now, what are you going to do next?'

'I don't know. I think I'll lie low for a while.'

Angie was vigorously shaking her head. 'That's the very last thing you must do.'

'Really?'

'You know what they say when you fall off a horse? Get back on. You've got to get out there and let them all see you. You've got to go to restaurants and night spots. You've got to dress well and laugh and look like you haven't a care in the world. If possible, you should get some guy to squire you around.'

'And how exactly am I supposed to do that?'

'Oh, c'mon, Kirsty, you must have a little black telephone book. If necessary, rope in somebody's brother. The last thing you must do is hide away. Then the gossips will really think that Hennessy dumped you.'

'You're dead right,' Kirsty said. Already she was trawling through her head for a potential partner. Cecily had a salesman called Clive, who was gay. He might fit the bill.

'You know what? I think you're in the wrong job. You should have been an agony aunt on the problem page of the *Bugle*. You'd be perfect. Just talking to you has cheered me up. However, there's one potential danger. Suppose I run into Samantha O'Leary?'

'That shouldn't be a difficulty. You just smile sweetly and

be so nice that she'll think she's done you a favour by taking Hennessy off your hands.'

Kirsty sighed. 'I could never do that, not in a million years. I don't possess sufficient self-control.'

'Well, you can't avoid her for ever. You're bound to run into her somewhere. She pops up all over the place.'

'That doesn't mean I've got to talk to her. The very sound of her name made me feel sick even before this happened.'

Talking about Samantha O'Leary was making her very uncomfortable. She was sorry she had mentioned her. Just then, her phone rang. She dug it out of her bag and saw her mother's number. She had been so wrapped up in her troubles that she hadn't called her all day.

'I'm ringing about the concert,' Helen began.

'Yes?'

'I wonder if you've had an opportunity to take my suggestion on board?'

'Which one?'

'That young model with the blonde hair, Samantha O'Leary. Could you give her a ring and ask if she can help us out with the publicity?'

Kirsty stared at the phone in horror. She groaned and switched it off.

'What's the matter?' Angie said.

'That was my mother. You'll never guess what she wanted me to do.'

'What?'

'Ask Samantha O'Leary to publicise her concert.'

* * *

Helen stared at the silent phone in her hand. Unless she was very mistaken, Kirsty had cut her off. It was most unlike her to behave like that. And she hadn't even had an opportunity to talk about the concert tickets she wanted her to sell.

She had sounded stressed, poor girl. She was working too hard, that was the problem. Helen decided to leave her alone and not add to the pressure. Later, when things had calmed down, she would have a serious talk with Kirsty and persuade her to go off for a nice holiday.

Meanwhile, she would push on with the publicity drive on her own. There were lots of people she knew who could help.

Chapter Twenty-six

'Tell me more about the man who taught you to play the piano,' Mrs Gilbert said to Antonio. They were seated in the parlour of her house, in a street near the church. He had come again to play, not because he felt the need to practise but because he liked listening to the sound Mrs Gilbert's piano made. Afterwards she had invited him back to her home for tea.

'His name was Señor Alvarez. He was the music teacher at the school in Ronda, where I was born. He was a wonderful man, so kind and encouraging to me.'

Mrs Gilbert nodded as Antonio continued the story he had told Helen and Anne.

'Did you have a piano at home?'

'My parents were too poor to buy one. My father was a carpenter. But Señor Alvarez invited me to his house and allowed me to play his piano.'

'You were very fortunate to meet him.'

'Yes,' Antonio agreed. 'It was a stroke of good luck.'

'But even that wouldn't have been sufficient if you didn't already have the talent. That was the real stroke of luck, Antonio. I suspect that Señor Alvarez saw it too. That was why he encouraged you.'

'He said I had the music in my head.'

'And so you do. All the great musicians and composers have it. But it isn't enough to keep it. You must give it away. You must allow others to hear it. A pearl is useless if it is locked away in a box and nobody can see it.'

Antonio smiled. He liked this friendly little woman. She was very similar to Helen. 'That is an interesting way to put it. But you mustn't talk like that.'

'But it's the truth. And that's why your concert is so important. I think it is a wonderful gesture on the part of Mrs O'Neill to organise it for you. The more people who get a chance to hear you, the better.'

'And you learned from your mother?'

'Yes. She was a great music lover. I used to practise for hours.' She laughed at the memory. 'But all that practice could never give me what you have, Antonio. You have a gift that is allowed to very few.'

'Is your husband still alive?'

'He died ten years ago.'

'That is sad. What did he do?'

'He was a bank manager.'

'Do you have any children?'

'Two daughters. They're both married and have children of their own but, unfortunately, none of them is interested in the piano.' She paused. 'Do you have any family, Antonio?'

'No. I was an only child. Both my parents are dead.'

'And you never married?'

He shook his head.

'Why not? You're a handsome man. I'm sure there must be lots of women who would be happy to marry you.'

He looked at the floor. 'I earn barely enough money to keep myself. How could I keep a wife and family?'

'What do you do?'

'I play for guests at a holiday complex in Marbella. But it only lasts for the summer. In the winter, I play in bars in Málaga.'

'I'm surprised that no one recognised your talent before Mrs O'Neill came along,' Mrs Gilbert said.

He was about to tell her that he hadn't been able to go to music college but stopped himself in time. He was beginning to sound as if he was complaining, he thought. 'I don't feel sorry for myself,' he said. 'I think I am very fortunate.'

Mrs Gilbert's face broke into a broad smile. 'That is the right attitude, Antonio. And things do change, you know. Nothing stays the same for ever.'

Antonio glanced at his watch and stood up. 'I have to return to Howth,' he said. 'Helen will think I got lost.' He shook Mrs Gilbert's hand and thanked her for the tea.

'You must come again,' she said, as she walked with him to the front door. 'It's been wonderful talking to you.'

'I also have enjoyed it,' he said. He gave her a polite nod, then began to walk up the street.

What a very interesting young man, Mrs Gilbert thought. I do hope his concert is a success. I wonder if there is anything I can do to help him.

***

It had taken Robbie Hennessy three days to recover from the debauchery of Crazy Joe's nightclub. After finding Samantha O'Leary's note, he had made sure his phone was switched off, gone straight back to bed and pulled the duvet around him. He was in a deep hole. If Kirsty ever got wind of this, it was goodnight, Irene. She'd never forgive him, not in a million years.

He spent the remainder of the day sipping cups of tea and swallowing paracetamol while he sweated and shivered and tried to get his jumbled thoughts in order. His big mistake was going to Crazy Joe's. He could see that now. But he had just been handed that fat bonus cheque and Kirsty had refused to celebrate with him. That had triggered it. If she'd only been a little more accommodating, none of this would have happened.

And now he had Samantha on his case and she was threatening to contact him. She was a nice girl but she wasn't Kirsty. What was he going to do when she started calling? He'd have to find some excuse to palm her off and make sure that Kirsty never found out. Otherwise it was curtains.

Then there was his boss. Robbie wasn't sure if he'd bought his story about food poisoning. His boss wasn't a fool and took a dim view of people taking days off work. He was particularly down on anyone who missed time because of drinking. At ClickOn, the employees were expected to party and be at their desks, bright as buttons, the following morning.

If he did nothing else, he'd have to drag himself into the office in the morning. He'd promised his boss he'd be there. A loud groan escaped his lips. Please, God, get me out of this mess and I'll never get drunk again, he prayed. At last, he fell into a fitful sleep and didn't wake till seven o'clock the next day.

He got up, had a shower, shaved and dressed in clean clothes then forced himself to eat some breakfast to settle his stomach. He still felt terrible but at least the burning needles in his head had stopped and the shaking had diminished to a mild tremor.

That day, he worked steadily at his desk, hoping his boss wouldn't stop to talk to him and that Samantha wouldn't ring. Somehow he managed to get through until finishing time, when he went straight home and got into bed again.

On the third morning he felt much better. He examined himself in the bathroom mirror. The colour had returned to his cheeks and his eyes had regained their lustre. He was over the worst, and the knowledge gave him a further boost. He even made a point of seeking out his boss and apologising for not showing up for work.

'Did you see the doctor?' his boss asked, his eagle eye examining Robbie's face for telltale signs.

'He said it was a twenty-four-hour bug that was doing the rounds. He gave me a script for medication.'

'Make sure you don't pass it on to anyone else,' his boss grunted. 'We've got targets to meet.'

As the day progressed, Robbie found his old confidence returning. He had a tuna roll for lunch and ate it at his desk. He even managed to make some sales. At home time, he was actually feeling good again. He decided to go off on his own and have a beer at the Rusty Nail in Westmoreland Street to celebrate his recovery. Just the one, he told himself. It will do me good.

He found a quiet seat in the snug and took out his mobile phone. It had been silent for three days. When he switched it on, he found a string of messages, six of them from Samantha

O'Leary asking to see him again. He felt a slight shudder run down his spine. He'd have to find a way to let her down gently but not just now. This was going to be a delicate operation and he needed time to work out a plan. The last thing he needed right now was another woman on the warpath.

As he checked through the messages, he realised there wasn't a single one from Kirsty. A terrible thought came into his head. What if someone had seen him with Samantha in Crazy Joe's and passed on the information to her? She'd be spitting blood.

He'd better call her. He'd give her the spiel about food poisoning. But before he did that, he'd have another drink. He called the barman and asked for a double whiskey. Then he picked up the phone, took a deep breath and prepared to ring.

'Hello,' a voice answered.

'It's Robbie. I'm sorry I haven't been in touch with you for a while but I've been struck down with food poisoning and haven't been able to get out of bed for the past three days.'

There was silence.

'Are you still there?' Robbie asked.

'Of course I'm here. What do you want?'

'I've just explained. I want to apologise for not getting in touch with you.'

'Is that all?'

She sounded very strange. Something warned Robbie to tread carefully.

'Yes. But now I've recovered. I was just wondering if you might want to come out with me tonight. We've still got to celebrate that contract I pulled off, remember.'

There was a long, excruciating pause. 'That's very kind but the answer is no. You and I are finished, Robbie. I never want to see you again. In fact, I wish I'd never met you in the first place. Now will you do me a favour? Please don't ring my number again.'

There was a click and the conversation ended.

Definitely something odd, Robbie concluded. She seems to have lost it completely. That was women. He would never understand the way their minds worked. Ah, well, if Kirsty wasn't interested, there was always Samantha. It was time to give her a call.

Chapter Twenty-seven

'So, how many tickets have we managed to sell?' Anne asked. The two women were ensconced in the drawing room at Avalon once more, totting up the figures for the concert. Antonio had gone to St Matilda's to play Mrs Gilbert's piano. It was Monday morning and the concert was scheduled for two days' time.

'Ninety-six,' Helen said gloomily.

'Is that all?'

'Mark has sold his thirty tickets but Deirdre has only managed ten.'

'What about Kirsty? You were expecting big things from her.'

'She hasn't sold any.'

Anne looked surprised. 'Not even one?'

Helen shook her head.

'That's odd. I would have thought with all her contacts she would have sold fifty at least.'

'I didn't give her any,' Helen confessed. 'When I spoke to her she sounded stressed so I decided to back off and leave her alone.'

'Stressed?' Anne gave her a quizzical look. 'How do you mean?'

'You know, on edge. I think she's been under a lot of pressure recently with her business and I didn't want to add to it. Once the concert is over, I'm going to have a heart-to-heart with her, try to persuade her to slow down. She's worn out, poor child.'

'Well, that's a pity,' Anne said. 'Are there any other people we can try? What about all the committees you're involved with? Surely they can take a few more.'

'I've called them all and I'm sorry to say most of them have let me down. Maybe we priced the tickets too high. With all this austerity, people don't have much spare cash. Perhaps we should have charged only ten euros.'

'Nonsense,' Anne said. 'You wouldn't buy a cup of coffee and a cake for ten euros in some places in Dublin. There's nothing wrong with the price.'

'And nobody's heard of Antonio,' Helen added feebly. 'That's another reason. If he was better known, I'm sure we wouldn't have this problem.'

'Now you're talking absolute rubbish. That's precisely why you wanted to give the concert in the first place, so that we could bring him to greater attention. You're just making excuses, Helen. The reason people aren't buying tickets is because they're too damned mean.'

Helen wasn't enjoying this conversation with her friend. 'I suppose you're right. I feel sorry for Antonio. He's going to be very disappointed. And poor Mr Watt was relying on the proceeds for his church organ.'

'We'll just have to redouble our efforts,' Anne said firmly. 'At this rate the church is going to look half empty and you did say you were going to fill it by hook or by crook. Have you had any luck with the publicity campaign you were planning?'

Helen lowered her eyes. 'Not really. I was relying on Kirsty for that. I thought she might have been able to drum up support from some of her fashion industry friends, but when I mentioned that model, Samantha O'Leary, the phone went dead.'

'That's most unlike her,' Anne said. 'She must really be under pressure. Well, there's nothing for it but to roll up our sleeves and get stuck in again. What if we asked the shopkeepers in the village to stick some of the flyers in their windows?'

'And I'll ring the *Northside News* and see if they can't run a piece about the concert,' Helen added. 'They're always very accommodating when it comes to local charities.'

'Yes,' Anne said. 'That's a good idea.'

'And there'll always be latecomers. Some people don't make up their minds till the last minute.'

'Helen, I have to go. I promised Cynthia Burgess that I'd meet her for lunch. I'll ring you this afternoon.'

'Try to sell her a ticket,' Helen said, as Anne made for the door.

'I already have,' Anne replied. 'She's taking two. Now don't despair. You know what they say in showbiz?'

'What?'

'It's not over till the fat lady sings.'

* * *

Helen listened to the front door closing. She had a bad feeling about the concert. It wasn't just that ticket sales were so poor. It was also because she hadn't managed to persuade one influential person to attend and she needed them there to get

Antonio's career launched. Indeed, some of them had behaved disgracefully.

None of the producers she knew in RTÉ had even come to their phones, leaving her to explain her mission to their secretaries, and Helen could tell from their voices that they were bored. The same thing had happened when she'd rung the Arts Society and asked to speak to Victoria Mulcahy, whom she'd considered a certainty to help.

But the worst villain of all was Archie McGonagle of the Garden Theatre. She had actually managed to speak to him. But when she started to explain about Antonio's concert, he had immediately cut her short, telling her he was leaving that afternoon for a long trip to New York. And when she turned on the television the following evening, there he was being interviewed live on RTÉ News.

Well, it just showed she'd placed too much trust in some people. Perhaps she should have listened to Anne. Her friend had raised objections when Helen had proposed bringing Antonio to Dublin but she had been so carried away with the idea that she had just brushed them aside. Now the concert was only a couple of days away and she was facing the stark reality that it could be a disaster. No wonder she was down in the dumps.

Then there was Kirsty. She hadn't spoken to her for several days. Kirsty had always been a wonderful daughter. She had nursed Helen through her illness, waiting on her hand and foot till she recovered. Now she was in danger of making herself ill because she worked so hard on her fashion business.

She wondered if it was such a good idea to leave off speaking to her till after the concert. Maybe she should call her right away. But she would have to be tactful. She wouldn't even mention the concert in case it upset her. Yes, she decided, she would ring now. It would be lovely to hear her voice again.

* * *

Kirsty was gazing out of her window at the yachts moored in the harbour. She'd had a busy morning dealing with clients, who were still clamouring for Penny Muldoon's creations. Business was booming. But it was the only bright spot in her life just now. Otherwise, she was feeling miserable.

Dumping Robbie Hennessy hadn't brought her any of the satisfaction she had anticipated. Instead of pleading and begging for another chance, he had taken it in his stride, as if he couldn't have cared less. Now, she was beginning to feel bored. She had been confined to her apartment for the whole weekend. Apart from one phone conversation with Angie, she hadn't spoken to anyone. Her meals had consisted of oven-ready food she'd fished out of the freezer. And for entertainment, she'd watched old movies on television.

Now it was Monday and she was feeling very sorry for herself, alone once more without a partner, while all her friends were wrapped up in relationships. Angie had suggested they go clubbing but, apart from the fear of running into Robbie or Samantha O'Leary, she just couldn't summon the energy to get involved again. Maybe it was her destiny to remain single, but Kirsty was certain she was going to hate it.

Then there was her mother. They'd had no contact since the night Kirsty had cut short their phone conversation. It had given her an excellent excuse not to get involved in the crazy concert Helen was organising for Antonio. Privately, she was hoping the event would be a washout; otherwise, he might stay for ever. What she wanted most was to get him out of

Avalon and back home to Spain. But now, on top of everything else, she was feeling guilty.

She knew Helen had been relying on her to publicise the event. And she could have done it easily with a few quick phone calls. She knew lots of wannabe models and designers who would have been delighted to oblige. They were all publicity mad, just dying to get their faces into the papers. Most of them had agents who spent their time feeding gossip to the entertainment editors for headlines like *Why I'm so happy with my new body* and *How I met the new man in my life.*

But she had done nothing. And now it was probably too late. If the concert wasn't a success, Helen would take it very badly. She had thrown herself into it and she wasn't used to failure. Damn, Kirsty thought. None of this would have happened if Antonio hadn't charmed his way into her life. There would be no concert, no tickets to sell and Kirsty wouldn't be feeling any guilt.

At that moment her phone rang. She picked it up and heard her mother's voice. 'I was thinking of you, darling,' Helen began. 'I hope you're all right.'

'Oh, Mum, what a coincidence! I was thinking of you, too. It's so nice to hear your voice.'

'How are you feeling?'

'I'm fine.'

'I'm sorry for not ringing sooner but I've been very busy.'

'Oh, Mum, you don't have to apologise. It's my fault. *I* should have called *you.*'

'Well, you have a business to run and I don't. Are you really fine? I'm worried about you.'

'Why?'

'You're working too hard. You never stop. And that's not good. You should take a break.'

'Mum!'

'Well, I *am* concerned about you! I'm your mother, and sometimes I can see things that you can't. You've been under too much strain, recently. You've lost your vitality. Something's been bothering you. Now please don't deny it. Have you had a fight with your boyfriend?'

Kirsty started. Had her mother developed psychic powers? Could she read her mind? 'What gave you that idea?'

'Just intuition. Now, you mustn't allow yourself to get upset over these things. You're a young, attractive woman. Just remain patient and the right person will come along. They always do.'

'Tell you what,' Kirsty said, deciding to get off this dangerous subject. 'I have important negotiations with some clients right now but once they're out of the way, I'll take a break.'

'Will you really?'

'Yes. I'll go off on a little holiday. That's a promise.'

'Oh, that's great news,' her mother said. 'I'm so pleased. It will do you a world of good. You could stay at Puebla Maria. It's got everything you could want – a pool, gardens and a beautiful restaurant. And it's almost in the middle of Marbella. That holiday I had there was a tonic. Now, I've taken up too much of your valuable time. I'll leave you alone and let you get on with your business. But, remember, you can ring me anytime and talk. I'll always listen. I love you and I want you to be happy.'

'I love you too, Mum.'

Kirsty put the phone down. Talking to her mother had bucked her up and made her feel much better. And then another thought struck her. Helen hadn't mentioned the concert. She wondered why.

Chapter Twenty-eight

The following morning Kirsty was up early, anxious to get back to work. She had given a promise to her mother and she intended to carry it out. When everything settled down, she would take a break, go off somewhere sunny and just chill out. Maybe she'd persuade Angie or Penny Muldoon to go with her. She'd forget about Robbie Hennessy and Samantha O'Leary.

Their relationship wouldn't last anyway. He would soon grow tired of her bimbo talk and constant attention-seeking and then he'd be ringing Kirsty again. But this time, he wouldn't find it so easy to smooth-talk his way back into her affections. The door would be firmly closed. She should thank her lucky stars she'd got rid of him.

She would use the holiday to take stock of her life and where it was going. Her mother was right. She was young and she *was* attractive. She could easily find another man, if she put her mind to it. There were loads of them out there. And this time she would make sure to choose the right one – someone she could fall in love with and who would love her back.

She would find someone caring and respectful, who didn't drag her off to noisy nightclubs and didn't think it was great fun to guzzle Bombay Fizzs all night long till he was legless. Someone who would remember her birthday, who didn't wake her with his awful snoring, someone sensible and intelligent, who didn't let her down in public with his loud voice and stupid jokes. He was out there somewhere. She just had to find him.

She was startled to find that Antonio's handsome face had suddenly appeared at the forefront of her mind, as if by magic. I'm going bonkers, she thought, vigorously shaking the image away. She returned to her work with renewed energy, and seemed to fly through her tasks. At one o'clock she decided to ring Cecily Moncrieffe. 'I've got some sketches that Penny has been working on for her next collection. I thought you might like to see them.'

'I sure would,' Cecily replied.

'Okay, I'll drop them in the post.'

'No, I've got a better suggestion. Why don't I call over and see you? There are some things I want to discuss.'

Kirsty had a bright idea. She had been stuck in the apartment for the past three days. She needed to get out into the world again before she caught cabin fever.

'Stay where you are. I'll come to you.'

'When can I expect you?'

'Half an hour. I'm on my way.'

* * *

Cecily ran her business from her main boutique on Grafton Street. Kirsty left the car in an underground garage and walked the short distance to the shop. It felt good to be out on the streets once more, seeing real people going about their everyday business.

When she arrived, Cecily was waiting. 'Let's go and have coffee,' she said.

Cecily left her deputy in charge and they walked to a pastry shop further along the street. They found a table near the back and gave their order.

'I really like these,' Cecily said, poring over the portfolio of sketches Kirsty had brought. 'This young woman is really very good.' She went through them slowly, occasionally stopping to examine one that particularly appealed to her.

'She's excited at the prospect of working with you,' Kirsty said.

'The feeling is mutual. Ms Muldoon has talent. Are there any more like her in your stable?'

'I've got several. Caroline Malone is very good. She specialises in clothes for the younger woman. Then there's Emma Dunne – she's not long out of college but she's got definite flair.' She mentioned several more names.

Cecily closed the portfolio and looked across the table at Kirsty. 'This brings me to the matter I wanted to discuss with you. I've been thinking recently about a scheme that might benefit us both.'

'Go ahead. I'm listening.'

'What would you say to working exclusively for me? It would save you the hassle of trying to sell your clothes to different clients. My shops are well established, have a guaranteed high-end clientele and a top-drawer reputation.'

Kirsty's heart skipped a beat. Cecily's proposal was something she had already considered herself. But it had come sooner than she'd expected and had caught her off-guard. She tried to conceal her surprise. 'How would it work?'

'Simple. We'd agree a contract for a fixed term during which I would have exclusive rights to your clothes. I've already got similar arrangements with several of the top designers, like Alice Kennedy and Patricia Dunleavy. They deal only with me. I promote their brands. If customers want their clothes, they have to come to my shops.'

'Go on,' Kirsty said.

'The benefits are obvious. From your point of view, you get guaranteed space in my boutiques and the knowledge that your clothes will be worn by the best people. That can only enhance your name and reputation and grow your business. It's a win-win situation for both of us.'

'It would mean you have a monopoly,' Kirsty replied. 'You could fix the prices and I'd have nowhere else to go.'

Cecily gave a dismissive wave of her hand. 'That would be very short-sighted of me. As soon as the contract expired you'd be off to someone else. I'd be cutting my own throat. Anyway, you've already agreed a contract for Penny Muldoon's designs.'

'But that's only for eighteen months. And what happens if you don't like my other designers' work? Where do they go then?'

'Why are you so negative?' Cecily demanded. 'I'm sure I'll like their stuff or I wouldn't make the proposal. Anyway, I usually work with the designers in advance so they know exactly what I want.'

'I'll need a bit of time to consider this,' Kirsty said.

'Of course. I didn't expect you to agree immediately. But I should tell you that opportunities like this don't come along every day of the week. Think hard about it but don't take too long. I expect to hear from you in a day or two. And, remember, you and I work well together. There's no reason why it shouldn't continue.'

Kirsty was anxious to get away but Cecily detained her with more scandalous gossip about her rival Trixie Lefarge and some young Moroccan boyfriend she had taken under her wing. It was four o'clock before she got back to Howth.

She knew the deal that Cecily was proposing was a wonderful opportunity. It would lift her business to a new level and increase her income stream, which meant she could pay her young designers more and attract new ones. They would be delighted when she told them.

But there were downsides too. Kirsty would lose some of her independence and put a lot of power into Cecily's hands. If she was going to take up the offer she would have to insist on certain guarantees. And before she signed anything, she would need to talk to her solicitor, Gavin Tierney, and get his advice. She rang him at once and made an appointment to see him the following day.

Next she checked her text and phone messages and found nothing urgent. Outside her window, the sun was shining on the harbour. She decided to go for a walk along the cliffs. The fresh air would do her good and give her an opportunity to think. She pulled on a pair of jeans and a warm sweater and set off.

She started along Balscadden Bay, then began the long climb to the Summit. She soon found herself pausing for breath and realised she was out of shape. She needed to cut down on the comfort food and the wine and take more exercise. But the scenery was stunning. Today the sky was clear and she could see across the bay as far as the Wicklow hills.

And it was peaceful, which allowed her to consider Cecily's proposal. Allure Fashions had finally reached the crossroads she had seen coming. The choice was to continue to plod away, slowly building the business, or make the big leap forward that Cecily was offering. She turned the options over in her mind, and by the time she reached the top, she had come to a decision.

She would accept Cecily's offer but limit the term of the agreement to three years. If everything worked smoothly, they could renew the contract when it expired. There would be an argument with Cecily over money but it was a good battle to be in and would be resolved in the end. Kirsty knew there were many small suppliers who would trade places with her in a heartbeat.

She sat down to rest. She was excited to have made her decision. But before she did anything, she would summon her designers and put Cecily's proposal to them for their agreement. They had always operated as a team and Kirsty was anxious to continue in this way. It had been the cornerstone of her success.

On the way back down the hill, she decided to pay her mother a visit at Avalon. When she arrived, Antonio surprised her by opening the front door. He was dressed in jeans and a white T-shirt. Beneath the thin fabric of his vest, she could see the outline of his taut stomach muscles. '*Buenas tardes*, Kirsty.' He grinned. 'I saw you coming up the drive. You are looking very good today.'

She gave him a tight smile. 'I'm here to see my mother.'

'She is on the patio. I am about to make some tea. Would you like some?'

'No, thank you.'

She walked through the house and out to the back where she found Helen sitting in the sun. She had a sheet of paper in her hands and a worried frown on her face. When she saw Kirsty, the frown disappeared and was replaced by a warm smile.

'It's so good to see you,' she said, and started to rise from her seat.

'Don't get up,' Kirsty replied. She dragged a chair across and sat down beside her. 'The garden's looking very well. More of Señor Antonio's work, I suppose?'

'Yes, I've come to rely on him quite a lot, you know. He insists on doing everything, including the cooking.'

No doubt he does, Kirsty thought. That's all part of his plan to lull you into a sense of false security. But he's reckoned without me. I'll soon put a halt to his gallop.

At that moment, Antonio appeared again with a tray containing a teapot, cups and saucers. He put it down on a little table and poured for Helen. 'Are you sure you don't want some?' he said to Kirsty. 'You haven't changed your mind?'

'No, thank you.'

'I'll leave you alone to talk,' he said, and returned to the house.

Helen took a sip of tea. 'That's good, so refreshing.'

'You looked worried,' Kirsty said.

'Did I?'

'Yes, what's bothering you?'

Helen gave a loud sigh. 'Anne and I have been working very hard for Antonio's concert. I don't mind admitting that I'll be glad when it's over.'

'When is it?'

'Tomorrow night.'

Kirsty sat up. She had been so consumed with her own affairs she had completely forgotten that the concert was looming so close. 'How is it going?'

Her mother stared at the ground. 'Not very well, I'm afraid. I'm sorry to say that a lot of people have let me down. That blackguard, Archie McGonagle, lied to me and said he couldn't support us because he was off to America. And the following evening, I saw him live on television. As for Victoria Mulcahy of the Arts Society, she wouldn't even take my call. I'd been relying on her. That's the sort of thing I've had to deal with. But we'll push ahead anyway. I promised Antonio a concert and I intend to keep my pledge.'

'How many tickets have you sold?'

'We have it up to a hundred and twenty. We got some publicity from the local shops and the *Northside News*, which brought in extra sales.'

'And how many were you aiming for?'

'Ideally we would have liked to fill the church.'

'How many is that?'

'Two hundred, but a hundred and fifty would be respectable. You see, it's not just about Antonio. We're giving the proceeds to the vicar, Mr Watts, for his organ fund.'

'What time is the concert?'

'Eight o'clock at St Matilda's in Rathmines.'

'Right,' Kirsty said, standing up quickly. 'I have to go now. But I'll see you tomorrow night. I'll definitely be there.'

* * *

The whole way home, her heart was heavy with remorse. She had promised to see her mother at the concert and hadn't the courage to admit that she hadn't even bought a ticket yet. She was one of those who had let Helen down. She had been so wrapped up in her own problems that she had forgotten about her mother. How selfish was that?

Now she was determined to make amends. She didn't agree with the concert, and she didn't want Antonio to stay a moment longer at Avalon than was absolutely necessary. But she wasn't going to stand idly by and see her mother humiliated.

As soon as she returned to her apartment, she sat down at her desk and rang Anne O'Malley. 'I want to purchase fifty tickets for tomorrow's concert,' she said.

'Fifty? Are you sure?'

'Yes. I was talking to Mum and she tells me sales have been slow.'

'That's putting it mildly. They've ground to a halt.'

'Well, I hope to remedy that a little. I'm going to give these tickets to my friends and encourage them to come. But, Anne, I want your word that you won't tell Mum anything about this. I don't want her to know.'

'Of course not.'

'So when can I have the tickets?'

'I can drop them down to you this evening.'

'Excellent. Can I give you a cheque?'

'Sure. That's a thousand euros.'

A few minutes later, Kirsty was ringing her friends. She started with Cecily Moncrieffe and continued through her extensive contacts in the fashion world. It was ten o'clock by the time she had finished and she had secured promises to attend from several well-known designers and catwalk models. She sat back and poured a glass of chilled Chablis. She felt a little better after her evening's work. Hopefully, the concert wouldn't be a disaster, after all.

Chapter Twenty-nine

Charles Ponsonby-Jones was fond of telling his friends that he had the best job in Irish journalism. He was the music critic of the *Gazette* and spent his time going to concerts and recitals where he was both feared and respected in equal measure. Wherever he turned up, he was given the best seats and people always made a fuss of him. 'Where else would I get a job like this?' he would often say. 'I do something I thoroughly enjoy and get very well paid for it.'

Charles was a small, plump man, with a bald head and bushy eyebrows, who dressed impeccably in neat suits and bow ties. He was a legend in Dublin music circles because of the enormous power he wielded. A good review by Charles could ensure a successful tour for an orchestra or an opera singer. A rave review would result in a sell-out concert and extra performances. A poor one could mean that the whole enterprise had to be cancelled. It was little wonder that promoters and concert-hall managers were afraid of him, and music lovers paid close attention to every word he wrote.

Charles was used to being courted, flattered and showered with gifts of wine and books, particularly at Christmas time. He was always given first interviews with visiting celebrities and invited to the best parties. But he jealously guarded his independence and prided himself on never allowing these favours to cloud his judgement. When he sat down to write his reviews he relied entirely on his instincts and impeccable taste. If he liked a performance, he said so. If he didn't, he made that clear in the article he wrote.

He had never married and lived with an ageing cat, called Pickles, in a small bachelor flat in Stoneybatter, which was packed solid with reference books, CDs and rare vinyl recordings of opera singers and other musicians. Pride of place in his study was given to an expensive music system. This was where he liked to spend his free time, sitting in a comfortable armchair with his eyes closed and Pickles sleeping on his chest while he listened to virtuosos, such as Jussi Björling and the violinist Fritz Kreisler.

His love of music went back to his youth when he had had ambitions to become a concert pianist. He had attended music college for several years, studied hard and spent long hours practising on the piano in his elderly aunt's front parlour. But gradually the sad reality dawned on him. He had some talent but not enough to become a first-rate pianist. So, rather than be second best, Charles had become a critic instead, quickly rising to the powerful position he now occupied on the *Gazette*.

He was in fine form as he sauntered along Blackhall Place towards the river. He had slept well, the sun was shining and this morning he had received a fat cheque for a *Sunday Times* article. As he turned onto Arran Quay, he thought of the day that lay ahead. He would stop off for lunch at his favourite

Italian restaurant in Temple Bar, then go into the office. There was some correspondence to catch up with. Meanwhile, Bernadette, his assistant, would have provided him with a list of this evening's engagements. He would choose one that appealed to him and ask her to make the arrangements.

He was whistling a Rossini aria as he pushed open the doors of Bella Italia and Giovanni, the Neapolitan waiter, came forward to greet him. 'Ah, Mr Ponsby-Jones, how good to see you. I hope you are well today. We have a nice table waiting for you by the window.'

Charles smiled to himself. After all the years he had been coming here, Giovanni had never learned to pronounce his name correctly. 'Thank you, Giovanni, I'm in excellent condition,' he said, as he settled down at the table and spread a sparkling white napkin across his lap. 'Now, I'd like you to bring me a menu and a glass of your best Chianti.'

It was three o'clock when he left Bella Italia, having consumed a fine lunch of veal scallopini with *fedelini* and a green side salad. He strolled through Temple Bar and emerged onto Westmoreland Street, then went into the office. Bernadette was waiting with his list of potential engagements. 'It's a bit thin tonight,' she said, as he sat down at his desk looking out on the street. 'There's a choral recital in the National Concert Hall at eight o'clock and a colliery band in Liberty Hall at seven.'

Charles wrinkled his nose. 'I'm not keen on choirs, and as for colliery bands, I'd run a mile to avoid them. Just leave the list with me and I'll go through it myself.'

He spent the next hour dealing with the pile of letters that had built up, then turned his attention to the engagements. Bernadette was quite right; it was very sparse. He let his eye run down the list till one caught his attention: Piano recital by Spanish pianist Antonio Rivera at St Matilda's Church, Rathmines. He'd never heard of him – or of St Matilda's Church, for that matter. 'Where did this piano recital invitation come from?' he asked Bernadette.

'It arrived in the post. And a lady rang to mention it, a Mrs Gilbert. She said the pianist wasn't well known but he was very good. She also said she knew you and asked if you might like to come.'

Lucy Gilbert! Of course he knew her. They had been students together at music college. She had been Lucy Stewart then. Charles smiled at the memory. He'd had rather a soft spot for Lucy. He might even have asked her to marry him if Harry Gilbert hadn't whipped her away from right under his nose.

Hmm, he thought. It would be nice to do her a small favour for old times' sake. Besides, there was nothing else pressing tonight. He turned to Bernadette once more. 'Would you please call her and say I'd be delighted to accept her invitation?'

* * *

It took the taxi driver some time to find St Matilda's Church, but when he finally deposited her outside it at a quarter to eight, Kirsty was pleased to see a crowd already forming at the entrance. She was surprised to notice a small group of photographers standing on the sidelines with their cameras at the ready. Who had tipped them off? It must have been one of the publicity-mad models or their agents, anxious to get their faces into the papers, she decided.

She joined the queue and made her way to the door where a tall man in a clerical collar smiled, shook her hand and introduced himself as John Watt, the vicar. Beside him, a small grey-haired woman took her ticket and gave Kirsty a programme in exchange. 'I'm Lucy Gilbert. So glad you could come. I hope you have an enjoyable evening. Just go in and find a seat. The recital will begin in fifteen minutes.'

Kirsty took the programme and entered the church. It was already half full and she immediately spotted two of the models she had invited, Bette McCoy and Polly McGurk, looking glamorous as they chatted with Daphne Mansfield, one of the city's leading boutique owners. When they saw her they waved and blew air kisses. In a corner she saw two more of her invitees, simpering, posing and doing their best to attract attention.

She was startled to hear someone call her name and turned to see her mother rushing down the aisle to greet her. Her eyes were gleaming with pleasure. 'I'm so relieved,' she said. 'We've sold all the tickets! Anne tells me there was a last-minute rush. The vicar is over the moon and so am I. I was so worried that people wouldn't come. I would have hated it if Antonio had had to play to an empty church.'

'Well, you can relax now,' Kirsty said. 'There's a crowd outside waiting to get in. It may be standing-room only.'

'I don't know half of them,' her mother went on. 'Anne tells me some of them are personalities. I wonder how they heard about it.'

'Social media,' Kirsty said. 'That's how it works, these days. People send messages to each other on Twitter if they hear of something exciting.'

'Well, thank God they did. Anne and I have seats in the front row. Why don't you come and join us?'

'Are Mark and Deirdre here?'

'Only Mark. He's sitting with us too. Deirdre couldn't come because of her boys. But she did buy a ticket.'

Why am I not surprised? Kirsty thought, as she followed her mother down the aisle to the front row.

Anne smiled when she saw her and squeezed Kirsty's hand. 'It looks like the concert's going to be a great success,' she whispered. 'Your mother is a wonder when she puts her mind to something. She never gives up.'

'Don't be so modest,' Kirsty replied, with a conspiratorial grin. 'You had a big hand in it too.'

Anne blushed.

Mark leaned over to her. 'Good to see you, Kirsty. You're looking very well. How is your business? Is it turning over all right?'

'It's turning over so fast I can scarcely keep up with it. I have a very important proposal on my desk right now, which is taking up a lot of my time.'

'That's a good complaint to have. Remember, if I can help in any way, with negotiations and stuff like that, don't hesitate to call.'

'I might just take you up on that.'

There was a slight pause and she thought her brother was going to ask why Robbie Hennessy wasn't with her but, thankfully, he turned to talk to Anne. Kirsty used the opportunity to examine her surroundings. St Matilda's was a beautiful old church with a high ceiling and large stained-glass windows. Right up beside the pulpit, a small stage had been erected and on it stood a piano and stool. Kirsty looked around for evidence of loudspeakers and a sound system but there was none. Clearly, Mr Watt and her mother were confident that the acoustics would carry the music.

By now, the church was filling quickly. People were squeezing into their seats and some had resorted to standing in the side aisles to get a better view of the stage. At precisely eight o'clock, the lights dimmed and a single spotlight came on to highlight the lone piano. Mr Watt walked out onto the stage and stood for a moment till the chatter died away and the audience fell silent. Then he began to speak.

'Ladies and gentlemen, as the vicar of St Matilda's, it is my great privilege to welcome you to our little church tonight. The proceeds of this concert will go to the organ restoration fund for which I am most grateful to you all. I believe you are about to have an experience that most of you will never forget. I have had the honour of hearing our young Spanish visitor play and I can tell you that he is a musician of truly exceptional talent. So, without further ado, I would ask you to welcome Señor Antonio Rivera, who has travelled from Ronda, in the province of Andalucía, to be with us tonight.'

There was a polite round of applause and Antonio walked out onto the stage.

Kirsty's mouth fell open. He was dressed in a black dress suit with white shirt and black tie. His dark hair was carefully groomed and his complexion gleamed in the light. She had never seen such a handsome man. Several other women clearly shared her view for she heard sharp intakes of breath as Antonio bowed politely to the audience, sat down and prepared to play.

There was a moment of anticipation and then the first notes soared out over the audience. Kirsty's chest tightened. Till now she had never heard Antonio play but she immediately recognised the quality that had so caught her mother's imagination. She glanced at the programme and saw that he was playing Beethoven's Sonata No. 8 Opus 13. The audience was silent, spellbound, as the music filled the church, echoing back off the ceiling. When the piece ended, the audience applauded enthusiastically.

Immediately Antonio began to play Brahms' Rhapsody in B Minor. Once more the church fell silent as the music swelled from the stage to encompass the audience. As the last notes died away, he rose again and bowed. This time he was smiling, clearly pleased that he had won the confidence of his listeners.

When the recital ended two hours later, he had played six pieces and, to Kirsty's untutored ear, each one had sounded better than its predecessor.

It was a triumph, there was no doubt about it. The audience rose from their seats and gave him a prolonged ovation while Antonio stood under the heat from the spotlight and wiped the sweat from his brow with a white handkerchief. Kirsty was forced to concede that she had been wrong and her mother had been right. Antonio was a gifted pianist, possibly a musical sensation.

But this realisation didn't change her opinion of him. In her eyes, he was still a trickster whose hidden agenda was to exploit her gullible mother. And, if anything, his triumph tonight had only tightened his hold over her.

Kirsty had been too slow. She had allowed Antonio to establish himself in Avalon where he was busy making himself useful by doing household chores and burrowing deeper into Helen's affections. She could see it all so clearly now. Tonight's success would boost his confidence. He would make the house his base to develop his musical career. With every passing day, it would become more difficult to dislodge him. She had to stop him. If she didn't act soon, it would be impossible.

By now, people were leaving their seats and pressing forward to the stage to shake Antonio's hand and ask him to sign their programmes. But Kirsty didn't join them. Instead she hurried from the church and out into the cool air, anxious to get away from the adoring crowd.

But in her haste to leave, she failed to notice the little plump man with the bald head who, like her, was hurrying away from the church.

Chapter Thirty

Helen didn't get up till nine o'clock, and when she did, she was still sleepy. It had been an amazing night and it hadn't ended with the concert. It had taken half an hour for all the stragglers to leave the church as people kept pressing forward to congratulate Antonio and shake his hand. Then Mr Watt had insisted that they stay behind and join the members of the vestry committee in a small sherry reception to celebrate Antonio's performance.

Helen was anxious to get home but decided it would be rude since Antonio was the guest of honour. So, with Anne, she had followed Mr Watt to the vicarage where they spent another forty-five minutes while people kept telling Antonio how wonderful he had been and he smiled shyly. It was after midnight when they finally got back to Avalon, and Helen had been so tired that she had gone straight to bed.

The next morning, after she had showered and dressed, she made her way to the kitchen, where she found a note from Antonio saying he had gone for a walk. She looked out of the window and saw it was another bright day. Where does he get the energy? she wondered, as she put the kettle on to boil and made a mug of coffee. She buttered some toast, took it out to the patio and let her eye travel along the lawn to the sea gleaming in the morning light.

What a wonderful experience it had been to sit in St Matilda's and hear Antonio play. How proud he had made her feel. His performance had been flawless, and so moving, the reception from the audience overwhelming. It just proved how right she had been to rescue him from Puebla Maria and the ungrateful diners who didn't appreciate musical genius when it was sitting right in front of their noses.

Everyone she had spoken to had thoroughly enjoyed the evening, especially Mr Watt and his wife, who wondered if Antonio might be persuaded to give another concert. Helen was delighted at the idea but someone else would have to organise it. She hadn't the stamina to go through it all again.

Despite Antonio's amazing success, though, she still had one regret. Not one of the important people she had tried to interest in the venture had turned out to support her and she needed them to help launch his career. They had managed to pack the church but Helen knew it would take a bigger concert and possibly even a television appearance before the general public woke up to his enormous talent. And that would require professional organisation well beyond her limited capability. It was going to be a long process, but they had made a start – and a very successful one at that. She should look on the bright side. They would use last night's event as a foundation to build on. Antonio had demonstrated his amazing musical talent and had proved what he was capable of. Once she had recovered her energy, she would sit down with him and Anne and plan the way forward.

At that moment, she heard the bell ring. She got up to open the front door and found Anne outside, bristling with excitement. 'Have you seen this?' She pressed a newspaper into Helen's hands.

'The *Gazette*. What about it?'

'Last night's concert. Did you know Charles Ponsonby-Jones was there?'

Helen was vaguely familiar with the name. 'Is he a reporter?'

'He's much more than a reporter. He's their music critic and the very best in the business. Surely you've heard of him.'

'I don't remember inviting him,' Helen said. 'How did he find out about it?'

'God knows. But he was there and he has written the most amazing article. When I saw it, I knew I must bring it to you at once. Let's go inside and you can read it for yourself.'

They went into the kitchen and, picking up her glasses, Helen sat down at the table and began to read.

It is rare in the life of a music critic to be in the presence of genius but that was my good fortune last night. In a small church in Rathmines I listened to a young man play the piano in a manner that recalled the great artists of the past.

His name is Antonio Rivera and he is from Ronda in southern Spain. He gave a recital before a small invited audience. It is no exaggeration to say that he amazed his listeners with the range of his skills and the passion of his playing. I have no hesitation in declaring that Señor Rivera is a musical prodigy who is destined for major success on the world stage.

Those who heard him play last night will treasure the experience and, in years to come, will tell their grandchildren that they were present on the night Rivera played in Dublin.

The article went on to review the concert in glowing terms and mention the musical pieces that Antonio had played. When she had finished reading, Helen's hands shook as she took off her glasses. 'What a nice man to write such kind words. Antonio will be delighted when he sees this.'

'Kind? Are you mad? That is a review any musician would kill for. Charles Ponsonby-Jones is the most respected music critic in Ireland and he isn't in the habit of being kind to performers. So, if he says something's good, people sit up and take notice.'

'Perhaps I should ring and thank him?'

'No,' Anne said. 'That may not be a good idea. Later Antonio could write him a short note. But don't you see what this means, Helen? You were hoping to bring Antonio to the attention of some important people. Well, I can't think of anyone more important in the music world than Charles Ponsonby-Jones.'

'What should we do now?'

'I'm not sure – I've never been in this situation before. But I know one thing for certain. This is extremely good news.'

Just then, Helen's phone rang. She picked it up and pressed it to her ear.

'Have I got Helen O'Neill?'

'Speaking.'

'This is Archie McGonagle of the Garden Theatre. I wonder

if I could have a brief word with you about Antonio Rivera. You're acting as his agent, aren't you? The last time we spoke you were enquiring about the possibility of a concert. Well, thanks to a gap in my schedule, I now have a window of opportunity.'

Helen caught her breath. 'You told me you were going to America.'

'Yes, Helen, that's correct.'

'And then I saw you on television.'

'I'm afraid there was a mix-up and I had to change my plans but I'm still here in Dublin and very anxious to open discussions with you. When would suit you best? I could come and see you right now, if that's possible.'

'I'm not sure I want to talk to you, Mr McGonagle. I think you behaved very badly.'

'But I've just explained. It was a misunderstanding. I'd be prepared to give Antonio a two-week run in the theatre, beginning next week. I think I can guarantee full houses. That's a thousand bums on seats for twelve nights. If it goes well we could extend it. We can sit down immediately and agree the terms.'

'I'm not available right now,' Helen said.

'At least promise you won't talk to anyone else till you've spoken to me,' McGonagle pleaded.

'I'm sorry, but I'm in no position to do that. Antonio is the subject of a lot of enquiries right now. We have to decide what is in his best interest.'

'But, Helen, the Garden Theatre can seat a thousand people and I'm giving you a guarantee to sell it out.'

'And I must remind you that when you were given the opportunity to present Antonio you turned it down. Now you have to excuse me. I have another call coming in. I may get back to you in due course.'

'Please listen to me, Helen.'

She switched off her phone, turned to Anne and grinned. 'I bet Archie McGonagle will think twice before he ever lies to me again.'

No sooner had the call ended than the phone was ringing again. This time it was Victoria Mulcahy of the Arts Society. She began, in a sweet, flattering voice, 'Hello, Helen, I've just been reading Charles Ponsonby-Jones's review in the *Gazette* and it appears I missed a really interesting performance last night.'

'Yes, you did, Victoria.'

'I'm terribly sorry I wasn't there but I didn't know anything about it.'

'That's because you wouldn't take my call when I rang to tell you.'

'Really? I don't remember that.' Victoria sounded taken aback.

'It was ten days ago. I was trying to drum up support for Antonio's concert and naturally I rang you. You were one of the people I was relying on. But you were too busy to talk to me.'

'In that case I apologise. I'll have a word with my assistant. Now, first of all, I must congratulate you on the success of your concert. It appears that you pulled off a remarkable triumph. Our members are very keen to hear Antonio Rivera play and I'm calling you to organise a private recital. This would be strictly for members of the society, you understand. If Señor Rivera is free on Saturday evening we would be delighted to have him play for us at our concert rooms. We would cover his expenses, of course.'

'No,' Helen said.

She heard Victoria Mulcahy gasp. 'What did you say?'

'I said no. If you had taken my call last week, we would have been delighted to oblige but now things have moved on. My phone is hopping with people who want to hear him play. I've just spoken to Archie McGonagle of the Garden Theatre about a two-week run.'

'But I thought we were friends,' Victoria said.

'So did I,' Helen replied, and terminated the call.

She turned to Anne, who had been listening intently. 'The cheek of her. She wasn't around when I needed her and now she wants Antonio to play for nothing to entertain her members. Well, she can go and whistle for all I care.'

It continued like this for the next hour. Immediately after Victoria called, one of the RTÉ producers rang to ask if Antonio would be available to do an interview for the one o'clock news. Next the *Irish Times* was on the line and then the *Independent*.

At that moment they heard the front door open and Antonio came into the room. He bent to kiss Helen's cheek, then greeted Anne. 'I've just had a lovely walk along the beach and look what I picked up.' He took a copy of the *Herald* from his pocket and spread it out on the table. The front page was taken up with a large photograph of a pouting young woman smiling into the camera.

Supermodel Petal Maguire, attending last night's Dublin gig by piano maestro, Antonio Rivera

Dublin's music fraternity turned out in force last night for a concert given by the brilliant Spanish piano player Antonio Rivera. But only the crème de la crème were invited to this top-secret performance. Little is known about Rivera, who is notoriously reclusive. But one of those lucky enough to attend the event said it was the best concert held in Ireland this year. It is not known if Rivera plans any more appearances.

Helen put down the paper and looked from one face to the other. This was something she hadn't bargained for. She'd had a bright idea to bring Antonio back to Dublin and, in some vague way, launch his career. But apart from organising a concert, she hadn't really planned how this was going to happen. She had simply supposed that it would occur by itself. And now, by a complete fluke, Antonio had become the centre of a media storm and people were beating down her door to get to him. What was she supposed to do?

The phone was ringing again. Helen turned to Anne in desperation. 'This is getting out of control. We need help.'

Chapter Thirty-one

'Switch off the phone,' Anne commanded. She drew out two chairs and they all gathered round the table. Then she turned to Antonio. 'While you were out, we had one call after another from people wanting to talk to you and offering concert bookings. The phone hasn't stopped ringing.'

His face broke into a broad smile. 'I'm so pleased. That is good news, yes?'

'Of course it is. But Helen and I aren't equipped to handle it. And neither are you. Now that you've got recognition, thanks to Mr Ponsonby-Jones – you won't have heard of him but he's an influential music critic – everything has changed.'

'How do you mean?'

'We had a man called Archie McGonagle offering to put you on at his theatre for two weeks. It's one of the biggest auditoriums in Dublin. But how do we know how much to ask for? He'll want you to sign a contract and we know nothing about legal matters. How can we be sure he won't swindle you? Then we've had all these newspapers and television producers looking for interviews. Have you ever talked to a journalist before?'

'No,' Antonio confessed.

'How will you know what to say?'

'I will simply answer their questions.'

Anne shook her head. 'You can be very naïve, Antonio. Some journalists will try to trick you. They will ask you difficult questions, perhaps about your personal life and things you don't want to talk about. Believe me, it isn't something you should do without being prepared.'

He looked disappointed. 'But this publicity will bring more people to hear me play. Isn't that what we want?'

'Of course, but it has to be controlled. We have to take charge of the agenda. The problem is that none of us has any experience in these matters and there is too much at stake.'

'So what are we to do?'

Helen had been sitting silent. Suddenly, she spoke. 'I've got a suggestion.'

'What?' Anne asked.

'Why don't we ask Mr Ponsonby-Jones?'

* * *

The music critic of the *Gazette* was finishing his morning coffee and preparing to set off into the busy streets of Dublin in search of lunch before the restaurants began to fill. He had read his review of last night's concert and was very pleased with the way it had been presented.

He was still savouring last night's event. It had been the experience of a lifetime, something he would never forget. And to think that Antonio Rivera was unknown, even in his native Spain. Well, perhaps his review would bring the young pianist to greater attention. If he succeeded in doing that, Charles Ponsonby-Jones would be quite proud. He reminded himself to drop a note to Lucy Gilbert to thank her for the invitation.

Just then, his phone rang and when he picked it up, he heard a voice he didn't recognise.

'Mr Ponsonby-Jones?'

'Speaking.'

'I'm sorry to disturb you. My name is Helen O'Neill. I organised last night's concert in St Matilda's. I'm calling to say how pleased we are with your wonderful review this morning. I'd like to thank you.'

'There's no need, dear lady. I was simply doing my job. I hope it was of some help to you.'

'Oh, yes, indeed. It was enormously helpful. Everyone is delighted. Antonio asked me to tell you how grateful he is.'

A thought occurred to the music critic. Now that he had her on the line he would try to find out a little more about the mysterious pianist. 'How exactly did you get to know Antonio?'

'I met him on holiday.'

'Really?'

'He was playing the piano in the restaurant of the resort where we were staying.'

'The resort restaurant?'

'Yes.'

'How amazing.'

'I thought so too,' Helen agreed. 'I thought it was a terrible waste of talent. And many of the diners there didn't even pay him any attention. Some of them laughed and chattered while he was playing. That was when I decided to bring him back to Dublin with me and introduce him to an audience who would appreciate him.'

'Very commendable. Where was he trained?'

'He wasn't. His parents were too poor to pay for him to go to music college. That was why he couldn't get work with an orchestra and had to play in hotels and bars.'

Charles Ponsonby-Jones caught his breath. This story was fascinating. The more he heard of it, the more intriguing it became. To think that an untrained musician could give the magnificent performance he had heard last night was incredible. Perhaps he should look again at the young pianist. Perhaps he should sit down with him and hear his story from his own lips. It would make a splendid article for the features page of the *Gazette*.

'Another reason why I'm ringing is because we need some advice,' Helen continued.

'What sort of advice?'

'You see, since your article appeared today we've had a lot of calls from people asking for interviews and so on. RTÉ want to talk to Antonio and several of the newspapers. And Archie McGonagle wants to put him on for a two-week run at the Garden Theatre. We've been overwhelmed. We just don't know how to handle it all.'

At the mention of Archie McGonagle's name, Charles bristled. 'You haven't agreed to anything, have you?'

'No, we're totally inexperienced and we're afraid of making a mistake.'

'You've done the right thing in coming to me. I'm ashamed to say this but there are a lot of unscrupulous people out there who would think nothing of exploiting Antonio.'

'So what should we do?'

'Leave it with me. Antonio's career must be handled with extreme care. He's not like a run-of-the-mill entertainer who can perform just anywhere. You wouldn't exhibit the *Mona Lisa* in a bingo hall, would you?'

'I don't think so.'

'Well, Antonio falls into the same category. He's an artist with a very precious gift and he requires special treatment.'

'That's my view too,' Helen said.

'Let me consider this and I'll get back to you, Mrs O'Neill. I'll put my thinking cap on and come up with a plan. In the meantime, turn down requests for interviews and don't agree to any offers, no matter how attractive they appear. And, for God's sake, don't sign anything.'

'Certainly, Mr Ponsonby-Jones.'

'Why don't you call me Charles? It's easier.'

* * *

'What did he say?' Antonio asked eagerly, as Helen finished the call and sat down again at the table.

'He said we should do nothing.'

'*Nothing?*' Anne was clearly astonished. 'I'm very disappointed. I was certain he would help us.'

'Let me finish,' Helen replied. 'He said there were a lot of people out there who would think nothing of exploiting Antonio and on no account to sign anything or give interviews. He said Antonio was like the *Mona Lisa* and you wouldn't hang her in a bingo hall.'

'Is that all?'

'Good God, will you let me finish?' Helen replied, exasperated. 'He said he would consider the situation and come back to us with a plan.'

'When?' Antonio asked.

'He didn't say.'

Anne and Antonio exchanged a glance.

'So that means we just have to wait?'

Helen shrugged. 'I'm afraid it does.'

* * *

As he set off for his morning walk into town, Charles Ponsonby-Jones's thoughts were still on his conversation with Helen. Antonio's future was at stake. If he fell into the wrong hands he would regret it for ever. One false step and he could find himself at the mercy of shysters who would line their pockets at his expense with no concern for his long-time career.

He had seen it before. He had seen artists paraded in front of ignorant audiences as if they were performing seals in a circus. And when the audiences grew tired of them, they were dumped on the scrapheap. Archie McGonagle would have Antonio playing the piano like a trained chimpanzee if he thought it would draw in the crowds. It must not be allowed to happen. Antonio's gift was too great to be squandered for the sake of a quick buck.

Charles was reminded of Chopin or the young Mozart, who was playing harpsichord and violin when he was only five. They were child prodigies blessed with unique musical talent. But, of course, they had come from families steeped in classical music whereas Antonio was untrained, although he played the piano like an angel. That made him even more special. When he made his formal début, it had to be handled properly.

Antonio needed a good manager, someone who wasn't motivated solely by greed but had the young pianist's interests at heart and knew how to deal with the media to best advantage. There were several people he could think of but the best was David Wheeler, who managed some of the biggest names in the music world. He lived in London and, by good fortune, Charles knew him personally.

He would ring David and invite him to Dublin to hear Antonio play. And he would also sit down with the pianist and have a long chat with him. He would find out all about him and then he would write a lengthy article for the *Gazette*. That would bring him to the attention of the right people, who understood the finer subtleties of music. In fact, he would do it this very afternoon as soon as he had had lunch.

With his mind made up, Charles Ponsonby-Jones stopped outside a French restaurant at the corner of Merchant's Quay and studied the menu in the window. The confit of duck sounded particularly appealing. It would go nicely with a glass or two of Pinot Noir.

He pushed open the door and entered the warm interior.

Chapter Thirty-two

Kirsty had gone to bed as soon as she got home from the performance. But it was a long while before she was able to get to sleep. Her mind was still wrestling with the problem that had consumed her all evening. Now that Antonio had given his successful concert, her mother's project was complete. She had done what she had promised. Now Kirsty had to get Antonio out of Avalon and back home to Spain as quickly as possible. Otherwise he would stay there for ever. There was no time to lose. But how was she going to do it?

Since his arrival, she had been watching as he had settled into the house and made himself at home. Avalon was *her* house, the place where she had grown up. It infuriated her to see him flatter her mother and hear about him cooking the meals and trimming the lawn. He behaved as if he owned the place! It was driving her to distraction to see him strutting around the house as if he had lived there all his life.

She was convinced that her mother's decision was the product of an irrational mind, despite what Dr Humphries might say. It all went back to the shock of Kirsty's father's sudden death and Helen's nervous breakdown. There was no other way to explain the crazy plan to bring a complete stranger back and install him in the family home, not to mention all the effort she had expended on the concert.

But she also knew she was whistling in the wind. Neither of her siblings agreed with her and even Anne O'Malley, who was normally a rock of common sense, was part of the conspiracy. The only person who could see her point of view was Robbie Hennessy, and he was off cavorting with that idiot Samantha O'Leary.

Kirsty felt like weeping from frustration.

She had contacted Benny Taylor's detective agency several times and always got the same response: 'We're working on it but we haven't got any dirt on him yet.' She knew it was a waste of time. Taylor wasn't going to find anything. It meant she was on her own and had only one option left. She would have to confront Antonio and tell him in no uncertain terms that he wasn't wanted and would have to leave.

* * *

The phone woke her at eight o'clock. Cecily Moncrieffe was on the line. 'That was a wonderful concert last night,' she began. 'What an amazing talent that young man has and how stunning he looks. If he didn't play the piano so well he could have a successful career as a male model. Thanks for inviting me.'

'Don't mention it.'

'Now, to get straight down to business, have you had an opportunity to consider my proposal?'

'Yes,' Kirsty replied, wiping the sleep from her eyes. 'I'm in broad agreement but there are some items we need to discuss further. And I also need time to consult with my designers.'

'Okay, but can you do it quickly? I'm anxious to get it nailed down. If you're not interested, there are several others who are.'

'I'll start working on it immediately,' Kirsty said, and terminated the call. Now Cecily was threatening her. Usually she was as nice as ninepence but she could be a dragon when it suited her. She hopped out of bed, had a quick shower and began contacting her designers to invite them to a meeting at midday. When that was done, she had breakfast and began to prepare.

The first to arrive was Emma Dunne, a pretty, dark-haired girl who had been working with Kirsty for eighteen months. During this time she had made a considerable impression on the fashion world with her imaginative ideas. Kirsty predicted a bright future for her. She brought her into the lounge where the meeting was to be held. 'Coffee?' she asked.

'Yes, please.'

'How'd you get here?'

'I drove.'

'Traffic okay?'

'Yes. Now, tell me what this is all about, Kirsty. You sounded very cloak-and-dagger on the phone.'

'I'll explain everything when the others arrive. Just make yourself at home while I get the coffee.'

The kettle was just coming to the boil when she heard the doorbell ring again and Caroline Malone turned up, every bit as curious as Emma. By the time midday arrived, all six of her designers, including Penny Muldoon, were sitting in Kirsty's magnificent lounge, with its stunning views across Howth harbour.

'Right,' she began. 'I'm sure you're all wondering why I invited you here so I'll put you out of your misery as quickly as I can. I have received an interesting proposal from a leading womenswear retailer. They want Allure Fashions – us – to work exclusively with them. I'll outline the terms in a moment. For my part, I'm inclined to accept the proposal, provided I can reach agreement on prices and duration of contract. But before I proceed, I want to make sure that you guys are all on board.'

'Can you tell us who the retailer is?' Emma Dunne asked.

'Yes. It's Cecily Moncrieffe. But I'd prefer you to keep that information to yourselves for the time being. Some of you have already done business with Cecily, including Penny, who has a similar exclusive agreement with her. I've always found her very fair to deal with.'

Penny nodded.

'Will she interfere with our work?' Caroline Malone asked.

'I think that's too strong,' Kirsty replied. 'She'll probably want to consider your ideas beforehand so she can decide if she's interested. And she may make suggestions for improvement. I think that's okay. But you'll be entirely free to design the clothes you want to make. I honestly don't see any problems in that area.'

They kicked the proposal around for another forty-five minutes, and Kirsty asked for a show of hands. Everyone was in agreement.

'Good,' she said. 'I'll now sit down with Cecily and sort out the finer details. I'll keep you posted on how things turn out.

And, remember, you can call me at any time if you want to talk about anything.'

They left in a buzz of chatter. She went into her office and rang Cecily. 'I'm ready when you are.'

'Good. Can you be at my place in Grafton Street at ten o'clock in the morning?'

'Of course,' Kirsty replied.

She checked the time. It was ten past one. She would spend the rest of the afternoon planning for tomorrow's meeting with Cecily. She hadn't forgotten her plan to confront Antonio. It would have to wait. As soon as she had finished with Cecily, she would turn her attention to him. And this time she would crush him.

* * *

Charles Ponsonby-Jones paid off the cab and watched it speed away towards Howth village. Then he walked up the drive towards the house. He had called Mrs O'Neill as soon as he had finished lunch and told her of his plan to invite David Wheeler to Dublin and also to interview Antonio for the *Gazette.* She had suggested that he come out to Avalon at once. And now here he was.

Helen, Anne and Antonio were waiting for him at the top of the drive. Immediately, the women began to ply him with questions. Will Mr Wheeler know what to do about all these phone calls they'd been getting? Would he be able to handle Archie McGonagle, who was very insistent and kept ringing them about putting Antonio on at the Garden Theatre?

Charles raised his hand to silence them. 'David Wheeler will know exactly what to do. He's had years of experience in these matters. But I must counsel you that he hasn't agreed to anything yet. He hasn't even heard Antonio play. However, I have no doubt that, when he does, he'll be very impressed.'

'Will he take care of everything?'

'Yes, provided he agrees to become Antonio's manager.'

That seemed to allay their concerns.

'In that case, we'll leave you alone with Antonio and you can get on with your interview,' Helen said. 'You can use the drawing room. It's quiet in there.'

Charles sat down with Antonio, took a notebook from his briefcase and prepared to write. Outside the window, he could see a well-tended garden and beyond that the blue of the sea. It was a nice house, very similar to the one where he had been brought up in County Wicklow.

He glanced at the young man sitting across the table from him, waiting patiently. He looked so humble, without a trace of the arrogance or superiority that Charles often found in artistic people. And yet he possessed such talent.

'Tell me about growing up,' he said. 'Where were you born? How did you first learn to play the piano?'

Antonio cleared his throat. 'I was born in Ronda. It is a small town in the mountains in southern Spain. My music teacher at school was a Señor Alvarez. He taught me how to play.'

'And did you find it difficult?'

Antonio shook his head. 'I loved it from the very beginning. It was never a chore for me to play, always a pleasure. Señor Alvarez used to say I had the music here.' He tapped his head and smiled.

Charles was frantically taking notes as Antonio spilled out his story. This was going to be a very easy interview. Antonio was so open and honest. There was no hint of guile or subterfuge. Charles barely had to prompt him. It was like talking to a child.

'Keep going,' he said. 'Tell me about the first time you played in public.'

It was five o'clock when Charles finally closed his notebook and stood up. He had got all the information he required to write his piece. Already he knew it would be a sensation, the best article he had ever written, full of wonderful quotes and anecdotes. When it appeared it would make waves throughout the music world.

'I'll arrange for a photographer to come out tomorrow morning and take your picture.'

'What time?' Antonio asked.

'Around eleven o'clock. You don't need to dress up. Just wear something casual. I think we should take it here beside the window with the garden outside.'

'Okay,' Antonio said.

The women were waiting when they came out of the drawing room.

'Have you finished?' Mrs O'Neill asked.

'Yes.'

'And when will we know about Mr Wheeler?'

'I'll ring him as soon as I get back to the office. I'll let you know what he says.'

'You've been very kind, Mr Ponsonby-Jones. May I offer you some tea?'

He smiled. 'I told you to call me Charles. And, yes, I would like a cup of tea, no sugar and just a spot of milk. Would you mind calling a taxi to take me back into town?'

* * *

David Wheeler had just finished dinner at his home outside London when he heard the phone ring. It was evening. He'd had a frantic day arranging a concert tour for an Italian opera singer, and now he was considering a short stroll across the common to clear his head.

His wife looked into the study where he was tidying some papers. 'It's for you, my love, Charles Ponsonby-Jones.'

Charlie Ponsonby-Jones! David hadn't heard from him for ages. He wondered what his friend wanted to talk about. 'I'll take it,' he said, and picked up the phone. 'Charlie, you old devil, what have you been up to?'

'Quite a lot,' Charles replied. 'How are you? Busy as usual?'

'You can say that again. I'm putting the finishing touches to Enrico Manzini's concert tour. I needn't tell you how stressful it is. Enrico can be very temperamental.'

'I remember the time he walked off the stage at the Royal Albert Hall because some poor man in the audience had a fit of coughing. That caused a sensation.'

David laughed. 'So, what can I do for you?'

'It's not so much what you can do for me. It's what you can do for a young Spanish pianist I've just been interviewing. He gave a recital last night and I've never heard anything like it. He is truly amazing. And, unlike Enrico Manzini, he's not the least bit temperamental. Quite the opposite in fact. He's all sweetness and light.'

'Tell me more. Where did he train?'

'That's another incredible thing. He has no formal training. He learned his art from a music teacher at school. He just has this most unusual gift. And he needs a manager, David. Already the sharks are circling. He needs someone like you who can guide him and keep him out of trouble.'

'Um,' David said. 'When can I hear him play?'

'Whenever you like. He's staying in Dublin with a woman who discovered him playing in a hotel restaurant in Marbella and took him under her wing.'

'A hotel restaurant?'

'Yes.'

'Now you've got me really interested. I could drop over to Dublin in the morning. Can you fix up a meeting?'

'It would be my privilege,' his friend replied. 'Just call me when you've booked your flight and I'll take care of the rest.'

* * *

Charles said goodbye to David Wheeler and immediately rang Helen O'Neill. 'David Wheeler is arriving in the morning to hear Antonio play. Would you contact Lucy Gilbert and ask if we can borrow her piano again?'

* * *

Lucy had just finished reading Charles Ponsonby-Jones's review for the second time. She had read it first thing that morning over breakfast and savoured every word, then put it aside to enjoy again with her evening meal. It was the most positive review he had ever written – and she had read most of them. Normally he was very sparing in his praise, which was why he was so highly regarded as a music critic. He didn't dish out the accolades willy-nilly. You had to be really good to get a promising word from Charles.

She was absolutely delighted for Antonio. A review like that was bound to cheer him up and boost his confidence. And he badly needed it if he was ever going to get the recognition he deserved. She was glad that she'd sent Charles an invitation to the recital although there had been no contact between them since their college days.

That had been a happy time in Lucy's life and she remembered it with great affection. It had been the late sixties, the era of flower power, and they had all been young and carefree, full of hope and ambition. They had believed they were invincible and nothing could ever harm them. And here she was now, on her own, her husband dead and her children married.

She smiled at the memory. How things had changed. Back then, Charles had carried a torch for her although he had never plucked up the courage to ask her for a date. And, eventually, Harry had come along and swept her off her feet. Charles had never married, and she had heard recently from a friend that he was now living in a flat in Stoneybatter with his cat, his books and recordings.

Asking him to the recital had been something of a gamble. What if he hadn't liked Antonio and had given him a bad review? That could have knocked poor Antonio back completely. But it had been a risk worth taking and it had paid off. This morning's review was brimming with praise. It would be read by the music Mafia and they would sit up and pay attention. The next time Antonio gave a concert people would be queuing up for tickets.

She thought again of the handsome, dark-haired young man and his self-effacing charm. She had coaxed his story from him and learned of the tough life he had led in the little town in the mountains. But despite the hardship, he was remarkably cheerful and uncomplaining. And, of course, he had the fantastic musical gift that, thanks to Charles's review, would now reach a wider audience.

She was about to clear away the dishes when her phone rang. She picked it up and pressed it to her ear.

'Lucy Gilbert?' an unfamiliar voice enquired.

'Speaking.'

'This is Helen O'Neill from Howth.'

'Oh, Helen, how are you? Have you read Charles Ponsonby-Jones's marvellous review in the *Gazette*?'

'Indeed I have. That's the very reason I'm calling you. You see, Charles has arranged for a man called David Wheeler to come from London tomorrow to hear Antonio play and we were wondering if we could borrow your piano again.'

'That's fantastic news. Of course you can have the piano.'

'Where is it?'

'It's still in St Matilda's. Mr Watt was going to have it returned to me tomorrow. I'll ring him now and ask him to keep it one more day.'

'That's even better. I hope it's not an inconvenience?'

'Not at all. We won't be using the church again till Sunday. What time will Mr Wheeler be coming?'

'I don't know yet but I'll let you know as soon as I find out.'

'Excellent. Just do that and I'll pass the information on to Mr Watt.' Lucy turned off her phone. David Wheeler. She knew his name. He was one of the most powerful figures in the music world. He managed some of the biggest names in the business. Things were certainly looking up for Antonio if David Wheeler was coming to hear him play.

Chapter Thirty-three

Helen was up early the following morning. She had barely slept a wink with excitement. As well as David Wheeler, they were expecting a photographer from the *Gazette* at eleven o'clock. Antonio seemed to be taking it all in his stride. He hadn't batted an eyelid.

She went down to the kitchen to make breakfast and found him already there, boiling eggs. 'Just go and sit outside,' he said. 'This will be ready in a few minutes. Would you like tea or coffee?'

'I think coffee, please, this morning.'

'Coming up,' he said.

'Your English is improving every day, Antonio.'

'You think so? I just repeat what I hear people say.'

Helen went out to the garden. It was cooler today and there were clouds gathering. But it was pleasant to be outside in the fresh air with the roses in bloom. A few minutes later, Antonio joined her with a pot of coffee, toast and the boiled eggs. They began to eat.

'The man who is coming today, David Wheeler, is a very important person. If he likes you, he can do a lot to promote your career. He can arrange for you to play at major concerts. He can strike deals with record companies. You will travel the world and thousands of people will hear you.'

'I understand how important he is.'

'You seem very relaxed, Antonio. Aren't you excited?'

He shrugged. 'Of course I'm excited. I know this is a big opportunity. But I don't want to build up my hopes. What happens is outside my control. You told me once that I might look back with regret if I turned down your generous invitation. But if it doesn't work out, I won't be disappointed. I will still be able to play the piano, Helen. I will always have that consolation.'

She laid her hand on his. 'You're very philosophical, Antonio. I don't know if I would be able to remain so calm in your situation. But I admire you for it. And, of course, you're right. Whatever happens, you will always have your wonderful gift.'

The photographer arrived at ten to eleven. Antonio had shaved and put on a white open-necked shirt with black trousers. The photographer fussed while he arranged him in several poses beside the window till he got one that seemed to please him. Then he began snapping. When he had finished, he brought Antonio out to the garden, placed him sitting near the roses and took some more. It was after twelve when he left.

Almost at once, the phone rang and Charles Ponsonby-Jones was on the line to announce that David Wheeler would be arriving at Dublin airport at one o'clock. He would meet him and take him straight to St Matilda's. Helen rang Lucy Gilbert to give her the news, then turned to Antonio, who was standing beside her. 'He's on his way. Are you ready?'

He nodded.

'So let's go.'

They picked up Anne and drove out to Rathmines where they found the vicar and his wife waiting with Lucy Gilbert. Mrs Watt invited them back to the rectory to wait for the arrival of the visitors. They sat around in the parlour and made small talk, each person aware of the momentous importance of the forthcoming meeting but no one daring to speak of it directly. Meanwhile, Antonio seemed to have withdrawn into himself and sat quietly leafing through a church magazine he had found on the vicar's bookshelf.

The call, when it came, sounded like a grenade going off in the tense room. Helen opened her phone and clamped it to her ear while the others watched in silence.

'Hello?' She nodded. 'Okay.' She closed the phone and spoke to the others. 'They'll be here in five minutes.'

* * *

They went outside to meet the visitors. The clouds had parted and now the sun was peeping out again as they gathered on the pavement outside the church. Helen nervously checked her watch as the minutes ticked away. Eventually, they saw a taxi appear out of the traffic and the driver pulled to a stop beside Mr Watt. The door opened and Charles stepped out, quickly followed by David Wheeler.

Helen stared at him. He was a tall, confident-looking man in his early fifties with silver hair brushed across a broad forehead. Charles paid the taxi fare and the driver sped away. He led David Wheeler to the little group standing on the pavement and introduced them. David shook hands, and when he came to Antonio, he stared into his face. 'So you're the pianist I've heard so much about?'

'Yes,' Antonio replied.

'I'm told you're very good.'

'I like to play. It is what I enjoy most. As for being good, that is not for me to say.'

David smiled. 'Well said, Antonio. We'll soon find out.' He turned to the others. 'Shall we go inside?'

They filed into the little church. The sun was now streaming in through the windows and tiny specks of dust were dancing in the light. The church seemed more silent and solemn now that it was empty of people. Helen allowed her gaze to travel down the aisle till it came to rest on Lucy Gilbert's Steinway.

David waited till everyone was seated, then invited Antonio to play. All eyes followed him as he began the slow walk towards the altar, his footsteps echoing in the silence. When he came to the piano, he turned to the little audience and bowed. Then he drew out the stool and sat down. He flexed his fingers and, a moment later, the opening bars of a Mozart concerto floated up to the roof. David sat back and closed his eyes.

Once the piece was finished, Antonio launched into a lively polka and followed it with a selection from Bach's Goldberg Variations. He played solidly for half an hour, and when at last he stood up, a gentle ripple of applause rose from the listeners and quickly grew to a crescendo. It had been another triumph.

David bounded out of his seat and went to greet him as he came back down the aisle. He took Antonio's hand in his firm grasp. 'That was absolutely superb. Everything I've heard about you is true. You really do have a magnificent gift. How soon can we talk?'

Sitting nearby, Helen and Lucy exchanged a joyful glance.

* * *

They all filed out of the church and Mr Watt locked the doors.

'I can't believe this is all happening so quickly,' Helen said to Anne. 'To think that such a powerful man as David Wheeler is prepared to take Antonio under his wing. It's like a dream come true. I wish I'd brought my camera.'

Suddenly she was struck by an idea. She had half a dozen bottles of champagne in the cellar left over from a birthday party. Here was a chance to open one or two – and it would give David Wheeler and Antonio an opportunity to talk. She turned to the little group, still milling around outside the church. 'Listen, everyone. I'd like to invite you all to my home in Howth for a little celebration. It's not far. We could be there in half an hour.'

David exchanged a glance with Charles Ponsonby-Jones. 'What do you think?'

'That sounds like a splendid idea,' he replied. 'You're not returning to London till tomorrow morning, after all.'

The ladies got into Helen's car while the three men said they'd follow in a taxi. Thirty-five minutes later they were turning into the drive at Avalon.

Helen immediately got busy. She rang a local restaurant to order some food, then went down to the cellar and rescued a couple of bottles of champagne.

Meanwhile, in the drawing room, her guests had wandered over to the window to admire the garden and the view. Anne helped Helen fill the glasses, then called them all together and Helen proposed a toast. Then she got out her camera and began taking pictures.

Oh, I'm so happy, she thought. This is a moment to remember for ever. Another thought occurred to her. She hadn't heard from Kirsty since the concert. She should include her too. She took out her phone again and made the call.

* * *

Kirsty had just returned from her meeting with Cecily Moncrieffe. It had begun pleasantly, then descended into a bruising encounter, the two women arguing over the terms of the proposed agreement. Several times, Kirsty had been tempted to get up and walk away.

But she had stuck it out, and they had managed to reach a compromise. The agreement would last for three years and would then be subject to review. She had also managed to wring concessions on the financial side of the package. All in all she felt she had done a good day's work. But now she was exhausted. She needed a long soak in a warm bath.

Just then, the phone rang. When she answered she heard her mother's voice and a babble of conversation in the background. 'Where are you?' she asked.

'I'm at home.'

'It sounds like you're having a party.'

Her mother laughed. 'Well, I am, in a way. That's the reason I'm ringing. You won't believe the amazing stroke of luck that Antonio has just received. A man called David Wheeler has come over from London. He's a major figure in the music world and he's interested in managing his career. I have them here in the house and we're having a little celebration. I thought you might like to join us.'

The mention of Antonio got Kirsty's attention. Here was the chance she had been waiting for. If she was able to get him alone at this party, she could confront him.

'I'll be with you in twenty minutes,' she said.

She had a quick shower, got dressed and started up the hill in her Aston Martin.

* * *

Anne O'Malley opened the door, and when Kirsty entered the house, her mother appeared with a glass of champagne. She looked around but could see no sign of her quarry. 'Where's Antonio?'

'He's in the drawing room, talking to David. Let me introduce you to Charles Ponsonby-Jones, the music critic. He brought David over and wrote the wonderful review of Antonio's concert that's in the *Gazette*.'

A chubby man in a bow tie smiled and shook her hand.

'And this is Lucy Gilbert, who kindly loaned Antonio her Steinway piano to play.'

'I'm pleased to meet you,' Lucy said. 'Your mother tells me you're a fashion designer.'

'She's exaggerating. I'm just the person who sells the clothes that the designers create.'

'It sounds very interesting.'

'Most of the time it is. But it can have its moments,' Kirsty replied, thinking of the fractious session she'd just had with Cecily.

'Do you enjoy it?'

'Enormously.'

'Well, in my experience, that's the most important thing.'

At that moment, the drawing-room door opened and she saw Antonio emerge. He didn't look at anyone but kept his head down as he made for the garden. This was the moment she had been hoping for. She steeled herself, apologised to Lucy and started after him.

***

She found him at the bottom of the lawn, looking out at the sea. He turned round when he heard her approach and his face broke into a smile. 'Kirsty, it's you.'

'I understand you've had some success with your music. Congratulations.'

'Thank you. But it is not as simple as you might think.'

'Oh? Why not?'

'David wants me to move to London. He says there are more opportunities there.'

She could barely believe her ears. If Antonio moved to London, her worries would vanish. She could relax.

'But that's fantastic news. David is right. You must go, Antonio.'

She looked into his eyes and felt her heart begin to melt but his next words quickly brought her back to earth. 'I don't want to go. I want to stay here.'

She stared at him He had just confirmed everything she had suspected from the very start. She felt her anger rise. 'I agree with David. I think it's time for you to leave.'

A shadow fell across his face and his lips trembled.

'My mother has achieved what she set out to do. She said she would bring you to the attention of the public and she has done that. There is no longer any reason to stay in this house.'

'But I like it here. I like Avalon. Your mother and Anne have been so kind to me.'

Kirsty's voice hardened. 'Do I have to spell it out for you,

Antonio? You have outstayed your welcome. Now it's time to go.'

He was visibly shocked. 'Why are you saying this?'

'Because I know what you're really up to. My mother is ill. She had a nervous breakdown when my father died and you have taken advantage of her. You have burrowed your way into her trust, with your sad tales of your impoverished childhood in Spain. You're trying to swindle her.'

At these words, his face turned pale. 'This is not true. I have no interest in her money. It means nothing to me.'

'I'm warning you, Antonio. If you don't leave Avalon voluntarily, you will leave me no choice but to go to the police.'

He hung his head. 'Very well.' He started to walk away, then stopped and turned back to her. 'You have never liked me, Kirsty. I have known it from the beginning. Always you have been cold to me. Why is that?'

She made no reply. She stood watching the sun begin its slow descent into the ocean. At last she had done it. She had confronted Antonio and sent him packing. She should have been savouring her triumph. But instead she felt something like sadness creep across her heart.

Chapter Thirty-four

Robbie Hennessy was staring out of his apartment window at the river rolling by. He had just got home from the office. Now he was thinking about what he was going to do for the rest of the evening and privately hoping that Samantha O'Leary wouldn't ring. He'd been out with her for five nights in a row and he was exhausted. It was all right for Samantha. She could sleep till noon but he had to get up for work each morning. Tonight he was looking forward to a quiet evening at home, watching football on the box.

He was growing restless. Samantha was starting to get on his nerves. Their evenings were a giddy round of nightclubs, boozy parties and champagne receptions, anywhere there was a camera. They hadn't spent a single night together in a quiet little restaurant since they'd met. Everything had been conducted in the glare of the spotlight. It was beginning to get him down.

He knew she didn't care about him. The only person Samantha cared about was herself, and who was talking about her and how many times she got her picture in the papers. She was like a gramophone record, all me, me, me. She had got herself into a real funk a few days ago over some bloke that Robbie had never even heard of, some Spanish piano player called Arturo Rivers or something. He had given a concert and Samantha hadn't been invited. Apparently, there was an article about it in the *Herald* that she kept going on about, as if it was the biggest thing since the Rolling Stones had played Slane Castle in 2007.

She was outraged that Bette McCoy and Polly McGurk had been there and she wasn't. How come they'd got invited? Why did they get their photos taken? Yap, yap, yap. She kept rabbiting on like it was a gigantic conspiracy this Spanish bloke had cooked up against her. For God's sake, the poor guy couldn't have invited every wannabe model in Dublin – there'd have been no room for the audience.

There'd been another situation when some eighteen-year-old model had got a contract to promote a perfume brand and Samantha had gone bananas, ringing up her agent and given him dog's abuse because it wasn't her. She was a schemer, too. She liked to play the little girl lost but Robbie knew that inside her pretty blonde head a calculating machine was working overtime.

What a miserable existence, he thought. How does she live with herself, constantly looking over her shoulder and watching her rivals to make sure none of them stole a march on her? She never relaxed. No wonder she was hyper. He could see the writing on the wall. Pretty soon he would have to tell her the truth. He was going to have to let her go and he dreaded her reaction. There would be fireworks.

The truth was, he missed Kirsty and wished they had

never broken up. Of course, she had her faults too. She could be cutting and dismissive sometimes, and she was always lecturing him. But at least she wasn't mad, like Samantha. And she could hold a sensible conversation without the word *me* popping into every sentence. If he hadn't got plastered that night in Crazy Joe's he'd still be going out with her. Ah, well. He sighed. That was Fate. No point crying over spilled milk.

Just then his phone rang. When he picked it up he heard the voice he'd been expecting.

'Hi, honey, it's little me. Have you had a busy day?'

'Actually, I had a very busy day and now I think I'll watch a bit of television and catch an early night.'

'But you can't do that, sweetie.'

'Why not?'

'I need you tonight. There's a new nightclub opening in Leeson Street and I've got an invitation. It's called Sugar Daddy's. It's going to be the social event of the year.'

'You said that about the record launch you dragged me to last night.'

'This one's different. Everyone will be there, all the celebs and the snappers.'

'Why don't you give it a miss, Samantha? You can't spend your whole life going to nightclub openings. Why don't you follow my example and have an early night? You'll feel better in the morning.'

'Are you crazy? People would think I wasn't invited. I've got to be there. They're expecting television cameras. I could be on *Six One*.'

'Then why don't you go without me?'

He heard her gasp. 'Now I know you've gone off your head. If I turned up on my own, it would be death. They'd say I couldn't get a partner. How would I ever live it down? Now look, Rob, darling, you've got to be sensible about this. I really need you tonight and I'm not taking any refusal.'

Robbie closed his eyes. His resolve was starting to crack.

'Please,' she begged. 'You don't want my enemies talking about me. You've no idea how much they'd love it. You've got to stand with me on this one.'

'What time?'

'It's opening at ten o'clock. Could you pick me up at nine? I want to get there early.'

'Okay,' he said wearily. 'But I'm warning you. Tomorrow night I'm taking a break. I haven't got the stamina for this.'

'Thanks, darling. I'll make it up to you.'

Robbie turned off the phone and uttered a loud groan as he set off for the bathroom to have a shower. Why hadn't he told her to take a hike? Now she had rolled him over once again. She was using him, he could see it clearly. She had more or less admitted it. Their relationship had nothing to do with romance and everything to do with propping up Samantha's image. She really was the limit, he thought, a conniving, self-seeking, publicity-mad egomaniac. The sooner he got rid of her, the better.

* * *

She was waiting for him when he turned up at her apartment at nine o'clock. She was wearing a short white silk dress with a plunging neckline, displaying lots of cleavage. And she'd got her hair done *again*. That was the second time in three days. She settled beside him on the back seat of the cab and gave him a quick peck on the cheek. 'Thanks for coming. How do I look?'

'Like a million dollars. I see you've got your hair done.'

'Yes,' she said, raising a hand to her forehead and tossing the curls a little. 'Do you like it?'

'It's fantastic. But you got it done only two days ago.'

'Oh, for God's sake, Robbie, you guys are all the same. You know nothing about the work we women have to put in to take care of ourselves.'

'I thought it looked fine the way you had it before.'

'Well, it just shows how much you understand.' She broke off the conversation to give the driver directions, then turned again to Robbie. 'I'm really looking forward to this gig. *Le tout* Dublin is going to be out tonight. If I missed it, I'd never forgive myself.'

'Don't you ever get tired of all this razzmatazz, Samantha? Don't you ever look forward to a nice romantic meal together, just you and me, without all the cameras and the limelight?'

'Are you kidding? That's old-fashioned. Nobody does that any more. Anyway, there'll be plenty of time for romance tonight when we get home,' she said, with a lascivious gleam in her eye. 'I promised I'd make it up to you.'

Suddenly she lowered her voice so that the driver couldn't hear: 'I just heard a bit of information today. Remember that concert last week that I wasn't invited to?'

'You mean the gig where the Spanish guy was playing the piano?'

'That's right,' she replied, her face darkening. 'The one where Petal Maguire got her picture on the front page of the *Herald*. I discovered who organised it.'

'Who?' Robbie enquired.

'Your ex's mother, Helen O'Neill. I couldn't figure out why

I wasn't asked when the others got invited. Now the whole thing makes sense.'

Robbie scratched his head. He hadn't a clue what she was talking about.

'Don't you see?' Samantha went on. 'That Kirsty bitch kept me off the invitation list for spite because you threw her over for me. That was her way of getting revenge.'

'You're off your head,' Robbie said. 'She'd never do a thing like that.'

'Wouldn't she? You don't know those snobby cows like I do. Well, I'll tell you something. She'll be one sorry sucker by the time I've finished with her. She'll regret the day that Spaniard ever left Madrid.'

They were turning the corner at St Stephen's Green and Leeson Street was coming into view. Suddenly, she sat forward and gave a little cry of joy. 'Look at the crowd outside. There must be fifteen photographers there already and it's only twenty past nine. Now don't be rushing me inside. Just take it easy. I want them all to get a good look at me.'

The cab pulled up outside the nightclub. Robbie paid the driver, got out and opened the door for Samantha. She stepped onto the pavement and gave a coy little smile for the newsmen. Immediately the cameras started clicking. Poking above the crowd, Robbie could see a microphone and a television camera.

'Miss O'Leary, look this way, please.'

Snap, snap, snap, went the cameras, as Samantha stood and posed with a look on her face as if she had just died and gone to Heaven. Then she began her slow progress to the front door, where a couple of burly security men examined her invitation before letting them in.

'I think I need a drink after that,' she said, taking a chilled glass of champagne from a waiter in a black dress suit. 'How do you think it went, Robbie? Did I look all right?'

'You looked brilliant. You looked like the Duchess of Cambridge arriving for a garden party at Buckingham Palace.'

Samantha beamed with pleasure. 'Did I really?'

'I've just said it. Now let's find somewhere to sit down.'

'Oh, no,' she replied, in horror. 'Nobody sits down at an event like this. The whole idea is to circulate.'

She looked frantically round the room till she spotted a plump, red-headed figure standing in a corner with a strange-looking young man in a blazer and cavalry twill trousers. She grasped Robbie firmly by the hand. 'Over here. Come and let me introduce you to a friend of mine.'

The red-haired woman stared at them as they approached. 'This is Susie Kelly,' Samantha said proudly. 'You must have heard of her. She works for the *Trumpet*. She's the top journalist in the country.'

'Right,' Robbie said.

'And this is my new boyfriend, Robbie Hennessy. He's big in the world of social media.'

Susie Kelly was studying him closely. Beside her, the youth in the blazer was looking bored.

'We're madly in love,' Samantha went on. 'We're thinking of running off to Las Vegas to get married.'

Robbie opened his mouth to speak but Susie Kelly beat him to it.

'Really?' she said. 'Tell me more.'

Chapter Thirty-five

'Antonio's gone,' Helen said.

Kirsty sat up straight. She'd been at her desk since seven thirty putting the finishing touches to her agreement with Cecily Moncrieffe before it went to her solicitor. Now it was half past eight and her mother was on the phone telling her Antonio had left.

She tried to keep her voice steady. 'To London?'

'No. He's gone back to Spain, and the sad thing is that he didn't even say goodbye.'

'Good Lord.'

'I'm shocked,' Helen continued. 'His room is empty and all his belongings are gone. Just when he was on the verge of gaining recognition, he decides to take himself off. All that effort washed down the drain. I must say I'm very disappointed.'

Kirsty was taken by surprise. He had left sooner than she'd expected. Perhaps her threat to go to the police had frightened him. However, Helen seemed to be taking it badly.

'Just stay where you are,' she said. 'I'm coming to see you.'

She locked the apartment and got into her car. Ten minutes later she was turning into the drive at Avalon. She found her mother in the kitchen, sad and depressed. 'Have you had any breakfast?' Kirsty asked.

Helen shook her head. 'I've no appetite. To leave without saying goodbye, why did he have to do that?'

'Let's make a nice cup of tea,' Kirsty said, putting the kettle on.

Once the tea was ready, she poured two cups and sat down at the kitchen table beside her mother. 'Now just start at the beginning and tell me exactly what happened.'

Helen took a deep breath. 'Shortly after you left last night, the party broke up. I thought Antonio was a bit low, particularly after the great success he'd had with the concert. He said he was tired and was going to bed. Then he did a strange thing. He came to me, shook my hand and thanked me for everything I had done for him.'

'And then what?'

'I got up this morning and found his bedroom empty and this on the table.'

She gave Kirsty a handwritten note.

Dear Helen,
I have decided I can no longer stay with you and must go home at once. I am sorry to be leaving so soon. I have always received great kindness and hospitality in Avalon, particularly from you and Anne. I will always have happy memories of my stay with you in Dublin.
With gratitude,
Antonio

As Kirsty stared at the note, an uneasy feeling stole over her. She hadn't foreseen the way her mother would react.

'I don't understand,' Helen continued. 'Until yesterday everything was going so well. David Wheeler wanted to take him back to London. He was on the verge of great things and then he just threw it all away.'

'Don't blame yourself, Mum. You did everything you could to help him. He says so in this note. Perhaps it was best for him to go. He could hardly expect to stay here for ever with you lashing out money on him.'

'But I spent hardly anything. He wouldn't allow it. He kept insisting on paying for groceries and stuff. And, look, he also left this.' She gave Kirsty a small bundle of notes. She counted a hundred and fifty euros. 'It was probably all he had left. I know he didn't earn much playing in that restaurant. He probably kept enough for his plane ticket and gave me the rest. Oh, I feel so miserable about that poor boy. I feel like I've let him down.'

Hearing this, Kirsty's unease turned into guilt. 'You did nothing of the sort,' she said sternly. 'You must stop thinking like that. He told me last night that he didn't want to go to London with David Wheeler. Maybe events were moving too fast and he panicked. None of this is your fault.'

'Then why didn't he talk to me? I could have reassured him. David Wheeler is not unreasonable. They could probably have worked out something between them to allow Antonio to stay in Dublin.'

Kirsty was running out of things to say. She didn't dare tell her mother about the confrontation in the garden. Certainly not with the mood she was in. 'Do you want me to stay with you for a while?'

Helen shook her head. 'No, you've got your business to look

after. Thanks for coming to talk to me. I'm going to ring Anne and ask her to come over. She'll know what to do.'

Kirsty stood up. 'Okay. If anything else turns up, I'm at the end of the phone.'

She left and drove back to her apartment.

* * *

As soon as she was inside, she went straight to her office and tried to pick up her work again. But she couldn't concentrate for thinking about the dramatic turn of events. She was racked with remorse. She had acted too hastily. But what was done was done. She must put all doubts aside. She had succeeded in removing Antonio from Avalon. In time, her mother would get over her disappointment. Now Kirsty must put the matter out of her mind and get on with the business of Cecily's agreement.

Once this was wrapped up, she would take the holiday she had promised herself, go away somewhere sunny and forget all about the recent events. She was beginning to think of lunch when her phone rang again. This time it was Deirdre.

'I've just heard the sad news about Antonio,' she said. 'It's terrible. I can't believe he's gone like that. What do you think happened?'

Kirsty took a deep breath. Now her sister was getting in on the drama. 'Who knows? He changed his mind or maybe he just got fed up.'

'I think he was threatened,' Deirdre said.

Kirsty started. 'Threatened? How do you mean?'

'Somebody told him to leave – somebody who didn't want him here. Why else would he pack up and go without even saying goodbye to anyone? And just when he was about to make his big breakthrough. It doesn't make sense.'

Kirsty was chilled. She tried to keep her voice steady. 'I don't follow you, Deirdre.'

'It's obvious. Another musician must have warned him off, some guy who was jealous of him. Don't think it doesn't happen. I've been told by people in the business that professional rivalry is rife in the music industry.'

'I hadn't thought of that, Deirdre. You might be on to something. Have you mentioned it to Mum?'

'Sure I have, but she's too upset to listen. My big regret is that I didn't get to see more of him. He was such a nice, gentle guy and such a handsome man. I didn't even get to his concert, tied up with the boys as usual.'

'You might have another chance. Who says he won't come back?' Kirsty said. 'Stranger things have happened.'

'You're right, and if he does, I'll make sure to see him more often. I have to run – Tommy's screaming for his lunch. You don't know how lucky you are not having kids.'

There was a click and she was gone. Kirsty heaved a sigh of relief.

She took a short break for lunch, then continued working till four o'clock. She emailed the agreement to her solicitor, Gavin Tierney, and finally stood up from her desk. The sun was out again so she decided to go for a walk along the pier and stretch her legs.

She should be feeling free as a bird. Antonio was gone and with him the threat that had never been far from her thoughts since her mother had first said she was bringing him back from Spain. But instead of feeling joy, she felt like a child with a guilty secret.

The doubts were creeping back. What if she had been wrong about Antonio? What if all those little jobs he had carried out, like painting the tree house, had been simple acts of kindness from the goodness of his heart? It would mean she had done him a terrible injustice, driven him out of Avalon on a mere suspicion. It would mean she had forced him to throw over the chance of a promising career at the one thing he was passionate about – playing the piano.

She shook her head. She had to stop thinking like this or she would drive herself crazy. She had acted in her mother's best interests. Antonio was gone. There was nothing more to be done. She reached the end of the pier and turned back. Twenty minutes later she was opening the door of her apartment once more and facing into a long, boring evening alone.

It was on occasions like this that she hated being single, when she had time to spare and no one to share it with. She was alone with no male companion to talk to, no strong, masculine arms to wrap around her, no lover to whisper sweet nothings in her ear. Was this to be her fate, never to have an enduring relationship, never to find love?

She changed into some casual clothes, then settled down on the settee with a glass of wine. She watched television till half past ten and then she went to bed. But sleep didn't sort her problems and when she woke the following morning she was still feeling down. She decided to eat breakfast out. There was a café near the railway station. She would go there.

* * *

Kirsty opened the door and was met with a blast of warm air. She found an empty table in a corner and ordered bacon, eggs, toast and a mug of coffee. Someone had left a newspaper on the table. She picked it up. It was a copy of the *Trumpet*, a rag she hardly ever read. While she ate, she turned the pages.

When she came to the gossip column, her heart stopped.

There, looking straight at her, was a photo of herself taken from some publicity material her company had put out. Across the page was another photo, this time of Samantha O'Leary. Splashed across the top was a huge headline:

FASHIONISTA LOSES MAN TO PASSIONISTA

Beneath, grinning insanely, like an ageing crone who was about to devour a newborn baby, was a picture of the gossip columnist, Susie Kelly. Kirsty swallowed hard and began to read the report.

> The big buzz among the demi-monde of Dublin's fair city is the recent coup by stunning model and wild child Samantha O'Leary, who has stolen hunky Robbie Hennessy away from fashion queen Kirsty O'Neill.
>
> O'Neill, who is the owner of Dublin design company Allure Fashions, used to be the favourite squeeze of handsome Hennessy, a leading light in the social media firm ClickOn. But not any more. Recently hot Robbie has been seen squiring blonde bombshell O'Leary around the city's night spots. Close friends tell me they are madly in love and are planning a wedding in Las Vegas.
>
> Meanwhile, O'Neill has gone into hiding and was unavailable for comment last night but observers are predicting handbags at dawn should the two divas cross paths any time soon.

Chapter Thirty-six

Kirsty's hands trembled as she put down the paper. Every line in the report was a lie, including the words *the* and *is*. She had not been dumped by that rat, Hennessy. *She* had dumped *him*. She had *not* gone into hiding. She had *not* been unavailable for comment. The vindictive old crone, Kelly, who had written this bilge, had never even bothered to contact her.

As for handbags at dawn, that was a joke. She wouldn't lower herself to speak to Samantha O'Leary, never mind get into a row with her over Robbie Hennessy. The suggestion that he was in love with Samantha and was planning a wedding in Las Vegas was a figment of someone's fevered imagination, unless he had completely taken leave of his senses.

She was so angry that she couldn't even hold her coffee mug. Everyone who read this would be laughing at her. And soon the whole town would be talking about it. She thought briefly of suing the *Trumpet* for libel but that would mean giving the lies even more publicity. What was she going to do?

She couldn't finish her breakfast. She paid the bill and

hurried back along the seafront to her apartment, went in and locked the door. She needed to think but her brain seemed to have shut down. All she could see was the grinning face of Samantha O'Leary and that dreadful headline: FASHIONISTA LOSES MAN TO PASSIONISTA. She became aware that her phone was ringing. Instinctively, she lifted it and pressed it to her ear.

It was Penny Muldoon.

'I'm calling to sympathise with you. I've seen that awful piece in the *Trumpet*. It's shocking but I want you to know that nobody believes a word of it. Your friends are all behind you, Kirsty. Don't let it get to you.'

'Thanks, Penny, I appreciate it.'

'What did you do to her anyway?'

'Who?'

'Susie Kelly.'

'Are you kidding? You don't have to do anything to her. She's just an evil old witch, who gets her kicks from writing outrageous lies about people. I told you about her that night we were eating in Malibu.'

'Yes, you did. Well, try to put it behind you. And, remember, we're all with you.'

The call ended but immediately the phone started ringing again. This time she felt the hairs on the back of her neck stand up.

'Hi,' a nervous voice said. 'It's Robbie. I'm calling to say I had nothing to do with that article this morning. I didn't even talk to Susie Kelly. It was Samantha who did it.'

This was the last straw. Kirsty exploded. 'How dare you ring this number? I told you the last time never to call me again. Now, do me a favour.'

'What?'

'Have a heart attack.'

There was a gasp. Kirsty terminated the call but a minute later the phone was ringing again.

'I'm warning you. If you keep this up, I'm going to call the cops,' she yelled.

'My, my,' a familiar voice said. 'You're really on edge this morning.'

'Cecily?'

'Yes, dear. I see you're making headlines for all the wrong reasons.'

'That story in the *Trumpet*? It's all lies. There's not one word of truth in any of it. I went out with Rob Hennessy for a while and got rid of him because he was a drunken bore.'

'I believe you, but it doesn't matter whether it's the truth or not. People who want to believe it will swallow it anyway. The point is, what are you going to do about it?'

'What can I do? If I sue them it will just make everything worse.'

'Well, there are several things you can do. You have to respond. I suggest you get on to Mags Smith in the *Tribune* and feed her a story. Mags will print it because she's a deadly rival of Kelly's. They hate each other's guts.'

'What should I say?'

'Something along these lines. "When contacted on a sun-kissed beach in the Costa del Sol yesterday, Kirsty O'Neill said she hadn't read the article because she was too busy enjoying herself with the wonderful nightlife. However, she did wish Samantha and Robbie well, saying they were made for each other." Anyone with an eye in their head will spot the little dig.'

'But I'm not on the Costa del Sol. I'm in Dublin.'

'That's the second thing you can do. Get there as fast

as possible. If you hang around here you're going to have a miserable time. Everywhere you go, people will be gawking at you and whispering under their breath. Take my advice. Disappear for a couple of weeks. When you come back, the whole thing will have blown over.'

'But what about the agreement we're negotiating? I just sent the final draft to my solicitor yesterday.'

'It can wait. When you get back, I'll still be here. And maybe in the meantime Robbie will have ditched Samantha or she will have ditched him. Do what I suggest and get the hell out.'

Kirsty thanked her, then turned off the phone. It was only half past nine and she'd taken three calls already. She thought about what Cecily had said. It sounded like good advice. If she stayed in Dublin she would continue to draw the attention of the gutter hacks. Every time she stepped outside the apartment, there'd be photographers jumping out of the bushes to get her picture. Besides, she was worn out with all the pressure. She had promised herself a break. If ever there was a time to go, it was now. She made up her mind.

She went into her office and began searching the web for flights. Where would she go? She looked out of the window at the dark clouds gathering over the harbour. She needed the sun. She thought of blue seas, waving palm trees and drowsy night skies filled with stars. Cecily had mentioned the Costa del Sol and her mother had too. She had raved about the place Kirsty had found for her at Puebla Maria.

But Kirsty had no intention of going there in case she ran into Antonio. It took half an hour to come across a place that looked promising, Hotel Geronimo in Fuengirola. It had a swimming pool, bars, restaurant and a fitness centre. It was close to the beach, half an hour along the coast from Marbella, and it had vacancies.

Next she had to check travel arrangements. This time her luck was in. An Aer Lingus flight was leaving at one o'clock, which would get her into Málaga airport for half past four. And there were two seats left. Kirsty took out her credit card and snapped one up. Then she returned to Hotel Geronimo's website and booked herself in for two weeks. She sat back in her chair and gave a sigh of satisfaction. Already the thought of sun and sand was working its magic.

By now she had calmed down a little and her energy was coming back. But there was still an awful lot to do before she could leave. First she had to inform her mother. She picked up the phone again. When Helen answered, she sounded as if she was still mourning the sudden departure of Antonio.

'Everybody's very upset,' she said. 'David Wheeler is naturally disappointed and Charles Ponsonby-Jones is shocked. He had to scrap the interview he had written when I told him the news. As for Lucy Gilbert and the others, they can't believe it has happened.'

'How about Anne?'

'She feels the same way. We put a lot of work into that concert and now it has all gone up in smoke. Anne keeps reminding me that she counselled me against it when I first suggested bringing Antonio back to Dublin. Now she's been proved right.'

The words she had spoken to Deirdre yesterday popped out of her mouth before she had time to think. 'You never know, Mum. He might come back. He hasn't phoned or anything?'

'No, not a word.'

'Try not to be too upset. You've got nothing to blame yourself for. You did everything in your power to help him and he threw it away.'

She heard her mother sigh. 'I suppose you're right. But it's little consolation.'

'Now listen, Mum, you'll be glad to know that I've decided to take your advice. I'm going on holiday to the Costa del Sol.'

That news seemed to cheer her mother up. 'I'm delighted to hear it. You've been working so hard. You'll feel much better when you come back. Are you going to Puebla Maria?'

'No. I tried but it was booked out.'

'That's a pity. Anne and I had a wonderful time there. So where are you going?'

'A place called Hotel Geronimo. It's in a town called Fuengirola.'

'I know it. We visited when we were down there. You'll really enjoy it. Are you going with – what's his name? Robert?'

'Definitely not,' Kirsty snapped, then checked herself. 'He can't come. I'm going alone.'

'I understand,' her mother replied. 'Now, you must keep in touch. I like to know how you're getting on.'

'I'll ring every day.'

'There's no need for that. Just call when you get an opportunity. Bye now and take care.'

What was next? Packing. And what would she bring? Already Kirsty was getting excited. She went into her bedroom and began selecting dresses, tops, shorts and sensible shoes for walking. And swimwear. She expected to spend a lot of time lounging by the pool. She began packing the clothes into her suitcase. When that was done, she went online and transferred several thousand euros into her credit card account in case she did some shopping while she was there.

By now, time was moving on. She went around the apartment making sure the lights and electrical equipment were switched off. She didn't want to return from Spain to find her beautiful apartment had burned down while she was away. Finally she sat down at her desk and rang Mags Smith, the gossip columnist at the *Tribune*.

'Hello, Mags, this is Kirsty O'Neill. About Susie Kelly's story in the *Trumpet* this morning. I want to give you a short response.'

'Fire away.'

'Before we begin, by the time you print this, I'll be on the Costa del Sol. I'd like you to report my response from there. Is that okay?'

'Even better, it will sound more exotic.'

'Exactly.'

She gave the short statement that Cecily had suggested earlier. 'Have you got that?'

'Yes, it's fine. Thanks for thinking of me. I never believed a word of that story. Everything that old wagon writes is a lie. She wouldn't know the truth if it bit her on the leg. This will be in my column in the morning.'

Kirsty switched off her phone with a smile of satisfaction. Then she gave the apartment a last-minute look-over, locked up and went downstairs. She got into her car and drove the short distance to the airport.

It was packed when she arrived. She checked in her baggage, passed through security and finally arrived in the departure lounge. She scanned the monitor. Her flight was leaving on time. She bought a coffee and sat down to wait. It had been a hectic morning but now she was leaving Antonio, Robbie Hennessy and the dreadful Susie Kelly behind. She could look forward to two blissful weeks on the Costa.

Half an hour later she was boarding the plane that was to take her to the sun.

Chapter Thirty-seven

Málaga airport was like a beehive when Kirsty emerged into Arrivals at four twenty p.m. Her flight had left Dublin on schedule and the pilot had even managed to shave a few minutes off the flying time because of favourable tail winds. Now she was eager to get to her destination. She grabbed her suitcase from the carousel, then made her way to the exit and out into the blinding sun.

The taxi rank was right outside the door. The driver took her case and stowed it in the boot while she opened the door, slid onto the warm leather seat and clipped on her belt. He was a slim young man in his late twenties and talkative. 'Where to?' he asked.

'Hotel Geronimo, Fuengirola.'

'Fu-en-kee-rola.' He corrected her pronunciation and grinned. 'You speak any Spanish, Señorita?'

'No.'

'So I will teach you.'

He started the car and they slid out of the airport. The first thing to strike her was the dazzling array of flowers: flaming geraniums, blood-red roses, purple violets. They seemed to be everywhere, in tubs, window boxes and hanging baskets. The driver was babbling away but Kirsty was only half listening. She was gazing out of the window at the sea, shining like blue silk, and the miles of golden sand that stretched as far as her eye could see. Yes, she decided, I'm going to like it here.

Soon they were on the motorway.

'*Buenos días*,' the driver said, catching her attention in the mirror. 'That means "good day". *Buenas noches* means "good night". You think you can remember that?'

'Sure,' Kirsty said.

'*Por favor* is "please", and *gracias* means "thank you".'

Kirsty repeated the words and the driver grinned. 'Excellent, Señorita. You are a very good student.'

'Where did you learn to speak English?' she asked.

'From passengers like you. I can also speak some German and French.'

'Your English is great.'

He shrugged at the compliment. 'It is not so good.'

She could see the ocean again, shining in the distance, and little white houses clinging precariously to the cliffs. She decided to change the conversation. 'What's the weather forecast?'

'Sun. How long are you staying?'

'Two weeks.'

'Sun all the time. Now it is June so already it is summer.'

'Good. That's why I came.'

Eventually, the car began to slow down. They had left the motorway and were coming to the outskirts of a town. Kirsty could see houses and tall apartment blocks gleaming in the afternoon light. A few minutes later, the driver swung onto an avenue and a large sign announced 'HOTEL GERONIMO'. He pulled up at the entrance, got out and opened the door for her. 'Now we have arrived.' He unlocked the boot, took out her case and deposited it at the front door of the hotel.

'How much?' she asked.

'Twenty-five euros.'

She gave him thirty and told him to keep the change. He seemed pleased and saluted her in gratitude. '*Muchas gracias, Señorita*. Enjoy your holiday and don't forget the words I taught you.' With that, he was off.

She paused to take in her surroundings. It was a large, modern hotel with a strip of green lawn in front and more tubs of flowers. Off to one side, she could see a garden with palm trees and flowerbeds and the shimmering blue water of a swimming pool. So far, it was living up to the online description she had read. She took hold of her case, pushed through the front doors and found herself in a large lobby with comfortable sofas and little tables where guests could relax. She marched across the marble floor to the reception desk and announced her arrival to a dark-haired young woman in a starched white blouse. 'Kirsty O'Neill. I have a reservation.' She produced her passport and placed it on the desk while the receptionist got busy on the computer.

'Yes, we have your reservation, Ms O'Neill. Room two six five. Would you care to register, please?'

She pushed a form across the desk and waited while Kirsty filled it in. Then she checked Kirsty's passport, smiled and handed her a plastic key with an information pack.

'Everything you need to know is in the pack. The dining room is along that corridor. We have several bars, one beside the dining room and another next to the pool. Do you need assistance with your case?'

Kirsty shook her head.

'The lifts are over there.' The woman pointed. 'And your room is on the first floor. Enjoy your stay at Hotel Geronimo, Miss O'Neill. If there is anything we can do for you, please do not hesitate to call me.'

Kirsty rode up in the lift and quickly found room 265. She opened the door and stepped inside. It was a large room, smartly furnished with a double bed, a wardrobe and a writing bureau, with a laptop computer and phone. Facing the bed was a large flat-screen television. A vase of fresh flowers and a bowl of fruit sat on a table in the corner. In another corner there was a bathroom. Large sliding doors took up one side of the room. She pulled them open and walked onto a sunny terrace with a little table and chairs.

She went to the rail and gazed out. She was looking over the hotel garden. There were a few people splashing about in the pool and others chatting at the bar. More were sunbathing on the lawn. She closed the doors again. Back in the room, she spotted a small fridge that she had missed. Inside was a chilled bottle of white wine and some glasses. What a pleasant surprise. She opened the bottle and poured a glass, then lay down on the bed and stared at the ceiling. This is bliss, she thought. Why didn't I do it sooner?

It was almost seven o'clock when she got up and by now she was hungry. It was time to plan the evening. She got undressed and had a shower, then put on a hotel bathrobe while she considered what to wear. The evening was warm so she would need something cool and casual. She started emptying her suitcase, hanging the clothes in the wardrobe until she found what she was looking for – a cool, knee-length dress. With it she would wear a light jacket and sandals.

While she was getting dressed, she thought about food. She could eat in the hotel restaurant but she had an urge to get out and explore the town. She brushed her hair and applied a little make-up, checked that she had sufficient cash and slung her bag across her shoulder. She glanced once more in the mirror. Now she was ready. She locked the door and began walking towards the lift.

* * *

It was a short stroll to the town and the streets were busy. The shops and restaurants were open again after the siesta and people were relaxing at pavement tables, chatting and drinking with friends. The information pack she had been given contained a street map and she used it to navigate her way. After walking for ten minutes she came to the beach, deserted now that the sun was going down.

She strolled past the tourist restaurants along the seafront, stopping occasionally to study the printed menus displayed on boards outside. She passed the port and the marina and at last found herself in the old part of town, a maze of small, narrow streets and shops that lay beyond, Plaza de la Constitución. There was an unmistakable buzz about the place. The little houses were decorated with window boxes and from the tiny bars came the sound of music and chatter. Eventually she stopped at a restaurant that appealed to her.

The board outside displayed a typically Spanish menu of fish and meat dishes. She entered and was led through the bar by a waiter in a white apron and shown to a table on a small patio at the back. She asked for a glass of wine, and when the waiter returned, she ordered grilled plaice and salad. She sipped the wine and studied her surroundings.

The patio held about eight tables and most of them were occupied. Along one wall a trellis was covered with cascading nasturtiums and small pots of white geraniums. Somewhere in the distance she could hear the lively rhythm of flamenco guitar. Above, the sky was darkening, and a few stars beginning to peep out. The waiter was back with her meal and she began to eat.

The plaice was thick and plump and had been grilled on a fire with cloves of garlic. The salad was stuffed with sliced peppers, tomatoes, cucumber and carrot and seasoned with oil and vinegar. She cut a piece of fish and put it into her mouth, then broke off a piece of freshly baked bread in a little straw basket on the table and gave a contented sigh.

She hadn't eaten since she'd left Dublin and now she was ravenous. She finished the meal, mopping up the juices on her plate with bread. When the waiter returned, he asked if she wanted dessert but she declined. She would buy an ice cream on her way back to Hotel Geronimo. She would save it as a treat.

By now, the streets and alleys of the old town were packed with people, singles, couples and families with children, eating and drinking at tables outside the bars. The lights were on and buskers were strolling through the crowds with guitars, stopping occasionally at a table to serenade a young couple with a romantic song. Kirsty wandered through the streets fascinated by what she saw all around her. It was nine o'clock and the town was throbbing. It might as well have been midday.

At last, she began to make her way back to the hotel. When she arrived she saw that the poolside bar was still open. She decided to have a nightcap. She chose a table outside and ordered a brandy. What a day she'd had, and what a wonderful world she had discovered, filled with music, laughter and colour. Now she knew where she would eat each night. She would return to the old town and take her pick from the myriad bars and restaurants in the narrow little streets.

The night air was warm and carried the heavy scent of flowers. From the nearby hedges, she could hear the cicadas chirping. She became aware that a young man was observing her with interest from the bar. He was tall and handsome with blond hair, possibly a German or Scandinavian tourist, alone like herself. The thought of a romantic interlude crossed her mind. It would be easy to let him know she was available. She just had to smile and he would buy her a drink and come across to her table. But something about his hair and build reminded her of Robbie Hennessy and she turned away. She finished her brandy and made her way back to her room.

There, she realised just how tired she was. She'd had a very long day. She got undressed and slid under the duvet. As she was slipping off to sleep, she remembered she hadn't called her mother to let her know she had arrived safely. She checked her watch. It was now eleven o'clock and Helen had probably gone to bed. She'd ring her in the morning. A few minutes later, she was fast asleep.

Chapter Thirty-eight

The morning sun filtering through the curtains wakened her. It was ten to eight. She had slept for almost nine hours and now she felt refreshed and full of energy. She went out onto the terrace and peered over the rail. The hotel was coming alive and the bar beside the pool appeared to be open. But the pool itself was empty of people. She put on her swimsuit, slipped into the hotel's bathrobe, made sure she had her room key and set off.

The grass was wet with dew and the birds were chirping madly in the bushes. Apart from a solitary gardener clipping the hedge, there was no one about. Kirsty had a quick shower, then walked to the deep end and dived in. The cold water shocked her but her body soon adjusted to the temperature. She swam for fifteen minutes, and when she emerged, she felt vibrantly awake. She dried herself and started back to her room.

On the way, she noticed a couple eating at a table outside the bar and caught the aroma of freshly brewing coffee. She decided to stop and have breakfast. A smiling waitress took her order for croissants and scrambled eggs, and while she waited, Kirsty stretched back in her seat to let the sun warm her face.

'Just arrived?' a voice enquired.

She sat up again. The man at the next table was speaking to her. He was small and chubby, middle-aged with a British accent.

'I arrived yesterday afternoon,' Kirsty said.

'You'll like it here,' the man's wife put in. She was about the same age as her husband and had dyed blonde hair. 'There's so much to do. We come every year, don't we, Jim?'

'Wouldn't miss it. Best little spot in Spain.'

'Where are you from?' his wife asked.

'Dublin.'

'We've been there – very lively place. We went to Glendalough. But the weather in Dublin's a bit changeable. That's why we come to Spain. It's more reliable here. On your own, are you?'

Kirsty wasn't sure she welcomed this interrogation but she knew the couple were just trying to be friendly. 'Yes,' she said. 'I've been working very hard recently and decided I needed a break.'

'You've come to the right place. There's plenty of entertainment for a young person like you, discos and nightclubs and things like that. We're too old, aren't we, Jim?'

'Wouldn't let us in.' The man laughed.

'Planning to do some sightseeing?' the woman asked.

'That's right,' Kirsty agreed.

'Then you must visit Mijas. It's a beautiful little village up in the hills. You can get the bus. Real Spanish, lots of things to see.'

'And donkey rides, don't forget to tell her about the donkeys,' her husband added.

Just then the waitress returned with Kirsty's order and the couple got up to leave.

'Jim and Valerie Wilson,' the man said, extending his hand.

'Kirsty O'Neill.'

'We're in room one five three. If you ever want to know anything, just give us a call. We'll be glad to help you.'

***

After breakfast, she returned to her room, sat down at the computer and went online to check the weather forecast. It showed a temperature of 22 degrees and clear skies. That was hot. She decided to change into a pair of shorts and a T-shirt. Then she took out her phone. It was time to ring home. She checked the code for Dublin and dialled her mother.

'It's me,' she said, when she heard Helen's voice. 'I've arrived. I'm in Fuengirola.'

'That's a relief,' her mother said. 'How was your flight? Did everything go smoothly?'

'Like a dream.'

'And what about your hotel, do you like it?'

'It's lovely. I've got a nice big room with all mod cons and I've just been swimming in the pool. I'm sorry I didn't call you sooner, but by the time I got settled last night it was too late and I didn't want to disturb you.'

'That's perfectly all right, darling. You don't have to apologise. Now, what are you planning to do today?'

'I haven't decided yet. I might put in a spot of sunbathing or I might go sightseeing. Or maybe I'll do both. That's the whole point of a holiday, Mum. You don't get tied down by schedules.'

'I couldn't agree more. You're there to relax.'

She wondered if she should ask for news about Antonio but her mother was speaking again in a subdued voice. 'There's something I think I should mention. Your sister rang last night and told me all about that dreadful newspaper article.'

Kirsty caught her breath. Deirdre could never keep her mouth shut. If anyone was going to tell Helen the bad news, it was sure to be her.

'I had a suspicion something like this was going on,' her mother continued. 'Remember I asked you if you'd had a row with your boyfriend that time you were feeling run-down? Anyway, I wanted to offer my support. Don't take it too hard.'

'I'm not taking it hard at all. I'm delighted to be shot of him. That report in the *Trumpet* is a pack of lies. It was *me* got rid of *him*.'

'He doesn't strike me as a very nice man. Imagine running off to Las Vegas to get married. How tacky can you get?'

Kirsty could feel her blood pressure starting to rise. Deirdre must have read the whole article to Helen. Or maybe she drove up to Avalon to deliver it in person. If she continued this conversation with her mother, she was going to explode. 'Listen, Mum, I have to go.'

'Okay, love. Now, remember what I said. Just put it all behind you. Who knows? Maybe you'll meet some nice person down there on the Costa.'

'Byeee!' Kirsty disconnected the call.

She thought of her earlier conversation with Jim and Valerie. They had mentioned the village of Mijas up in the hills and a bus that would take her there. She would go to Mijas. She put on a pair of runners, brushed her hair, checked her bag and set off.

It took her fifteen minutes to reach the bus station and discover that a bus was leaving ten minutes later. She bought a ticket and stood in line till it arrived, then found a seat beside a window. By the time it set off, the bus was packed with sight-seers like herself, cameras slung across their chests.

They left the bus station and soon began their slow ascent into the hills. As the bus climbed higher, the town began to fall away and soon they were out in the countryside with fields, trees, and herds of goats grazing on the short grass. As they drew closer to their destination, the road rose quite steeply, then suddenly levelled out and they had arrived in Mijas. The bus pulled into a square beside the bullring and they disembarked.

Kirsty gazed at her new surroundings. She was in a village of narrow streets, little whitewashed houses and more hanging baskets of bright red flowers. Across the square, she saw the donkeys that Jim Wilson had mentioned. They stood patiently in the hot sun, their necks garlanded with flowers and bells, while tourists posed for pictures.

A crowd had gathered across the street and she went to join them. When she squeezed through, she found herself looking down on a breathtaking view that stretched the whole way along the coast. Immediately below, she could see Fuengirola. She could pick out the spires of churches, even the façade of Hotel Geronimo, and Plaza de la Constitución where she had spent such a pleasant time last night. And right on the edge of the town was the sea, with yachts like toy boats bobbing serenely on the tide. She got out her phone and began taking photos.

There was a tourist office nearby. She went in, made some enquiries and emerged with a street map and guide. She set off to do some exploring. She walked along the main street and emerged into another square with bars and cafés doing a busy trade. She went down some steps and arrived in a street lined with souvenir stalls and quaint old antiques shops. After walking for half an hour she found herself at the end of the village and turned back again. By now, it was almost one o'clock. She decided to stop for lunch.

There was an abundance of places to choose from. After checking several menus, she sat down at a table outside a restaurant called Casa Pedro. When the waiter appeared she ordered a beer and asked what the special was.

'Today it is the paella of the house, Señorita. I recommend it.'

'I'll have it,' she replied.

It was a tasty dish of rice, chicken, prawns and peppers, accompanied by a green salad and a basket of warm bread. She finished the meal and felt a relaxing calm steal over her. The sun was casting shadows across the cobbles, and in a doorway a sleek black cat was dozing. She realised that since she'd arrived in Mijas, she hadn't once thought of Robbie Hennessy and the problems she had left behind in Dublin.

She returned to the bullring and waited for the bus to take her back. When she arrived at Hotel Geronimo it was almost four o'clock and the sun was still strong. She had thoroughly enjoyed her trip and now she felt like putting her feet up. She retrieved the paperback novel she had bought at the airport and sat reading on the terrace till the sun began to go down. Now it was time to plan for the evening.

She had promised to return to the old town so she had a shower and spent some time getting dressed before she locked up and set off. Tonight, she chose a different route, walking along the Paseo Maritimo till she reached the Moorish castle that guarded the entrance to the town. It was lit with floodlights. She took some photographs, then turned and made her way into the maze of narrow backstreets.

Soon she was in the grip of the magic, immersed once more in the laughter and music spilling from the cramped little cafés, and the heady aromas that wafted out from the busy restaurants. This time, she decided to choose a different place to eat and, after wandering for a while, she came across an Argentinian grill house. Inside she could see thick succulent steaks and strings of fat chorizo sausages cooking. It would play havoc with her cholesterol but what the hell? She was on holiday. She walked through the open door and was quickly shown to a seat.

The waiter immediately produced a menu but Kirsty already knew what she wanted. She ordered a fillet steak with salad and a glass of red wine.

'How do you want your steak cooked, Señorita?' the waiter asked.

'Medium, please.'

'You want fries with it?'

'Oh, no,' she said emphatically.

He nodded politely, took the menus away and ten minutes later returned with her dinner. She sliced the steak and immediately a rich juice oozed onto the plate. Inside the meat was pink and tender. She cut a piece, popped it into her mouth and closed her eyes. It was delicious.

When she had finished eating, she wandered through the narrow streets with their bustling bars and restaurants, stopping occasionally to watch a troupe of jugglers or a clown busking for coppers. Gradually, she left the confines of the old town and began to walk back to her hotel.

When she arrived, she saw the lights of the poolside bar were ablaze. She would have a nightcap again and unwind before she went to bed. There was a crowd of tourists at the counter and among them she saw the blond man who had been there the night before.

She took a seat at any empty table outside and asked for a gin and tonic. Tonight the bushes near the hotel were strung with fairy lights, which cast a romantic glow over the surroundings. When the drink came, she paid the waiter and sat looking out at the peaceful water of the pool. From the corner of her eye, she could see the blond man detach himself from the group and make his way towards her.

'Why is a beautiful woman like you drinking on her own?' he asked.

Kirsty stared up at him. 'Because I chose to.'

He smiled. 'Do you mind if I join you?'

She shrugged and he pulled out a seat and sat down. 'My name is Björn,' he said. 'May I ask what you are called?'

'Kirsty.'

'And where are you from, Kirsty?'

Close up, he was even more handsome. His blue eyes twinkled in a rugged, sunburned face.

'Ireland.'

'Ah, the green land of the giants. I have read all about Ireland.'

'Where did you learn to speak such good English?'

'At school. I am from Norway. All the children learn to speak English.'

So she had been right. He was from Scandinavia. 'And what are *you* doing here?'

'I'm with some friends. They have a yacht in the marina

and we sail around the coast. But the yacht is very cramped. While we are in Fuengirola I have decided to stay here at Hotel Geronimo. I like my pleasure,' he said, with a gleam in his eye.

He finished his drink and waved to the waiter for another. 'May I buy you one?'

Kirsty hesitated. She felt tempted. She was enjoying the company of this handsome Norseman. But if she accepted, he would interpret it as a sign of encouragement. Was she ready for what would follow? It was some time since she'd had a man other than Robbie in her bed and she missed the passion, the strong body pressed against hers, the endearments whispered in her ear. And who would know? She was alone here with no snooping gossip columnists to splash her business all over the papers.

She looked into his deep blue eyes and wavered. 'No,' she said. 'Thank you for your kind offer but I must go now. Perhaps another time.'

She saw the disappointment in his face as she stood up and walked away across the grass, back to her lonely bed in room 265.

Chapter Thirty-nine

Over the coming days, she settled into a routine. She woke around eight o'clock, went for a swim, then had breakfast at the poolside bar. She got to know Valerie and Jim, who shared a house in Brighton with their daughter, her husband and their two children. The trip to Spain was the highlight of their year. Over coffee and croissants they swapped gossip and shared tips about what to do and where to go.

After breakfast, she returned to her room and, once more, checked the weather forecast for the day. It showed remarkable consistency, as the taxi driver had predicted, smiling suns and temperatures in the early twenties. At ten o'clock, when she knew her mother would be up, she would ring her and have a chat.

But Helen was the only person she rang. She made a point of not calling Cecily Moncrieffe or Angie Dunlop for fear they might tell her something that would drag her thoughts back to Dublin and Robbie Hennessy.

She would spend the rest of the morning reading on the

terrace, and around one o'clock, she would go into the town and have a light lunch. She might spend the afternoon sightseeing along the coast. One day, she took the train into Málaga but found the city too hot and came back to Fuengirola.

She liked the evenings best when the sun had gone down and the air was cooler. She continued to enjoy the excitement of the old town but she sometimes went further afield, walking the short distance to the little resort of Los Boliches further down the coast where she never failed to find an interesting restaurant to have dinner. She ended the day at the poolside bar but she never saw Björn again. His yacht must have sailed to another port. The evening when he had made his overture to her had perhaps been his last in Fuengirola.

* * *

Before she knew it, a week had passed and she was halfway through her stay. By now, she was fully relaxed and enjoying the benefits of her holiday, which had lifted her spirits. When she returned, she would be ready to take up the reins of Allure Fashions with renewed vigour and energy.

* * *

One morning when she rang her mother, she got a surprise. They had been chatting about the usual topics: the weather and what Kirsty had done the previous day. As they were about to finish, Helen said, 'Have you been to Marbella yet?'

'No,' Kirsty replied. She hadn't ventured down to that part of the coast. Apart from her trip to Málaga, she had spent her time around Fuengirola.

'But you must. You can't go to the Costa del Sol and not visit Marbella and Puerto Banús.'

'Why? I'm quite happy where I am.'

'You'll be missing something if you don't go. And besides . . .'
her mother paused '. . . I believe that's where Antonio is.'

Kirsty's heart jumped.

'I've been giving the matter a lot of thought since you left,'
Helen continued. 'Antonio told me that the manager of Puebla
Maria promised he would keep his job for him should he want
to return. I'll bet that's where he's gone.'

'That's just guesswork,' Kirsty said quickly.

'Nonsense. Where else would he go? He had a job there. It's
the obvious place. Why don't you go and check? It's a short
distance on the bus. You could do it in a morning.'

Kirsty took a deep breath. She didn't want to disappoint her
mother but she was leaving her no choice. 'I'm sorry, Mum,
but I've no intention of looking for him. If he wants to contact
you he has your phone number. It seems to me that, wherever
Antonio is, he doesn't want you to find him.'

She switched off the phone. The call had shattered her
peace of mind. Now gloom had taken hold of her as she sat
staring at the sun creeping slowly along the terrace.

* * *

Today Kirsty was planning to go to the local market – which
Jim and Valerie had said was well worth a visit. It was held
each week at the fairground on the outskirts of town on the
road to Los Boliches. She applied sunscreen to her face and
arms, stuck a cap on her head and set off.

It took her twenty minutes to walk there, and when she
arrived, she found the place packed with locals and tourists
browsing through stalls selling everything from cheap clothes
to fresh fruit and vegetables brought in by the outlying farmers.

She joined the crowds, stopping occasionally to examine some item that caught her attention. But the only thing she bought was a bottle of branded perfume, which was selling for a knock-down price and which she suspected might be fake.

As she approached the top of the fairground, the crowds grew thicker and she could hear the clicking of castanets and loud shouts of encouragement. When she managed to squeeze through a gap, she saw two gypsy girls with roses in their dark hair, performing an intricate flamenco dance while a man sat on an upturned box, playing a guitar.

The women were twisting their arms sensuously to the rhythm and stamping their heels on a wooden board while their skirts whirled in a cascade of colour. Kirsty reached for her phone and began to take photos. When the women had finished, the audience roared their appreciation and tossed money into their basket, urging them to perform again. Kirsty moved on, eventually escaping from the crowds to find refuge at a shaded table outside a café where she ordered a *café con leche* and a crusty roll filled with tuna and corn. This would serve for lunch. The gloom of the morning still hung over her, and while she ate, her mind went back to the earlier conversation with her mother. She wished Helen hadn't mentioned Antonio. He was gone. Why couldn't her mother leave matters be?

Had she been a bit sharp with her, too dismissive? Should she have humoured her a little and let her down more gently? Her mother had made a good recovery from her breakdown but Antonio's sudden departure had affected her more than Kirsty had expected. She would never forgive herself if something like this was to tip her back into depression.

Guilt crept over her. What was she to do? Now that she had dislodged Antonio from Avalon, it would be crazy to seek him out and possibly pave the way for him to return. She could always say she had searched for him at Puebla Maria to no avail. But it was such an easy thing to disprove and would make Kirsty look bad if her mother discovered she had lied to her.

Another thought struck her. What if her mother was to ring Puebla Maria herself and find him there? What if she was to invite him back, possibly offer to pay his fare? What if Antonio was to ring Helen and tell her how Kirsty had ordered him out of the house and that was why he had left? What would she do then?

The more she thought about her dilemma, the more difficult it appeared and the more agitated she became. Whichever way she turned, there was danger. It was at times like these that she wished she had someone she could turn to for advice, someone she respected who would tell her what she should do. But she was on her own. However, there was one thing she was sure of. There was no way she was going looking for Antonio. She had come to the Costa del Sol to find peace and relaxation. She would be asking for trouble if she was to invite him back into her mother's life.

She finished her lunch and made her way back to the hotel. There was a group sunning themselves around the pool and Kirsty decided to join them. She went up to her room, changed into her swimsuit and wrapped herself in a bathrobe. She stuck the novel into her bag, walked across the hall to the lift, and a few minutes later she was laying her towel on a lounger and stretching out in the sun.

She languidly turned the pages of her book. She had bought

it on impulse at the airport but she wasn't really enjoying it. The plot was all over the place and the heroine was a wimp who was letting every man she met walk over her. Kirsty wished someone would take her by the shoulders and shake some life into her.

Eventually, she cast it aside, closed her eyes and faced the sun. It was so tranquil here. The only sounds were the humming of the bees around the flowerbeds and the chirping of the birds. She thought of the time, how quickly it had flown and how soon the holiday would end. Soon she would be back in Dublin, facing all the problems she had left behind, including the fallout from the *Trumpet* article. She could only hope that Cecily Moncrieffe was right and people would have forgotten about it by the time she returned. Meanwhile she was determined to squeeze the last ounce of enjoyment from her remaining days in Fuengirola.

She was feeling so relaxed that she found herself drifting off and soon she was fast asleep. When she woke it was six o'clock. The pool was deserted and the sun was sinking below the treetops. She decided to take a quick dip to revive herself. First she stood under the shower to wash off the sunscreen, then dived into the pool. When she emerged, she was wide awake again.

Tonight she was going for dinner to a restaurant called Granada that the Wilsons had recommended. They said the food was marvellous and they always made a point of eating there at least once whenever they were in Fuengirola. Kirsty had gone online to check it out and found a host of favourable comments. Now she rang and booked a table for eight o'clock.

Granada was a little way out of town on the road to Mijas. She began to get ready, putting on a dress, then doing her hair and make-up. At seven thirty she ordered a taxi and went down to the lobby to find it waiting. Twenty minutes later, she was being dropped off outside the restaurant.

It sat on a prominent position on a hill with stunning views over the landscape below. Kirsty was shown to a table beside the window where she could see right down over the town. Dusk was falling and lights were coming on to bathe the landscape in a romantic glow. The waiter asked what she would like to drink and she ordered a gin and tonic, then turned her attention to the extensive menu.

There were so many appetising dishes that it took her some time to decide. But finally she settled for a salad of bacon and cheese to begin and roast suckling pig for her main course. To accompany the meal, she chose a half-bottle of Rioja. While she waited she glanced around the room.

It was almost full and the few vacant tables that remained had cards marked 'RESERVED'. The clients appeared to be mainly visitors, like her, the men in suits and light jackets, the women in summer dresses. As far as she could see, she was the only solitary diner and already she was attracting glances. A buzz of conversation rose above the clinking of glasses and the scraping of cutlery.

By the time her salad arrived, she was quite hungry and she fell on it with relish. The bacon was warm and combined well with the cheese and crisp salad. But if the starter was enjoyable, her main dish was outstanding. Thin slices of succulent white pork rested in a light juice with potatoes, broccoli and sliced baby carrots.

By the time she had finished she was full, so when the waiter enquired about dessert, she politely refused. He took away her plate and returned a few minutes later with the bill and a complimentary glass of a local liqueur. She took a sip. It was warm and sweet, very pleasant. She left some notes on top of the bill including a generous tip for the excellent service. He seemed genuinely pleased and went off again to order a taxi to take her home.

It was half past eleven when she got back to the hotel and heard laughter from the pool bar spilling out into the night air. She went and sat on the terrace and watched the stars twinkling in the heavens. She'd had a fabulous dinner at the Granada, easily the best meal she had had since arriving in Spain. She'd had a swim, she had sunbathed and she had visited the market. All in all, it had been another wonderful day.

Chapter Forty

The following morning when she returned from breakfast, she saw the red light flashing on the room phone. It meant she had missed a call. When she checked the number, she saw it was her mother. Something was wrong. She sat down and rang her. 'Were you looking for me?'

'Oh, Kirsty, thank you for calling me back. I tried your mobile but you had it turned off so I decided to ring the hotel direct.'

'I was having a swim. Are you in trouble?'

'No, I'm fine. But I wanted to talk to you urgently.'

'Go on.'

'Now, I realise this is something of an imposition. I know you're on holiday and you just want to relax, but I wonder if you would do me a very big favour.'

'What?'

'Please don't jump down my throat when I tell you.'

'What is it?' Kirsty asked, beginning to lose her patience.

'I wonder if you would mind taking a trip along the coast to Marbella and checking if Antonio is there.'

Kirsty rolled her eyes. 'Mum, we've already had this conversation.'

'I know, but I'm concerned about the poor boy. I can't help wondering why he dropped everything just when he was on the verge of making his breakthrough and went running back to Spain.'

'But I've told you, Mum, I don't want to go looking for him.'

'Please do this for me. I'll bet he's back at Puebla Maria playing the piano for those ungrateful tourists. Why don't you go and check?'

'And if he *is* there, what am I supposed to do?'

'Just ask if he's all right. Tell him I'm thinking of him and wish him well.'

'He may not want to see me.'

'If he's there, I'm sure he'll be glad you've come. He's such a kind, gentle boy. Please do this for me. It will give me much peace of mind.'

'Let me think about it,' Kirsty said.

She went out and sat on the terrace. She could see the gardeners trimming the lawn and clipping the hedges. A man in a straw hat was settling onto a sun lounger to read a book. Some children were in the pool. She was beginning to get worn down by her mother's persistence. It was over a week since Antonio had left but instead of accepting it and moving on, Helen was still obsessed with him. She was like a dog with a bone, stubbornly refusing to let go. And now the problem had landed in Kirsty's lap again.

Dammit, she thought, this holiday is turning into a nightmare. Perhaps I should never have come here. Perhaps I should have gone to Tenerife or somewhere far away from Marbella. She had made her reluctance clear but still her mother kept insisting she go looking for Antonio. She resented the moral pressure she was under but it seemed she had little option. She gave a loud sigh. She would have to go to Puebla Maria and ask after him.

She went back into her room, rang the reception desk and asked about bus times to Marbella.

'There is a bus leaving the station every half-hour,' the clerk replied.

'How long is the journey?'

'About one hour, Señorita. It depends on the traffic.'

Kirsty thanked him. She checked the time. It was ten o'clock. If she left now, she could be in Marbella before midday. She remembered her mother saying that Puebla Maria was fairly central. It shouldn't take long to find it.

* * *

At the bus station, Kirsty discovered that the Marbella bus was leaving in a few minutes. She purchased a ticket and waited. At ten thirty, they set off. She watched from the window as the bus navigated the crowded streets of the town till it reached the Moorish castle, then joined the road going west. The route took them along the coast, past sandy beaches, but her mind was elsewhere, focused on what would happen when she finally arrived at Puebla Maria.

In her conversations with her mother, Kirsty had always dismissed Helen's insistence that Antonio was back playing the piano at the resort. But, privately, she suspected Helen was right. It was the obvious thing for him to do.

This thought brought her no comfort. She had no wish to meet him again after their showdown in the garden that night. But as the journey progressed, her attitude began to change.

She began to wonder how he was and how well he had settled back in Spain. She regretted the harsh measures she had been forced to take against him. In different circumstances, she might even have been attracted to Antonio. He was a very handsome man and had many fine qualities. By now, she was surprised to find she was actually hoping to see him again.

The bus ploughed along the road, past the resorts of La Cala and Calahonda, till it reached the suburb of Elviria. They had now arrived at the outskirts of Marbella where the traffic built up again and their progress slowed. Finally, the bus station came into view, and a few minutes later they pulled into a bay. It was now a quarter to twelve and the sun was high in the sky.

She looked around and saw a line of taxis, walked to the first and spoke to the driver. 'Puebla Maria hotel resort, please.'

'Certainly, Señorita.'

He opened the door for her and she got into the back seat. The hotel sat on an elevated position above the town. As they approached, Kirsty could see it was an exclusive resort, surrounded by walls and security gates. But once she had stated her business, they were allowed to drive up to the entrance. Three large coaches were already parked outside and disgorging guests.

'Do you want me to wait for you?' the driver asked.

'No, thank you. I'll make my own way back.'

'As you wish, Senorita.'

She paid him and he drove off. Kirsty stopped for a moment to take in her surroundings. The complex consisted of four large apartment buildings surrounding the central block where she now stood. There were several swimming pools, neatly trimmed lawns, a flowering shrubbery, palm trees, and ornamental fountains tinkling pleasantly in the background.

Her mother had been quite right to sing its praises. Puebla Maria was certainly very impressive.

She walked up the steps to the revolving doors and entered the hotel. At once, she was in a large lobby, similar to the one at Hotel Geronimo but much grander. A crowd of new arrivals was checking in at the reception desk and she joined the line. When her turn came, she spoke to the pretty blonde receptionist, whose identity tag gave her name as Luisa. Kirsty felt her heartbeat quicken in expectation.

'I'm enquiring about a man called Antonio Rivera. He's a pianist. I understand he might work here in the restaurant.'

At the mention of his name, the woman stared at her. Then she shook her head. 'I don't know him, Señorita.'

'Would it be possible to enquire for me?'

'What is your business with him?'

'He's a friend.'

Her manner seemed to change. She looked Kirsty over before speaking again.

'What is your name?'

'Kirsty O'Neill.'

'I'm sorry,' the receptionist said. 'You must talk with the manager. Only he can speak about staff matters. I can't help you and now I am busy.' She gestured to the crowd milling around behind her.

'What is the manager's name?' Kirsty asked.

'Señor Lopez.'

'Can I speak to him?'

'No, he is not here. You must come back again at three o'clock.'

'*Gracias*,' Kirsty said. She turned away with a sinking feeling.

This was an unexpected setback. The quest to find Antonio was turning out to be more complicated than she had imagined.

It was now a quarter past twelve. She had almost three hours to kill so she decided to spend the intervening time exploring the town. But this time, instead of waiting for a taxi, she decided to walk. It was all downhill, and provided she stayed out of the sun, she should be all right. She put on her sunglasses and set off.

Twenty minutes later she was in Plaza de los Naranjos, in the heart of Marbella's old quarter, an area packed with charming cafés, boutiques, craft shops and the Cathedral of the Incarnation. It was also the home of the tourist office. She called into the office and was given an information pack and a map of the town. She took it outside to a nearby bar and ordered a coffee while she plotted her route. Then she left some coins on the table and started walking again.

A short time later, she arrived in the bustling town centre with department stores, car showrooms, supermarkets and clothes shops. She crossed the main road and kept walking till the seafront came into view. Immediately she was struck by the lively air of the place. It was thronged with people – hustlers selling bootleg CDs and fake designer clothes, mime artists, people sunbathing on the beach. She continued along the Paseo Maritimo till she came across an attractive restaurant and decided it was time for lunch.

All the seats on the terrace were taken so she was compelled to go inside to a table at the back. She ordered the house special, chicken cooked with herbs and served with vegetables and rice. While she ate she thought about her earlier experience at Puebla Maria. Was it her imagination or had the receptionist reacted strangely when she had mentioned she was a friend of Antonio? And why would she do that? Was there something about Antonio that Kirsty wasn't aware of?

Well, she would shortly find out, if Señor Lopez was available and prepared to talk to her. She checked her watch. It was two o'clock. She called for her bill and paid the distracted waiter. Then she went out again to the sunny promenade. At least it had the benefit of a cooling breeze, unlike the streets further away from the sea. She came to a taxi rank, took the first available cab and asked to be driven to Puebla Maria.

This time she was rewarded. When she mentioned Señor Lopez, the receptionist lifted the phone, spoke briefly, then turned again to Kirsty. 'He is in his office. He will see you now.'

She was directed along a corridor to the left. She knocked and was told to enter. It was a smart office and the manager was sitting behind a large desk. He was a thin man with a moustache, dressed in a tight-fitting suit. She noticed the beads of sweat standing out on his forehead, despite the fan humming quietly in the background.

'Please sit down,' he said in perfect English.

Kirsty did so.

'You are Ms O'Neill?'

'That's right.'

'Are you the lady who took Antonio Rivera to Ireland?'

'That was my mother.'

'You realise that he left Puebla Maria in the middle of his contract?'

She began to feel uneasy. 'But I understood you gave him permission. I was told you guaranteed to keep his job for him if he ever wanted to return.'

'That is nonsense. He left us without even giving notice. He simply rang and told me he was going because he had been given a great opportunity in your country. He left us in a terrible mess and right at the beginning of the tourist season. We had no pianist to entertain our guests at dinner in the restaurant. I hired him when he was playing in back-street bars in Málaga and this was how he thanked me.'

Kirsty's face fell. 'Do I take it that he's not working here?'

'Of course not. How could I employ someone who behaved so badly?'

'I'm sorry to have taken up your time, Señor. I have been misinformed.'

She stood up and walked to the door. When she reached it she paused and turned around. 'He has left Ireland. I thought he might have come back here. Do you know where he might be?'

'No,' Señor Lopez replied emphatically. 'He could be begging on the streets for all I care.'

Chapter Forty-one

Kirsty left the hotel, her disappointment mingled with sadness. So Antonio had fled back to Spain with no job to return to. Her mother would be upset when she told her. And it was all Kirsty's fault. Guilt gnawed again at her conscience.

She took out her phone and called home. Helen answered at the first ring.

'It's me, Kirsty. I've just been talking to the manager of Puebla Maria and I'm sorry to have to tell you but Antonio isn't here.'

At once, she heard the disappointment in her mother's voice. 'Oh dear. Does the manager know where he is?'

'I'm afraid not. And I've got more bad news. Antonio told you he'd been promised his job back if he wanted to return. But that's not true. The manager said he had broken his contract and left the hotel high and dry. He was very angry about it.'

There was a shocked pause.

'That's terrible,' Helen said. 'I feel awful. I persuaded him to leave his job. If I hadn't encouraged him he'd still be there playing the piano.'

'Don't blame yourself. You were trying to help him.'

'I shouldn't have interfered. I can see that now. I was just being a busybody, trying to sort out everyone's life for them. But I couldn't resist. He is such a brilliant pianist and I felt his talent was wasted playing in that hotel restaurant.'

'Listen, Mum. I've done my bit. I told you this was a wild-goose chase. If you'll take my advice, you'll stop blaming yourself and put the whole thing behind you. Wherever Antonio is, I hope he's happy. But he's not here and I doubt you'll see him again.'

'I suppose you're right,' her mother said reluctantly. 'But it's not going to stop me feeling sad.'

When she got back to her hotel, it was almost five o'clock. There were still a few hours of sunshine left, so Kirsty changed into her swimsuit and stretched out on the terrace with her book. But she had barely settled down when her phone rang. She answered without looking at it, and heard Angie's voice. 'You didn't tell me you were high-tailing it to Spain.'

'Angie!' she gasped. The call had caught her off-guard. 'I wasn't expecting you. How did you know where I was?'

'I read about it in the paper. Mags Smith had a piece in the *Tribune,* saying you were down on the Costal del Sol fighting off the dashing *caballeros.*'

'I wish,' Kirsty said.

'So I decided not to bother you. I guessed you just wanted to escape from all that stuff Susie Kelly wrote about you and Robbie Hennessy.'

At the mention of his name, Kirsty felt her hackles rise. 'That was a pack of lies.'

'You don't have to tell *me.*' Angie laughed. 'Everyone knows that Samantha O'Leary is a publicity junkie. If she doesn't get her name in the paper she has withdrawal symptoms. How are you getting on down there? Enjoying yourself?'

'I'm having a great time. The sun hasn't stopped shining since I got here. I'm chilling out, charging up my batteries.'

'You're making me jealous. I could do with a few days lying on a beach. Now listen up, this is the main reason I'm ringing. Susie Kelly has another story in the *Trumpet* this morning. Are you sitting tight?'

'Sure.'

'The happy couple have broken up. Apparently they had a screaming row in Crazy Joe's club a couple of nights ago and some snitch has reported it all to the *Trumpet*.'

'*What?*' Kirsty sat bolt upright. 'That didn't last long.'

'Well, there you are. He should have held on to you. He didn't recognise a good woman when he had one. If he'd behaved himself, you might still be an item.'

'I doubt that very much.'

'Anyway, I thought you'd want to know. So when are you coming back? We have a lot to talk about.'

'I've got the best part of another week down here.'

'Why do some people have all the luck?'

'What are you talking about? This is the first break I've had since Christmas.'

'Well, make the most of it. Looks like things are going to heat up on the social scene by the time you get back.'

There was a click and Angie was gone.

Kirsty decided to let her hair down. Since arriving in Fuengirola, she had kept pretty much to herself, apart from her breakfast conversations with Jim and Valerie Wilson. Tonight she would put on her glad rags and go out clubbing. After dinner, she retreated to her room, and began to get ready.

She had a shower, then rifled through her wardrobe for something to wear. She chose a smart little party dress and a pair of heels, put on her make-up and brushed out her dark hair. She examined herself in the mirror. Satisfied with her appearance, she put on a light jacket and rang the desk to order a taxi.

On the way, she stopped off at the Bristol Bar on the seafront for an aperitif. The pub was filling with British holidaymakers and stag parties out on the town. She picked a seat near the door and ordered a gin and tonic. It wasn't long before she began to attract attention. Several single men smiled and waved from the bar but Kirsty wasn't interested. She finished her drink and headed out once more into the cool evening air.

By now, it was almost eleven o'clock and there was a lively buzz along the nightclub strip and queues forming outside the doors. A row of touts had taken up duty, dispensing vouchers for free vodka shots to anyone who entered. Kirsty chose the smartest-looking club, collected her vouchers and made her way inside.

At once, she was met by a wall of sound blasting out of the stereo system and flashing lights ricocheting around the cavernous dance floor. A pounding rhythm seized her. She walked out onto the crowded floor, shook her hair and began to dance. Around her, there was a seething mass of bodies, mainly young people in their twenties, dressed in jeans and T-shirts.

She was enjoying herself so much that she stayed on the floor for half an hour before making her way to the bar in search of a cold beer. As she stood at the counter, she became aware of someone speaking to her and turned to find a good-looking man in an open-necked shirt standing beside her.

'I asked if you'd like a drink.' He smiled.

She looked into his smouldering dark eyes. 'I was going to order a beer.'

He waved to the barman, who hurried over. 'Two Coronas, please,' he said. He turned back to Kirsty. 'You dance very well. I've been watching you. Where are you from?'

'Dublin.'

'On holiday?'

'Yes.'

He held out his hand. 'My name is Kurt.'

'Kirsty.'

'That's not an Irish name.'

'No, I think it's Scottish.'

She studied his face. It was strong, handsome and tanned. He spoke English well but with a slight accent. She reckoned he was older than the others, probably in his middle thirties. She could tell at once that he was an experienced man and confident.

'I would ask you to dance,' he continued, 'but I don't see much point. I would like to talk with you and it's impossible among that crowd.'

'So let's talk,' she replied. 'Where are *you* from?'

'Southern Germany. A little town in Bavaria called Königsberg.'

'Are you on holiday too?'

'No, I live here. I'm in the music business. This is my club.'

Kirsty stood back and took a fresh look at him. 'Really?'

'Why are you surprised?'

'I don't know. I've danced in many clubs but I've never met the owner before.'

'So, there is always a first time.' He grinned.

'How did you get involved in the business?'

'I bought the club from the previous owner. I was looking for an investment and this seemed like a good choice.'

'And is it?'

'The summers are excellent when the tourists are here. In the winter, it falls off a little. But I make a good return. Now you must tell me about yourself. What is your profession?'

'I have a company that designs exclusive womenswear.'

'So you are creative as well as attractive.'

She smiled. 'If you say so.'

'I do say so. You know it's true. You are the most attractive woman in the club tonight. Why do you think I am talking to you?'

This time she laughed. She was enjoying Kurt's company. He was much more interesting than most of the men she had met.

'You shouldn't be so modest, Kirsty. When you have beauty like yours, you should wear it with pride.'

They continued to talk for most of the evening. Once or twice, she glanced at his hands but there was no sign of a wedding ring. Only when she was thinking of going home did he ask her to dance. He turned out to be such a good dancer that the crowd formed a circle around them and clapped loudly when they finished.

By now, it was almost two o'clock and Kirsty was exhausted. 'I have to go,' she said.

'Where are you staying?'

'Hotel Geronimo.'

'I'll drive you.'

'No, I can get a cab.'

'I insist,' he said.

He had a red Ferrari coupé in a bay outside the club. They got in and fastened their seatbelts. It took him five minutes to drive through the empty streets to the hotel. He pulled into a lay-by and turned off the engine.

'Thank you for your company,' he said. 'I have enjoyed our conversation immensely.'

'Me too,' she said, and made to open the door.

But his hand stopped her. At the next moment, his strong arms were around her as he drew her close. She relaxed into his warm embrace as his soft lips touched hers and she felt her body ignite in a red glow of passion.

Chapter Forty-two

When she woke, she was still thinking of Kurt and his soft hot lips. On her night table was the scrap of paper, torn from his notebook, on which he had written his phone number so that she could contact him again. Kirsty got out of bed, drew the curtains and saw that the sun was already bright in the sky. It was a quarter past nine and this was the latest she had slept since arriving in Spain.

She put on her swimsuit and went down to the pool for her morning swim. She had slept well and now she felt vibrantly alive. When she stopped for breakfast she found that Jim and Valerie had gone home and in their place was a group of new arrivals.

But as she drank her coffee and ate her croissants, a strange thing occurred. Almost unconsciously, Kurt had disappeared from her thoughts and his place had been taken by Antonio. She realised with a shock that he had never been far from her mind since yesterday's visit to Puebla Maria and her interview with Señor Lopez. If Antonio had no job, where was he? What was he doing? And how was he surviving?

She was responsible for his plight, not her mother, who had acted from the kindness of her heart. It was Kirsty who had driven him out of Avalon and back to an uncertain future in Spain. What was more, she had done it without a shred of evidence against him. How had she been so cruel?

Of all the people who had known him, she was the only one who had held a low opinion of him. Everyone else had been impressed by his kindness, good manners and gentle ways. She could see it all so clearly now. She had been driven by spite and suspicion. She had wronged an innocent man. What was she going to do about it?

It took her a second to make up her mind. She had a duty to find him and try to put things right. But where was she to start?

* * *

It took Kirsty fifteen minutes to get to the station in time to catch the Marbella bus. From the window, she watched the resorts of La Cala and Calahonda flash by but her mind was elsewhere. She was trying to figure out what she was going to say and do when she got to Puebla Maria. This time, she was determined not to leave without getting some answers.

Eventually, the bus pulled into Marbella and the passengers descended into the baking sun. The row of taxis was waiting. She spoke briefly to the first driver and gave her destination, then climbed quickly into the back and they set off. A short time later, the imposing exterior of Puebla Maria came into view. They passed the security gates and came to a halt at the front door.

'Please wait,' Kirsty said. She ran quickly up the steps, pushed open the doors and was once again in the impressive lobby. It was almost deserted and, by good fortune, Luisa, the blonde receptionist, was on duty. Kirsty started towards her but Luisa saw her coming and pretended to be busy.

'I'm here to find out where Antonio Rivera has gone,' Kirsty told her.

The receptionist tried to ignore her but Kirsty repeated her demand in a louder voice, forcing the young woman to look up.

'Please, Señorita, you must keep your voice down. If Señor Lopez finds out you are here again, you will get me in trouble.'

'Then tell me where Antonio is.'

Now the receptionist looked frightened. 'I don't know.'

'Yes, you do. You're hiding something and I'm not leaving till you tell me.'

Other staff members were glancing in their direction. Luisa lowered her voice.

'One of the chefs told me he had gone to work in Málaga.'

'Where?'

She took a notepad, wrote something down and quickly handed it to Kirsty. 'Bar Cristal?'

'Yes. He is playing the piano there.'

'You're certain?'

'That's what I was told. Now, please, Señorita, you must go. I will lose my job if you stay.'

'Thank you,' Kirsty said. She folded the paper and put it into her pocket.

'Where do you go now?' the driver asked, as she got back into the cab.

'Málaga.'

His face brightened at the prospect of the lengthy journey and the hefty fare. He started the engine and they set off again.

They headed down the hill towards Marbella, then took the motorway. The signs for the various towns kept flashing past: Fuengirola, Arroyo, Torremolinos. After half an hour, the rooftops and spires of Málaga came into view, shining in the distance. At the approach to the city, the traffic began to build up and the driver had to reduce speed. It was a quarter to two when they finally arrived at the main railway station.

'I'm looking for this address,' Kirsty said, handing the driver the piece of paper.

'Bar Cristal? Do you know the street?'

'That's all I have.'

'It's impossible.' The driver raised his hands. 'Málaga is a large city, so many bars.'

Kirsty sensed his reluctance to go searching all over the city with her and his desire to return to Marbella. A street cleaner was passing by. The taxi driver wound down the window and spoke to him. Kirsty saw the man scratch his head and shrug.

'He says he doesn't know.'

But Kirsty was insistent. 'Who would know? What should I do?'

'The police. You should ask there. They will know.' He pointed along the street to a white building with the Spanish and Andalucían flags flying outside.

She thanked him, paid the fare and watched the cab speed away. Then she began to walk towards the police station.

A young man, in the smart blue uniform of the Policia Local, was on duty at the information desk. However, he spoke no English and Kirsty had to struggle to make herself understood.

Eventually his face broke into a broad smile of understanding. He opened a drawer, took out a tourist map and spread it on the desk. With a pencil he traced the route to the bar. It was about a mile away. He wrote down the name of the street, Calle Cervantes, folded the map and gave it to her.

'*Buena suerte, Señorita*,' he said, with a polite nod.

'*Buenas tardes*,' she replied. She left the station and started off again into the hot afternoon sun. It took her half an hour to walk to Calle Cervantes. By now, she was perspiring freely and her T-shirt was clinging to her skin. About halfway down the street, she saw a sign: BAR CRISTAL. She hurried forward only to have her hopes dashed. A notice on the door in Spanish and English stated that the bar was closed and wouldn't open again till five o'clock.

With a heavy heart, she turned and retraced her steps towards the station. It was now three o'clock, siesta time: the streets were empty and many of the shops and stores were closed. She had no choice but to wait till Bar Cristal opened. When she got to the station she was tired and thirsty but here, at least, the cafés were open. She went into the first she saw and sat down at a table. When the waitress arrived, she ordered a cold beer and a ham omelette.

Now that she was so close to finding Antonio, she began to rehearse in her mind what she would do and the questions she would ask. It was going to be embarrassing for both of them. The last time they had spoken, she had said some dreadful things. She had accused him of taking advantage of her mother, of setting out to rob her. She could still see the horror on his face.

She recoiled at the memory. How could she have behaved like that? How could she have said those terrible things? She wouldn't be surprised if Antonio refused to speak to her after what she had done. And she would deserve it.

But gentler images began to drift into her mind: Antonio smiling at her, his beautiful eyes twinkling as he spoke kindly to her. At the time, she had dismissed it all as mere pretence, Antonio attempting to ingratiate himself. But what if it had been genuine? What if he had really meant it? The thought of the callous way in which she had behaved filled her with revulsion. What a total bitch she had been.

'*Una cerveza, Señorita.*'

The voice of the waitress announcing the arrival of her beer shook her from her reverie. She finished it in three gulps and ordered another when the omelette arrived. It came with fries and the inevitable basket of bread. She hadn't realised till now just how hungry she was and fell on it with gusto.

As she ate, her spirits began to revive. Now she knew exactly how she would handle the situation when she met Antonio. He would want to know what she was doing in Málaga and why she had come to see him. She would explain that she was on holiday and her mother had asked her to locate him. That would break the ice.

She would then work her way round to the argument in the garden the night before he left. She would tell him she now believed she had been mistaken. She would apologise and withdraw her accusations. It would be tricky and she would have to be careful how she phrased things but she believed she could pull it off. Then she would ring her mother and tell her she had found Antonio and let the two of them speak. Her job would be done.

At a quarter to five she set off again for Bar Cristal, eager now to see Antonio. This time when she arrived, the bar was open and a man was polishing glasses behind the counter. She entered with a spring in her step.

'*Hola*,' she began, using one of the few Spanish words she had learned. The man smiled at her.

'*Inglesa?*'

'*Non, Irlandesa.*'

'Ah, an Irishwoman,' he said in perfect English. 'What would you like to drink?'

'Nothing, thank you. I'm looking for Antonio Rivera.'

The man stared at her for a minute and his expression changed. 'You have come too late,' he said. 'He left last night.'

Chapter Forty-three

Kirsty's heart sank. It seemed as if the Fates were conspiring against her. Each time she came close to finding Antonio, a fresh obstacle rose up to block her. 'I think I *will* have a drink,' she said. 'Could I have a glass of brandy, please?'

The man took a bottle from a shelf, poured a measure and placed it before her. 'Are you a friend of his?' he asked.

'More of an acquaintance. I was told he was working here.'

'He played in the evenings.' The man pointed to an old piano that stood in the corner of the bar. 'It was background music for the patrons, not that they paid much attention. How well did you know him?'

'Not very well.'

'He was a very good pianist. Years ago, people would come from all over Málaga to hear him. The bar would be packed and people listened – you could have heard a pin drop when he played. Then a man called Lopez hired him to work at a fancy hotel in Marbella. I didn't see him again after that. With Antonio gone, people drifted away and trade was bad. Then last week he returned and asked if I would take him on again. I told him I couldn't pay much. But he said it didn't matter, he was desperate. I don't know whether Lopez fired him. He never talked about it. But Antonio had changed. He used to be a happy-go-lucky guy, but now he seemed sad. He didn't smile any more. He just sat there and played the piano while the patrons talked and paid no attention. I felt sorry for him. Then last night he said he wouldn't be coming back again.'

A lump rose in Kirsty's throat. She pictured Antonio playing for a pittance while the customers ignored him. What a comedown for the man who had held the audience spellbound that night at St Matilda's Church in Rathmines. 'Did he say why he was leaving?'

'No.'

'Do you know where he went?'

The man shrugged.

'I need to find him,' she said. 'It's very important. I might be able to help him.'

'I never had an address for him,' the man continued. 'Or even a phone number. But I know he came originally from Ronda. He used to talk about growing up there as a little boy.'

'Where is it?'

'It's a town in the mountains about an hour's drive from Marbella. Maybe he's gone there.'

Kirsty finished her drink and paid him. 'Thanks for talking to me.'

'*De nada*,' he said, and continued polishing glasses.

She walked back to the station and caught the next train to Fuengirola. It was now clear that Antonio was in trouble. Any trace of doubt had vanished. He had told the bar owner he was desperate. She thought of him without money, hungry, maybe sleeping rough in shop doorways. She had to find him. By the time she turned into the gates of Hotel Geronimo, her mind was made up. Tomorrow morning she would hire a car and drive to Ronda.

* * *

It was eleven o'clock when she set off. On the back seat of the hired car was a bundle of flyers she had got printed up from the photo of Antonio she had on her phone. In Spanish the caption read: 'ANTONIO RIVERA. HAVE YOU SEEN THIS MAN? PLEASE CONTACT KIRSTY' and her number. She knew it was a long shot but it was the best thing she could think of. On the seat beside her was a map of the area, the route marked in pencil by the receptionist at Hotel Geronimo.

She headed west past Marbella till she came to San Pedro de Alcántara, then left the coast to begin the steep climb towards her destination. Soon she was in the Sierra Bermeja mountains. She had to slow down and drive carefully as she negotiated the twisting road through the rocky passes. It was a long forty-five minutes before she saw the rooftops of Ronda gleaming and another quarter of an hour before she arrived on the outskirts and parked in a little square.

She got out and stretched her legs. She was in a charming old town of cobbled streets, ancient churches and stunning Moorish architecture. But she hadn't time to admire her surroundings. She had a job to do. Her plan was to visit as many bars and restaurants as possible and distribute the flyers in the hope that someone might recognise Antonio and tell her where he was.

She started with a bar across the street. She marched inside and found a scattering of working men taking their lunch break. She ordered a coffee and showed the flyer to the young barman. He studied it politely, then shook his head and passed it to some of the customers along the bar. They crowded round to look but gave the same response. No one knew the man in the photo. However, the barman did agree to put the flyer on a noticeboard beside the door. Kirsty paid for her coffee and set off again.

Up and down the square she went, handing out the flyers. Then she began to work her way towards the centre of the town. But here she ran into a problem. Tourist coaches were disgorging their passengers and the bars and restaurants were packed. She found it increasingly difficult to engage the attention of the busy waiters. Still she persisted.

Three hours later, after she had visited about thirty venues without success, her hopes were fading and she began to doubt the wisdom of her quest. Was it reasonable to expect people to remember Antonio after so many years? It was a hopeless task, like looking for a needle in a haystack. She felt herself begin to despair. Then she got a break.

It was a tiny bar near the bullring. When she opened the door, she found herself in a gloomy little room with bullfighting posters and photos of famous matadors adorning the walls. It was empty, apart from a group of locals playing chess at a table in the corner. By now, Kirsty was tired and hungry. She decided to stop and have something to eat. She sat down at the counter and ordered a portion of tortilla and a glass of wine. While she ate, she produced her flyer and showed it to the waiter. He took it to the window and studied it carefully in the light. She saw him peer at it and slowly rub his chin. Then he took it to the group playing chess.

Immediately, they abandoned their game and bent their heads to examine the picture. A babble of excited conversation broke out and they turned to look at Kirsty. One of the chess players got up from the table and came towards her. He was about thirty with fair hair and a thin, sallow face.

'You speak English?'

'Yes,' Kirsty replied.

'I think I know this man.'

Her heart leaped.

'I went to school with him. His father was a carpenter. He mended carts and ploughs for the farmers.'

'I don't know about his early life,' Kirsty said.

'I think it is him,' the man continued. 'The face looks the same and the name, Antonio Rivera. That was his name too. They lived in a house here in Ronda.'

'Do you know where I can find him?'

'It is a long time ago,' the man said. 'Why do you want to find him? Is he in trouble?'

Kirsty paused in case she said something that would make the man suspicious.

'No, he's not in trouble. He is a pianist. I might have work for him.'

'That's right.' The young man was nodding eagerly. 'He played the piano. I remember at school the master gave him lessons. It is the same man. I have no doubt.'

'Can you help me?'

'I haven't seen him for many years. When he left school he worked for a while in his father's carpentry shop. Then he left to go to Málaga.'

'Are his parents still here? Can I talk to them?'

The man shook his head. 'The carpentry shop was sold and now his parents are dead. There is no one left.'

He turned to one of his companions and they spoke in rapid Spanish. Then he turned back to Kirsty.

'My friend says you should go and ask at the shop. The people there are called Hernandez. If anyone knows where he is, it will be them.'

'What is the address?'

'Calle Santiago, near the Barrio San Francisco. You can't miss it. It is the only carpentry shop there.'

Kirsty thanked him, paid for her meal and set off again into the crowded streets.

It didn't take her long to find the area the man had mentioned. Calle Santiago was a little cobbled street of workers' houses and bars. She hurried along, her eyes scanning the buildings till at last she saw what she was looking for. The premises stood at the end of the row with the name 'Hernandez' prominently displayed on the front. Her heart beat faster as she drew closer till she found herself looking into a dim little workshop with a strong smell of sawdust. A man wearing goggles and overalls was working at a machine. When she appeared in the doorway, he switched it off and raised his goggles. He spoke to her in Spanish.

'*Sí, Señorita*?'

Kirsty produced the flyer. He took it from her and studied it. 'You are looking for this man?'

'Yes. His family used to own this place.'

The man shook his head and gave back the flyer. 'I don't know him.'

'Can you help me? I need to find him.'

But the man just shrugged. 'It was a long time ago. Too

long.' He pushed the goggles back over his eyes and restarted the machine.

Kirsty turned away and began walking back to the centre of town. She had reached her lowest ebb since she had begun her search for Antonio. She had come so close and, once again, he had slipped through her fingers. Was there any point in continuing this fruitless quest, trudging from bar to bar, giving out flyers in the vain hope that someone would tell her where he was? Would it not be wiser to give up and accept the obvious – that she was never going to find him?

As she turned into the Plaza Duquesa she saw a figure cross the square in front of her. Her heart jolted and she caught her breath. Surely it couldn't be true. Surely not now, just as she was about to give up. She started to run but the figure was disappearing into the crowd. She began to shout like a mad woman. 'Antonio! Antonio!'

The figure stopped and turned in her direction. He was tall and dark with rough stubble on his face. He looked at her, then rubbed his eyes in wonder. 'Kirsty, is it you?'

She flung herself into his arms as the crowd parted and people stopped to stare. 'Oh, Antonio, I've been looking for you everywhere. Thank God I've found you at last.'

Chapter Forty-four

They stood staring into each other's eyes while the crowds flowed past. Kirsty was overcome with joy and relief. 'Look at you,' she said, pointing to his pale, thin face. 'What have you been doing to yourself? You look half starved.'

A flicker of a smile played around his mouth. 'I have been staying with a friend here in Ronda. He lets me share his room.'

'Have you no money?'

'A little. I had some savings but now they are almost gone.'

'The first thing we must do is get you something to eat.'

There were several fancy restaurants across the square. Kirsty walked with him to the first and they sat down at a table.

A snooty waiter appeared and glanced distastefully at Antonio's shabby figure but quickly changed his attitude when Kirsty spoke. 'Bring us the largest steak you have, please, and a dish of vegetables. Oh, and a half-carafe of wine.'

'*Sí, Señorita.*'

'Now,' she said, turning again to Antonio. 'Tell me why you left so suddenly without even saying goodbye. You broke my mother's heart.'

His dark eyes looked into hers. 'Don't you know, Kirsty?'

'Was it because of the argument in the garden?'

He shook his head. 'No, that was just anger. I could accept that. What I couldn't accept was your coldness. You wouldn't return my affection. All the time I stayed at Avalon was because of you. I wanted you so terribly and all you showed me was disdain. You never smiled at me. You barely spoke to me. The argument was the last straw. It convinced me that I was wasting my time. *That* was why I left.'

She felt like weeping. What he had said was true. She had behaved abominably towards him. She would have treated a dog with more affection than she had shown to Antonio. 'Please forgive me. What I did was terrible.'

'Of course I forgive you. I've just told you that I love you. How could I have bitterness in my heart?'

Tears welled in Kirsty's eyes. This man was so kind and generous while she had been so cruel. She found a handkerchief and wiped her tears. 'I had this crazy notion that you were a trickster trying to get my mother's money. That's why I was so against you.'

'But you should know that I'm not interested in money. Whenever I get funds, I intend to repay your mother.'

'And how do you intend to get funds?'

'I will find a way.'

'You lost your job at Puebla Maria. You tried playing the piano in Málaga and it didn't work.'

He glanced at her. 'How did you know that?'

'I've been trying to find you for the last two days. There is only one way for you to make money, Antonio, and that is by playing your wonderful music to large audiences. I want you to come back to Dublin with me. My mother will be overjoyed to see you. We'll contact David Wheeler again and he'll launch your career.'

'I will come on one condition, Kirsty.'

'Which is?'

'You tell me that you love me.'

She paused, then drew him close and kissed him hard on the mouth. 'Does that answer your question? Of course I love you. I've loved you from the moment I set eyes on you. But I was too busy finding fault with you to realise it.'

A smile lit his pale face. 'Then I will be happy to come.'

* * *

When the meal was over, Kirsty paid the bill and they set off to collect her car. Then they drove to the place where Antonio was staying, collected his belongings and began the slow journey back to Fuengirola. It was half past nine when they finally arrived at Hotel Geronimo and both were exhausted. They went straight up to her room, and while Antonio went into the bathroom to shower and shave, Kirsty sat down at the laptop to search for flights to Dublin.

There was one leaving Málaga the following morning at eleven o'clock. She booked two tickets, then rang Reception to say that she had to return urgently to Dublin and was cutting short her stay. When that was done, she began taking clothes from the wardrobe and packing them into her case.

The bathroom door opened and Antonio came out in a cloud of steam. He resembled a quintessential Adonis with the towel wrapped around his waist and the mass of thick black hair on his chest. She felt desire sweep through her. She took a step towards him and their mouths met in a passionate embrace. Next moment they were on the bed and his hands were frantically pulling at her clothes.

She closed her eyes and uttered a sigh of contentment.

Chapter Forty-five

Helen sat on the patio at Avalon with a cup of coffee and stared across the lawn. It was two days since she had heard from Kirsty and it was so unlike her not to ring. Kirsty was the reliable daughter, unlike her sister, Deirdre, who had a head like a sieve and was always promising things she never delivered.

Helen was sad. She still hadn't got over the way Antonio had left in such a hurry without saying goodbye, and then the news that he had had no job to return to at Puebla Maria. God knows how he was living. He might be begging on the street and sleeping on a park bench. That thought sent shudders down her spine. And it was all her fault. She was the one who had persuaded him to drop everything and come with her to Dublin. Why did she have to interfere? Why hadn't she left well enough alone?

And the tragedy was that he had been on the verge of success. The recital at St Matilda's had been a triumph. Everyone had been enthralled when they had heard him play.

David Wheeler had agreed to manage him and his career had been about to take off. And then he had thrown it away. Helen couldn't understand it. It just didn't make sense.

She missed Antonio. Things weren't the same since he had left. She missed him about the house, his cheeriness and his smile. She missed the way he insisted on doing little jobs for her. The lawn – now *there* was an example – needed trimming again and she couldn't summon the energy to drag out the mower. Perhaps she would call the man in the village and get him to come up and do it.

Well, there was no point in moping about it. She'd better get used to life without Antonio. She should put him out of her mind and get involved in her committee work again. She wouldn't be bored for long. She had plenty of things to keep her busy, friends to visit and talk to, although some of them had let her down over the concert. She hadn't forgotten that. Some had been slow to pay for tickets. Still, best not to hold grudges. Life was too short.

Just then, the phone rang. She went into the house and picked it up.

'Mum, it's me, Kirsty.'

'Thank God for that. I was beginning to get worried about you. Are you all right? Is the weather still good?'

'The sun is splitting the stones. I'm sorry for not ringing sooner but I've been very busy. Mum, I've got some wonderful news.'

'What?'

'I've found Antonio.'

Helen gasped. She struggled to speak, but eventually managed, 'You've found him?'

'Yes.'

'Is he well? Where was he? How is he surviving?'

'One thing at a time, Mum. I found him in Ronda and, yes, he's well. Better still, he's coming back with me to Dublin. He's agreed to talk to David Wheeler and put on another concert.'

Helen thought she was going to faint. 'When are you coming?'

'Today. I'll call you from the airport when we arrive. We should be at Avalon by two o'clock. Byeee.'

Helen had to sit down. Antonio was coming today. And he was putting on another concert. All this good news was more than she could handle. She needed a strong cup of tea. Then she would ring Anne and ask her to come over and help. There was so much to do.

Chapter Forty-six

The National Concert Hall was garlanded with flowers. From the ceiling, a single spotlight fell on the piano in the centre of the stage. In a few minutes' time, at precisely eight o'clock, Antonio would appear and the concert would begin.

Helen cast a nervous glance around the hall. Kirsty had told her that the tickets had sold out on the first day they went on sale but Helen wanted to check. Every seat appeared to be taken. She could see many important people she recognised from the papers: television personalities, actors, musicians, a sprinkling of politicians. Even the president was there. He had appeared five minutes ago and taken his seat further along the front row where Helen was sitting with Anne.

Beside them were Kirsty, Mark and Deirdre, who had insisted on getting in on the act. Mr and Mrs Watt and Lucy Gilbert were behind them, with some of Kirsty's friends: Angie Dunlop, Cecily Moncrieffe and the young designers who worked for Allure Fashions. Across the aisle, she could see

Charles Ponsonby-Jones and David Wheeler, their heads bent in conversation as they studied the programme.

Those two had been instrumental in organising the concert. Once Kirsty had told Charles that Antonio was back in Dublin and ready to perform, he had swung into action. He had contacted David and between them they had drawn up plans for this début concert tour. Then he had used his influential column in the *Gazette* to promote it.

After tonight, Antonio would give three more concerts in Edinburgh, Manchester and London. Later in the autumn, he would move to New York and several more cities in North America. The advance reaction was already very positive and David was predicting a successful tour.

And that was the amazing thing. While everyone else was agog with nerves and excitement, Antonio appeared to be taking it all in his stride. Each day he was bright and cheerful, without a hair out of place. He had gone over to Lucy Gilbert's house a couple of times to practise on her piano but that was the sum total of his preparation.

But there was one other thing that still intrigued Helen. Why had he bolted back to Spain that time? Despite several circuitous enquiries, when she had tried to coax the information from him, he had never divulged his reason. It remained a mystery. Perhaps he had just got homesick. Not that it really mattered. He was back again. He was staying at Avalon. And he seemed to be getting on famously with Kirsty, which was another surprise: the last time he was there she had barely spoken to him. At that moment, the lights dimmed and the master of ceremonies walked onto the stage. The hall fell silent.

'Ladies and gentlemen, it is my great honour and privilege to present to you a young musician who is already being hailed as one of the finest pianists of his generation. Would you please give a warm welcome to Antonio Rivera?'

The audience applauded generously as Antonio walked onto the stage, handsome as a matinée idol in his dark dress suit. He bowed politely and sat down at the piano. There was a pause, and then the strains of Liszt's Sonata in B Minor rose to fill the auditorium. There was a lump in Helen's throat.

* * *

When the concert ended, Antonio stood and bowed to the audience. People began to get out of their seats to applaud. It spread throughout the hall till everyone was on their feet and Antonio was receiving a standing ovation.

Helen turned to Kirsty, who was dabbing the corners of her eyes with a handkerchief. How odd, she thought. Unless I'm greatly mistaken, there is definitely something going on between that pair.

Chapter Forty-seven

Susie Kelly sat in her cubbyhole at the *Trumpet* office and pulled deeply on her cigarette. Of course, the management had a no-smoking policy but she ignored it by turning on the fan and blowing the smoke out of the window. Cigarettes for Susie weren't a luxury. They were a necessity. She couldn't get her brain in sync without a lungful of nicotine.

She was trying to compose a piece about Kirsty O'Neill, something cheap and nasty that would drag her down a step and put manners on her. But she was finding it very difficult. Everything that girl touched seemed to turn to gold. She was beautiful and had a body to die for. She had a successful clothes business that kept winning plaudits from the fashion editors. And now she had snagged the hunky Spanish pianist who had the music critics frothing at the mouth with praise. It was enough to make a gossip columnist sick.

She typed a few quick paragraphs and stared at them but they read like stale bread. She swore under her breath. This was like trying to climb Mount Everest in carpet slippers. It just wasn't possible. There were some people you couldn't write anything nasty about with any conviction and Kirsty O'Neill was top of the list. The last time she had tried it, Kirsty had leaked a counter-story to Mags Smith at the *Tribune* and the whole thing had backfired.

Susie felt perspiration trickle down her neck. Any minute now, the editor would be bawling for copy. It was time to give up on Kirsty bloody O'Neill and find another victim. She reached for the notebook where she jotted down scraps of tittle-tattle and gossip and frantically began leafing through it. At last, something caught her eye.

Samantha O'Leary, the publicity-mad wannabe fashion model who had been involved in a scene with her boyfriend in Crazy Joe's nightclub a couple of weeks ago, had checked herself into a detox clinic. That would fit the bill perfectly. Satisfied at last, she started hammering at her keyboard.

> Peroxide blonde bombshell Samantha O'Leary's love affair with Bombay Fizzs has finally caught up with her. A little bird has told me . . .

She finished the story, threw her eye over it and hit 'send'. Job done. Tomorrow morning, Samantha was going to wake up with enough publicity to keep her occupied for the foreseeable future. Susie stubbed out her cigarette, lit another and immediately launched into a coughing fit.

God, these cigarettes would be the death of her.

Acknowledgements

I would like to thank the following:

My family: Gavin, Caroline, Alex, Sam and Maura. Marc Patton for computer advice.

All at Hachette Ireland, particularly Ciara Considine and Joanna Smyth, and Hazel Orme.

The booksellers for their constant support.

And my loyal readers: You make it all worthwhile.

Also by Kate McCabe

The Spanish Letter

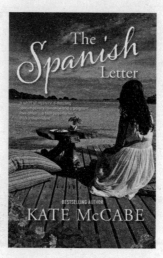

She thought she knew the men in her life . . .

Sandy Devine is a young woman who appears to have everything – a stellar media career, a stunning penthouse apartment overlooking Dublin's River Liffey and, after some stormy setbacks, the perfect romance with handsome A&R man Sam Ross. The pair are the envy of the Dublin social scene and it looks as if Sandy's future is bright.

But when her mother's health declines and she has to be hospitalised, Sandy discovers a letter in her mother's personal belongings, which unleashes a long-hidden family secret that forces Sandy to question everything she once took for granted.
As Sandy sets out on a voyage of discovery that takes her from Dublin to the Costa del Sol in search of her true identity, nothing can prepare her for what lies in store . . .

Out now in paperback and ebook

The Man of Her Dreams

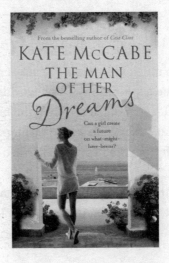

Piper McKenzie is young, beautiful and rich – the darling of the Dublin social scene. Married to handsome music promoter Charlie White and successful in taking over the family hotel chain, she looks to have it all. But when Piper discovers that her marriage is not what she thought it was, she's forced to question everything she has held sacred.

Then news comes that could have devastating consequences for the future of the family firm, concerning her wayward brother Jack and his self-interested wife Corinne. When Piper escapes to Spain with her young daughter to try to piece back together her world, her path once again crosses with Eduardo Delgado, a doctor she had a love affair with years earlier whilst on holidays. But can a girl create a future on what-might-have-beens? Or can a broken marriage be mended by second chances?

Reading is so much more than the act of moving from page to page. It's the exploration of new worlds; the pursuit of adventure; the forging of friendships; the breaking of hearts; and the chance to begin to live through a new story each time the first sentence is devoured.

We at Hachette Ireland are very passionate about what we read, and what we publish. And we'd love to hear what you think about our books.

If you'd like to let us know, or to find out more about us and our titles, please visit www.hachette.ie or our Facebook page www.facebook.com/hachetteireland, or follow us on Twitter @HachetteIre